Praise for *Murder on Page One*

'Ian Simpson is a real find. Murder on Page One is a beautifully crafted, gripping piece of crime fiction that holds the attention from page one until the very end.'

Alexander McCall Smith

'This well crafted, pacey, humerous whodunit from ex-judge Ian Simpson is an highly enjoyable read.'

Lovereading

'An enjoyable, witty page-turner brought to life by the well drawn, believable characters.'

Journal of the Law Society of Scotland

'The twists and turns keep pace with the rising body count in what is a highly enjoyable piece of crime fiction. A follow-up encounter with Inspector No would be most welcome.'

University of Edinburgh Journal

Murder on Page One

MURDER

ON THE

SECOND TEE

Matador
9 Priory Business Park
Wistow Road
Kibworth Beauchamp
Leicester LE8 0RX, UK
Tel: (+44) 116 279 2299
Fax: (+44) 116 279 2277
Email: books@troubador.co.uk
Web: www.troubador.co.uk/matador

ISBN 978 1783065 868

British Library Cataloguing in Publication Data.
A catalogue record for this book is available from the British Library.

Typeset in 12pt Minion Pro by Troubador Publishing Ltd, Leicester, UK
Printed and bound in the UK by TJ International, Padstow, Cornwall

Matador is an imprint of Troubador Publishing Ltd

MURDER

ON THE
SECOND TEE

IAN SIMPSON

For Richard and Graham

'Money can't buy friends but you can get a better class of enemy.'

Spike Milligan
Puckoon '63.

1

The first blow took Hugh Parsley by surprise. It fractured his right temporal bone and tore the middle meningeal artery. He stumbled and fell face down on the grass. A blow to the back of his neck cracked the occipital bone at the base of his skull. He was struck several times about the left temporal area. His brain, penetrated by bony fragments and squeezed by bleeding within the skull, ceased to function. Hugh Parsley was dead.

2

The man was on his front, arms outstretched, dark blood staining the closely-mown grass on which he lay. The little that could be seen of his face was a red, pulpy mess.

Detective Inspector Flick Fortune curled her lip as she looked down on him. Then her stomach heaved. She straightened up, swallowed hard, concentrated. All in vain. Her mouth filled and she ran to the bushes several yards in front of the second tee of St Andrews' historic Old Course. She bent over then spewed her breakfast into a spiky whin.

Meanwhile, earnest as a primary teacher at a school sports day, PC John Robertson laid blue and white tape in a circle round the body. The gentle breeze preparing to test the golfers on this dull, soft, late November morning tugged the unsecured tape giving it a mind of its own. When Flick returned, trying to look as if nothing had happened, Robertson scurried round the perimeter of his plastic circle trying to flatten the tape on the grass.

She felt the red tide spread up from her neck. Nearly polluting the crime scene of your first murder as an inspector was as unimpressive a start as you could get. She longed to scream at the gangly young constable that she had seen hundreds of bodies in the Met, but needing to explain was a sign of weakness, and for the next three weeks anyway the life inside her was to be a secret.

'Who found him?' she barked.

'A greenkeeper, ma'am. They go out while it's still dark to prepare the course.'

'Has anything been touched?'

'Macphail, that's the greenkeeper, says he didn't move anything, ma'am. But he did switch the green.' He nodded at the expansive first green, clear of the dew covering the rest of the course. From the direction of play it was flat with hummocks at the back. In front, the Swilken Burn flowed along a channel between wooden sleepers, ready to swallow a shot which was short or topped.

'Did he not think?'

'He said he didn't want to disturb him.' Robertson looked at the body, feet on the right extremity of the green, head and torso on the second tee and shuddered. 'Said he thought the guy was drunk.'

'What on earth …?'

'It's dark when they come out, ma'am, and he started sweeping the dew on the other side of the green. He says he went round him carefully then gave him a wee poke and saw he was dead.'

'Right,' she said quickly. The greenkeeper had ruined any evidence the killer had left on the green and she wasn't in the mood for his lame excuses. The corpse was much more interesting. He looked about forty-five, probably just under six feet, with thick, dark hair. He wore a golf jacket which had ridden up his back, dark grey slacks which retained their crease and black shoes sporting ornamental buckles. Some of the lining of his hip pocket protruded.

The call had come as Flick finished breakfast. It was Friday and her husband Fergus had suggested going out for dinner. Watching what she ate and not drinking, she had been unenthusiastic. Fergus's efforts to encourage her had been interrupted by the excited, very Scottish voice of the telephonist in the main office in Cupar. The relish with which she had announced a sudden death had been positively ghoulish.

Leaving Fergus with the dishes, it had taken Flick five minutes to arrive at the scene. Robertson had been there, clutching the crime tape and glancing uncertainly towards the first tee. He did not lessen her feeling that she was meeting this challenge on her own. In her rush she had forgotten gloves. She stuck her hands in the pockets of her padded coat and surveyed the humps and hollows forming the most famous golfing acres in the world. Behind them, pointing heavenwards, the roofs and spires of the Royal Burgh of St Andrews formed a jagged backdrop. Flick had not lived there long, but had already begun to think of it as home. Despite a history full of violent death, in this century it was a fine, safe place to bring up the child she was carrying. Visually unique, the golf course finished almost in the town itself, an irregular terrace of buildings, haphazardly designed, marking the boundary. This morning the whole scene had been painted over by a dark grey wash making everything monochrome and drab.

Perhaps the greenkeeper had not spoiled anything after all. Off the green the dew lay thick on the ground, undisturbed except by her feet and Robertson's. The body had almost escaped its pale shroud. She puzzled over this then remembered her physics; damp air condensed on hitting a cold surface, not a warm one. A shout of 'fore' from the first fairway disturbed her and a ball thudded into the turf, leaving a plug-mark in the soft green a few metres away.

'Stop these people, for God's sake,' she commanded.

Robertson picked up the ball and ran at the four approaching players, waving his arms and shouting. An animated dispute followed as the golfers saw no reason why a mere fatality should interfere with their game. Flick took a deep breath. Where on earth was the team supposedly coming from Cupar? It was just a few months since she had moved from London and policing the East Neuk of Fife was completely different to what she had been used to. Even the slobbish Inspector No seemed dynamic by comparison with some country 'bobbies'. She willed herself to be patient.

As the players reluctantly trudged back to the first tee, she looked round. In the opposite direction from the town, the five-star Old Course Hotel loomed over the seventeenth hole like a huge yellow cruise liner in a small port. A few people out on balconies craned for a better view. The news was bound to spread.

'They saw the point in the end, ma'am,' Robertson said, breathing heavily. 'They said they'd tell the starter not to let anyone else off the first tee. But we'd better talk to him soon. He won't be pleased.'

'We need more police here. You did tell Cupar it was a murder?'

'I said I thought it was. I didn't want to alarm them, ma'am. In case …'

'Well give me your radio …'

She was interrupted by a shriek of 'Hugh, Hugh!' A woman wearing sky-blue slacks and jumper was running across the golf course from the direction of the hotel. As she got closer, Flick reckoned she was in her mid-thirties. Her auburn hair was disheveled and she wore no make-up. 'Is he alright?' she gasped as Flick cut her off before she could see the full horror of the corpse's face. Speaking softly and with authority, Flick put her arm round her and steered her back towards the hotel, walking slowly. She caught a whiff of stale perfume.

The woman's name was Belinda Parsley and she spoke with the South of England accent that Flick often missed. She and her husband Hugh were guests in the hotel, attending a business weekend. The previous evening he had been up late with colleagues discussing work. She had gone to bed and fallen asleep. He had not been beside her in the morning and she had got up to look for him. She had heard someone talking about a body on the course.

'Is a doctor coming?' she asked.

'The man is dead,' Flick said quietly.

'Please, please tell me it isn't him,' the woman implored, straining to look behind her.

'What does your husband look like?' Flick asked, tightening her hold round her waist.

'Tall, nearly six feet. Dark hair. Handsome, well I think so …' She dissolved into tears.

'What was he wearing last night?'

'A shirt, no tie or jacket, grey slacks. They were new,' she sobbed.

'What colour were his shoes?'

'I can't remember. Black, I suppose.'

'Did he have black shoes with buckles on them?'

Belinda Parsley shook uncontrollably and twisted free. 'Oh no. It's him, isn't it? Dead? I can't believe it. No.' The last word came out as a long wail of anguish. 'Why won't you let me see him?'

Flick stood in front of her, arms out. 'We can't be definite, but I'm afraid it seems likely it's him. If it is, you will certainly see him later.'

'I want to see him now.'

'Please, Mrs Parsley, no. He's received some nasty injuries and this is a crime scene. We believe your husband was murdered.'

The distraught woman took a step back then stared at the body. Flick wondered if she was about to try to give her husband a last, bloody embrace, but to her relief Mrs Parsley stood still, composing herself.

'How did he die?' she asked, her voice catching.

'I believe he was assaulted, but we'll only know after the post mortem.'

'Did he suffer much, do you think?' She turned and locked her eyes on Flick.

This was part of the job that never got easier. 'It was probably quick,' she said, trying to sound authoritative, hoping she would not be proved badly wrong.

To Flick's relief, three marked police cars parked on the road beside the seventeenth green. Four uniformed constables and a plain clothes officer plus scenes of crime officers and a civilian photographer walked over. They had with them the white tent needed to shield the body and, after the photographer had taken some longer shots, erected it quickly. Detective Sergeant Lance Wallace, a stolid man in his mid-forties whose competence Flick respected, directed this operation.

'We need a pathologist,' she said to him.

'Dr MacGregor's coming from Dundee, ma'am. He should be here shortly.' Wallace spoke slowly in a matter of fact tone roughened by a Scottish accent that was not pronounced. Flick found his presence reassuring.

'I don't want the body touched.' She looked towards the first tee of the Old Course, round which a small crowd had gathered, some of them making aggressive practice swings. 'And I don't want to have any golfers here until we're finished. You go and tell the starter.' Aware of sounding shriller than someone in control should, she saw no reaction on Wallace's face.

'I'll have a wee word,' he said and set off unhurriedly towards the first tee.

There was one female officer present, Constable Amy Moncrieff. She had immediately gone to the sobbing woman. Flick wished she had more experience, but reckoned that even an inexperienced female officer would get more out of Mrs Parsley than any of the men.

'Take her to her room in the hotel, obtain a

photograph of her husband and encourage her to talk,' Flick instructed. Amy gently took the ashen-faced woman's arm and escorted her back to the hotel.

For the first time that morning Flick began to feel in control. She hoped the pathologist would arrive soon. Her husband, Fergus Maxwell, was a detective inspector in the Dundee police and had many tales about Dr MacGregor, whose flamboyant style in the witness box had left a deep impression on many juries. She looked forward to meeting him.

As she gazed round the historic links and towards the old grey town, she began to think seriously about the course of the investigation. Should she set up the incident room in the cramped and lightly-manned St Andrews office or eight miles away in the main office in Cupar? She would have to interview the hotel guests before any checked out. The staff too. In her own mind she was sure Mrs Parsley was a widow, but that had to be settled beyond any doubt. If the dead man had known his murderer, his work colleagues should all be regarded as suspects. His wife as well, though her reactions had seemed genuine.

A man wearing a long, brown coat and a Cossack-style hat approached from the direction of the town. He carried a bulky case, smoked a cigar and seemed in no hurry. 'Mrs Maxwell, I believe,' he said, bowing his head, 'or should I say Inspector Fortune?'

Flick shook his outstretched hand. 'Inspector Fortune today,' she said brusquely. 'And who might you be?'

'My name is Robert MacGregor, ma'am. I believe you

are in need of a humble pathologist, and I just happen to be one.' His twinkling eyes disconcerted her, never happy when being made fun of, even in a minor way.

'Oh good,' she said. 'Well, there he is.' She nodded at the tent, where flashes of light shone through the material as the photographer snapped away.

MacGregor took a puff of his cigar before exhaling. He then summoned PC Robertson to hold his coat, hat and cigar as he donned a white sterile suit and gloves. He picked up the bag containing his instruments, muttered 'Into the valley of death …' then drew aside the flap of the tent.

Flick was about to put on a sterile suit and follow him when the oldest of the constables, McKellar, shouted to her. He pointed into the Swilken Burn. In the opaque water she could make out something the shape of a golf club with a head like a branding iron. Nearby on the muddy bed of the burn lay a dark green pole about six feet long with a small mesh basket at one end.

'What's that?' she asked.

McKellar, a dour, angular man whose words were more respectful than his tone, smiled. 'It's a putter, ma'am. You use it on the green. The other thing's a ball scoop for wheeching your ball out of the burn.' He mimed a scooping action.

Cross with herself for asking, she snapped, 'Well fetch some polythene to wrap them. Then climb in and remove them. And be careful. The lab may be able to recover some evidence.'

'Right away, ma'am,' McKellar said in a sarcastic

monotone then ambled towards the cars. When he returned with the polythene sheeting he looked towards Robertson. 'Hey, Robertson, I've a wee job for …'

'PC Robertson has his hands full, McKellar,' Flick interrupted. 'And seizing the likely murder weapon should be done by an experienced officer. So take your shoes and socks off.'

She supervised as the disgruntled McKellar bared his feet and rolled up his trouser legs. He winced when his white feet touched the cold, brown water, but in lifting the items, even wearing gloves, he took care not to touch them more than necessary and placed them, almost reverently, on separate polythene sheets. Instead of climbing out of the burn he bent down to pick up a golf ball.

'A Titleist,' he said, 'with "HP" written on it.' Flick could see black marker ink on the ball. It was another pointer to the identity of the corpse.

Kneeling to examine the putter, she could see that the shaft was bent. It had a blue grip and a clumsy-looking head, with bars protruding backwards from either end of the blade. She knew golfers used some strange implements but this one looked extraordinary.

'Have you found the murder weapon?' MacGregor asked from behind her.

'Possibly,' Flick replied. 'What do you think?'

MacGregor squatted beside her and inspected the items closely. 'It's a mistake to make early assumptions, but my guess is that this putter was used on him. We'll know better once we have the lab report and the PM.'

He peeled off the sterile suit and put on his coat and hat. He took from Robertson his cigar, which had gone out, and clamped it between his teeth. Observing his red bow tie, Flick remembered Fergus telling her that after inadvertently inserting a conventional silk tie into a corpse's rectum along with the examining finger, MacGregor never again sported a tie that might dangle. She would have liked to have been a fly on the wall that day.

'He was battered to death, poor chap.' MacGregor sounded matter of fact. 'A number of heavy blows to the head, possibly with more than one weapon. Some of the blows were inflicted by something that did not have a smooth surface. Could well have been the back of that odd-looking putter. Died about one this morning, give or take an hour or so, but the injuries were probably sustained earlier. I'll do the PM this afternoon and I'll phone you afterwards. Could I have your mobile number?'

They exchanged numbers then MacGregor said, 'A pleasure to meet you, Inspector Fortune. I've always enjoyed working with your husband. He's an outstanding officer.' He lit his cigar and sauntered back to his car.

Flick looked at Robertson, who was wiping his hand on the leg of his trousers.

'That thing he smokes is disgusting, ma'am. It's all slobbery to hold, too.'

'You should have dropped it. I'd have backed you. By the way, was that a real dead animal on his head?'

'Oh, yes, ma'am. There's even a wee paw at the back.'

She pursed her lips but said nothing. Like many who had lived all their lives in cities, she strongly disapproved of blood sports. She wondered what Fergus saw in the pathologist.

Sergeant Wallace came up to her.

'They know we mustn't be disturbed, ma'am, but there are some very disappointed golfers, desperate to play the Old. I said they could go round by the Ladies' Putting Green and start.' In answer to her bemused look he pointed to the hilly putting green bisected by a path on the other side of the second tee. He added, 'They'll play the second as a short hole. Someone's coming to put tee markers down the fairway.'

'Well make sure it's a long way down the fairway. And if anyone sends a ball in my direction, I'll prosecute them under the Police (Scotland) Act,' she snapped. 'When the SOCOs are finished, they can have all their golf course back,' she added, not wanting to seem anti-golf.

'I made sure they know to give us a wide berth, ma'am.' Wallace smiled.

She looked at the tent and shook her head. 'Why, Wallace, Why?'

'Robbery or gay-bashing, depending on the gentleman's proclivities of course, or something else, though I doubt if it was premeditated. As vicious an attack as I've seen, ma'am.'

Flick nodded. 'Me too. It doesn't seem a likely spot for gay-bashing. It could have been a robbery that went wrong. I wonder if he has his wallet.' She went to the tent and asked the SOCOs to see if they could find it.

A female voice replied, 'Not here, ma'am, but there is a mobile phone.'

Flick turned to Wallace. 'Get the mobile checked and search these bushes for his wallet. And the burn, too. I bet the killer threw it away. And we'd better see if anyone with a window overlooking the course saw or heard anything.'

'You mean house to house, ma'am?'

'Exactly. Including people staying at Rusacks Hotel over there.' She gestured towards the road beside the eighteenth fairway. 'Find out if there have been any reports from the public that could be relevant. Can you think of anyone local who's mad enough or bad enough to do this?'

Wallace shook his head. 'No. I've been wondering about that and I can't see any of the St Andrews villains doing anything as brutal, unless it was personal of course.'

Well it's personal now, Flick thought. If I don't catch this killer everyone will think I'm rubbish.

* * *

After giving the men their instructions, Flick and Wallace walked over to the Old Course Hotel and round to the front door on the far side of the building. In the lobby they found Cupar's two detective constables, di Falco and Gilsland. They were both in their twenties, tall and bright with ready smiles. Apart from that they had little in common, but were firm friends. Suave, with Mediterranean good looks, Billy di Falco could have stepped from an Armani shop window. Gary 'Spider'

Gilsland might have bought his clothes at a charity shop closing down sale. A thick woollen pullover hung loosely from his skeletal shoulders and he wore his jeans as low-slung as was decent. Uneven tufts of ginger hair, a long way from forming a proper beard, sprouted from his face. In the elegant and stylish hotel lobby Gilsland was totally out of place.

Flick quickly up-dated the two detectives. She decided to send Gilsland to their base in Cupar to dust Parsley's mobile for prints then find out what he could from it. Spider, as everyone except Flick called him, was never happier than when engrossed in IT.

Before he left she took him aside. 'You look like a scarecrow, Gilsland,' she said quietly. 'Tidy yourself up before you come to work tomorrow.'

An expression of horror on his face, he said, 'Tomorrow, ma'am? But I had …'

'This is a murder. We have to move quickly, so no days off till we make an arrest. Sorry,' she added, remembering him talking about a family wedding at the weekend, 'but you'd have had to smarten up for the wedding anyway.' As he left, shoulders bowed, she felt a twinge of guilt.

As Wallace arranged with an under-manager to obtain a list of all guests staying the previous night, she went to see how Amy Moncrieff was faring with Belinda Parsley. Her room was situated in a wide, discreetly lit corridor on the first floor.

Amy answered Flick's knock and came out into the corridor. She showed the inspector a photograph of a smiling man on a foreign beach.

'It's him,' Flick said. 'But before we confirm it to her, have you found out anything?'

'Well, ma'am, she seemed to want to talk. Mr Parsley was a director of a bank in London, the Blue-something Bank. Mrs Parsley said he'd been very stressed, and there were issues with some of the other directors. They all came up here to thrash things out away from London, and took partners to make it look normal. They arrived on Wednesday night and spent yesterday morning working. In the afternoon most of them played golf. They split up for dinner last night, but there was a lot of discussion afterwards. Mrs Parsley went to bed. She takes sleeping pills and didn't realise anything was wrong till this morning.'

'Did she say what these issues with the other directors were?'

'No. She said her husband was still uptight at dinner. I got the impression that the directors had fallen out among themselves.'

'How?'

'She said Mr Parsley had been very particular who he sat with at dinner. They finished up at a table for four with their oldest friends in the bank, Simon and Eileen Eglinton. That's all I can tell you, ma'am.'

'You've done well, Amy. Stay with her and learn all you can.' She glanced at the photograph. 'We'd best get this over with.'

Belinda Parsley nodded when they told her then burst into hysterical tears. Flick left Amy to cope as well as she could and went to reception.

Jocelyn, the under-manager, was a devotee of

detective fiction and had been secretly thrilled by a murder inquiry touching her life. She was happy to help the police, even if these officers seemed quite ordinary. She wished Flick and Wallace had more pizzazz, or were at least eccentric. Bright, with a ready laugh, she enjoyed her job, but with her thirties looming sometimes felt in a rut. Brushing back her long blonde hair, she told the detectives that the bank was the Bucephalus Bank. They had taken eight rooms at two weeks' notice, rooms that would not have been available during the tourist season. Not all the guests in the group had come with partners, and the list Wallace had been given showed the room numbers of those who were in the party. The Parsleys had dined with the Eglintons the previous evening and had split the wine bill, one bottle of chablis and two vintage clarets. The group had booked in till Monday morning and no one had departed early. Jocelyn promised to let the police know should anyone attempt to do so.

Flick said, 'We'll also need to interview all members of staff who were on duty last night and all guests. Detective Sergeant Wallace will coordinate staff interviews, and I'll appoint an officer to speak to the guests, starting with those scheduled to leave today. We'll need forwarding addresses and contact details in case subsequent inquiries throw up something we need to check.'

Jocelyn looked doubtful. Police interviews, no matter how tactfully conducted, were upsetting to many people, and the Old Course Hotel prided itself on sending guests away happy and relaxed.

Flick had already decided to give di Falco the job of talking to guests. 'Don't worry,' she reassured Jocelyn, 'I know just the man to keep your guests happy. One more thing, we'll need to use one of your conference rooms to inform the rest of Mr Parsley's party about what's happened.' She looked at her watch. 'Would you send a message that I need to see them all, including partners, at nine-fifteen?'

'Oh, yes,' Jocelyn said with enthusiasm. This was more like Agatha Christie. She became even more excited when Flick called Billy di Falco over and introduced him. Broad-shouldered, with olive skin and jet-black hair, he gave Jocelyn a smile that showed off deep brown eyes and pure white teeth so regular that they almost looked false. Jocelyn showed him to a table and chair beside reception where she could see him, and without being too intrusive, he could interview guests when they checked out.

'Behave yourself,' Flick warned him as Jocelyn set up the gathering in the conference room she had allocated.

* * *

The room was spacious and well lit. Flick and Wallace arrived early and took their seats at one end of the large, oval table. Although she had never met one, Flick had developed a strong dislike of 'fat cats'. She regarded it as criminal that they should wreck the economy with greedy schemes and still pay themselves bonuses the size of the average worker's career earnings. If Parsley had known his killer, the murderer was probably about to enter the room. As the bankers came in, singly or in couples, she cast a careful eye over each of them. Few of them looked like fat cats, she thought. They seemed wary, careful not to sit immediately beside someone already at the table. By quarter past nine, seven persons, two couples and three women on their own, had gathered. No one spoke. Most avoided eye contact with the detectives and with each other.

A tall, thin man had an aloof bearing. He was with a large lady who wrinkled her nose as if smelling a bad smell. Both stared through the voile curtain as if there was something fascinating outside. The woman of the other couple wore designer trousers and blouse in lurid pink that clashed with the pale tone of the shirt worn by the man whose hand she fawningly grasped. She used her other hand to dab at her eyes, showing off her rings but not smudging her blue eye shadow. Her surgically altered face, smooth, tight and not quite symmetrical, was framed by a blonde bob.

A very thin woman dressed in black, her posture taut and upright, sat near no one. Stretched facial skin accentuated her enhanced lips. Bottle-fed, jet-black hair failed to conceal a scrawny neck. She poured herself a glass of mineral water. Although her hand shook, she looked round the others with eyes as cold as a lizard's. 'Blonde Plastic' and 'Black Plastic' respectively, Flick named these cosmetic disasters to herself.

A younger woman, fresh-faced and wearing a green tracksuit, her hair wet from a visit to the spa, unscrewed her water, poured some and gulped it down before setting her glass on the table with a defiant click. Flick observed her clean, neat nails, a contrast to the purple talons round Black Plastic's glass. The third woman on her own, also younger than the rest, began to doodle on the pad in front of her. Dressed in jeans and a tee shirt, she did not go with the others, Flick thought; she had the body language of an undergraduate who had gatecrashed a bad party.

Surprised by the lack of men, Flick allowed the tension to mount. At twenty past nine she looked at her watch and said, 'I am Detective Inspector Fortune and this is Detective Sergeant Wallace. Is everyone here?'

'Four of our number had an early time on the Old. I imagine they'll be well out on the course by now.' The speaker was the man whose hand was gripped by Blonde Plastic. Rotund, with a pasty face and crinkly, black hair swept back from a high forehead, his pink shirt was open at the neck. His oatmeal jacket looked expensive. He had taken the seat opposite Flick at the other end of the table. He did look like a fat cat, she thought, complete with trophy wife. Anywhere else, she would have assumed her ostentatious jewellery to be fake.

'Please give their names to Sergeant Wallace,' Flick said. 'And you are?'

'I'm Lord Saddlefell, acting chairman of Bucephalus Bank.' He spoke with a strong North of England accent.

'Thank you, Lord Saddlefell. I'm afraid I have to inform you and your colleagues that Mr Hugh Parsley is dead, and the circumstances of his death give rise to suspicion.'

The younger women, in the tracksuit and in the tee

shirt, both gasped. The thin, aloof man suddenly looked visibly distressed. The large woman beside him winced but continued to stare out of the window. Blonde Plastic sniffed and carefully lifted a tissue to her eyes. The faces of Black Plastic and Saddlefell were like stone: solemn, concerned, but not grief-stricken.

Saddlefell shook his hand free of his wife's and spoke again, his tone assertive. 'Am I right in thinking, Inspector, that Mr Parsley's body was found on the second tee this morning?'

'I don't know the source of your information, Lord Saddlefell …'

'One of our group playing golf was on the first tee when he heard that the greenkeeper had found a body. He texted us. Then we heard that Hugh Parsley was missing … This is tragic, tragic,' he added.

Flick tried to regain the initiative. 'Why are you here at all?'

'A conference, Inspector. A useful opportunity to discuss matters of mutual concern away from the pressures of everyday business.'

'And were there any divisions of opinion among you?'

The thin man screwed up his face and shook his head. Saddlefell replied smoothly, 'There always will be, Inspector, when you have a diverse group of independent minded, intelligent people. But yes, our chairman died recently and we planned to elect his successor here. And, to be quite straightforward with you, we have found it hard to agree on whether to lower the threshold of wealth for our clients. You see, we deal only with very high net worth clients, and we manage their financial affairs. We presently do not accept anyone who is not worth at least three million pounds. Some directors wish to lower this figure to one point five million, and we have yet to resolve that issue. You see, we are a niche bank. We say, rightly, that we carry great people, freeing them to get on with whatever business made them rich in the first place.'

'Hence Bucephalus, Alexander the Great's famous horse.' Flick nodded, pleased that a childhood memory had flashed back to her and noting a slight raising of Saddlefell's eyebrows. 'Do you want to be elected chairman?' she asked him.

'I have made myself available,' he replied stiffly. 'I don't know if anyone else will put their hat in the ring.'

The door burst open and four grim-faced men in golfing clothes walked in.

'That body on the second tee ...' the speaker was short, with a pot belly straining against a lime green sweater. A tiny mouth with fleshy lips was set in a round, flat, white face. His accent suggested an expensive education.

'Hugh Parsley, I'm afraid,' Saddlefell said quickly. 'These are the police,' he explained, gesturing at Flick and Wallace, 'and I have fully briefed them about why we are all here.'

The little mouth twitched. 'Was he murdered?' the first golfer demanded. 'The policeman beside the white tent said ...'

'Yes.' Glaring at him, Saddlefell interrupted again. 'I trust by some local madman,' he said, looking at Flick.

There was a moment of silence. One of the four golfers, who looked to be in his early thirties, with a thatch of luxuriant, dark hair and wearing a crazily patterned jumper, rushed to sit beside the woman in the tee shirt Flick thought of as the party gatecrasher and grasped her hand. She did not react. The youngest looking golfer, tall and darkly handsome, put his hand to his mouth as if he might be sick.

When she saw no one was going to say more, Flick brought the meeting to a close. 'Well thank you. This is a murder inquiry, and I hope not to cause too much inconvenience, but I would be obliged if you would all go to your rooms and stay there until either I or Sergeant Wallace have seen you. This may take most of the morning, but you will understand that it has to be done.'

Looking less than happy but raising no objection, the Bucephalus party filed out of the room.

Flick told Wallace to begin by interviewing whoever had served the Parsleys' table the previous evening. She decided to start with the Eglintons.

3

'Typical New Labour peer.' Eileen Eglinton ignored her husband's warning scowl. 'He made a packet,' she said meaningfully, 'then gave a lot to charity, muscular dystrophy I believe, and even more to the Labour Party. Now he's Lord Saddlefell of Tarn Howes.' Her clipped vowels suggested generations of real aristocracy.

Flick looked at her rather than her husband. 'Do you think he'll be the next chairman?' she asked.

Mrs Eglinton's size was emphasised by capacious dark green trousers and a loose-fitting maroon sweater. Her lower jaw protruded slightly and her brown, prematurely wrinkled complexion testified to a life spent outdoors. While downstairs she had stared out of the window, she now turned an unblinking gaze on Flick.

'I hope not. They'll elect Simon if they know what's good for them.'

'That's up to them, my dear.' Simon Eglinton, the tall thin man, had a head that was round, white and smooth. His wispy, straw-coloured hair needed attention from a hairdresser. He appeared to have checked the distress he had shown earlier. He looked steadily at Flick then put aside the putter with which he had been making practice strokes without a ball and sat on the edge of the bed, head bowed, hands clasped.

'Did Mr Parsley have any views on that matter?' Flick asked.

'Oh, Sauce was always loyal,' Mrs Eglinton said before her husband could answer. She occupied an upright chair beside the window. A copy of *The Times*, folded at the crossword, lay on the table in front of her.

'Sauce?' Flick asked.

Simon Eglinton got in before his wife. 'Yes. Hugh Parsley – HP. The sauce, you know. It was his nickname at school and he's never shaken it off.' He paused then added quietly, 'Never shook it off.'

'Simon and Hugh were at Eton together,' Mrs Eglinton explained.

'I gather you dined with the Parsleys last night?' Flick said, thinking that the dead man looked younger than his schoolfriend.

Mrs Eglinton was quicker than her husband again. 'Yes. We went to the Sands Grill on the ground floor. They do a decent steak.'

'Just the four of you?'

'The others went to the Road Hole Restaurant.'

'What did you discuss over dinner?'

'I banned business talk. The men talked golf, and we also discussed holidays.' Simon Eglinton, apparently content for his wife to field the questions, nodded agreement.

'How was Mr Parsley?'

'He seemed fine. A bit cross about not getting a time

on the Old this morning. They have a ballot, you know. He relaxed as the meal progressed.'

'How long was he married to Mrs Parsley?'

'About eight years. He was divorced then got in tow with Belinda when he was with Goldman Sachs. I believe she was a telephonist.' Mrs Eglinton pulled at her left ear. Flick noticed that while the skin of her left hand was rough, with short nails and nicotine staining, her right hand was much smoother, the nails manicured.

Mrs Eglinton smiled. 'I can see you're observant, Inspector. I'm left-handed and use it to do my gardening. In company, I hold my drink with my right hand.' She held up an imaginary wine glass. 'I enjoy a drink, but I'm passionate about my garden. We have a couple of acres.'

Years of competing in a man's world had left Flick's confidence shallow and brittle. Mrs Eglinton's easy self-assurance grated on her. She saw the compliment as patronising, however it may have been meant.

Abruptly she asked, 'Was their marriage happy?' She knew she sounded lower middle class but didn't care.

'I wouldn't say it was unhappy.' Ignoring Flick's raised eyebrow, Mrs Eglinton carried on, 'How is poor Belinda? Is someone with her?'

'She's as you might expect, Mrs Eglinton. And yes, a female officer is with her.'

'Well, I shall do what I can for the girl. She was never very comfortable with Hugh's colleagues. We're the nearest she's got to having friends at the hotel.'

'I've seen her talking quite happily to Mark Forbes,' her husband interjected.

Mrs Eglinton snorted dismissively.

'Where did Mr Parsley stand on the issue raised by Lord Saddlefell about lowering the threshold for clients to one point five million pounds?' Flick tried to keep any note of awe out of her voice.

Simon Eglinton coughed. 'This is very confidential, Inspector. I trust that what we tell you will go no further than necessary?'

'I understand.'

'Things have been difficult in our business since 2008. Terry Saddlefell has always been expansionist, while I believe in doing things as we have always done them, and I'm happy to say that the bank is doing well again. Hugh Parsley was in my camp. Oliver Davidson, one of the golfers, supports me. Saddlefell has Nicola Walkinshaw, that's the lady in black, and Mark Forbes on his side. Forbes was the golfer who spoke when they came in. Since our chairman Sir Paul Monmouth died in September, there has been an even number on the board – six, and none of us on our side is prepared to allow the acting chairman the deciding vote on an issue of this importance. We are all working directors. We have never had non-executives on the board. This weekend we have with us two of our senior employees to inform our discussions, and we intended to elect one of them to bring us back up to seven. I think Gerald Knarston-Smith is the obvious choice, and I have reason to believe that he is against lowering the threshold. I suspect that Sheila Anderson, the other candidate, may hold the opposite view. Gerald was one of the golfers. Sheila was in the tracksuit. I suppose now there will be two vacancies, but I intend to make sure any election is postponed until we know what happened to Hugh.'

'Do you know how Mr Parsley came to be on the golf course last night, sir?' Flick asked.

Simon Eglinton smiled. 'Hugh was always attracted to forbidden fruit, Inspector. At school, at university and during his first marriage.' He shook his head.

'Both marriages,' his wife corrected him.

He frowned at her then continued, 'The girls had gone to bed and we'd discussed some business in the library with Nicola and Sheila. It was late. "C'mon, Eggers," he said, "let's do some illegal putting." So we did. He got golf jackets, putters and balls from the club store and we strolled out of the hotel and round to the sixteenth green of the Old. It was ridiculous, with visibility practically zero, but we'd played on the Eden yesterday afternoon and Hugh's putting had been abysmal. I'd suggested a tip he was desperate to try, and so we went over to the first green where we could at least see something. The R and A is floodlit and there is some light from the town. We spent about ten minutes fooling about but it was still very silly. I said I was going in but he wanted to stay outside. We said goodnight and that was the last I saw of him.' His voice caught.

'Did either of you put a ball in the burn?' Flick asked.

Eglinton appeared puzzled. 'No. Not while I was there, anyway.'

'Could you describe his putter, please, sir?'

'Was that what was used …?'

Flick said nothing.

'Well, it was a hideous thing with a blue grip and metal bits sticking out the back. I told him he'd be better mashing spuds with it and getting a proper putter, like that one,' he indicated the traditional blade he had been handling, 'but he wouldn't listen. He said half the pros use things like his one.'

'Did you see anyone else out then?'

'No.'

'What did you do after you left Mr Parsley?'

Eglinton looked startled then smiled. 'Of course. You have to ask. I came to bed. And stayed here in this room. I imagine I got here about half past eleven. Is that right, dear?'

'I wasn't looking at my watch, but I suppose so,' his wife agreed.

'And you, Mrs Eglinton, what did you do after dinner?'

'I came up here. I'm reading a good book at the moment, a biography of Harold Macmillan, and I wanted to make some progress with it.'

'Did you leave the room at all after that?'

'Well, Inspector, I am one of those smokers the health police are trying to criminalise, so every now and again I sneak out to enjoy my perfectly legal pleasure.'

Flick winced. She blamed cigarettes for her mother's untimely death and was vehemently anti-smoking. 'Alright, but where did you go?' she asked, an edge to her voice.

Mrs Eglinton paid no attention to Flick's disapproval.

'Beside the front door. You meet all sorts there. The night before I was chatted up by one of the waiters.' She gave a vaguely equine snort.

'Did you go for a cigarette after your husband returned?'

She screwed up her face. 'Yes,' she said slowly. 'Yes, I did.'

'How long were you out of the room?'

'Ten, twenty minutes, maybe. I can't remember. I sometimes have two. And some fresh air.'

'Did you see anyone else from the bank party then?'

'No.'

'Do you remember your wife leaving the room, sir?' Flick turned to Eglinton.

'Yes I do. I decided to have a bath. My wife was back when I came out of the bathroom.'

'How long were you in the bathroom?'

'I can't remember. I had a good soak. It had been cold outside. Twenty minutes, maybe.'

'Did you go out again, Mrs Eglinton?'

'No. Not till breakfast.'

'Do either of you remember anything at all that might help us catch Mr Parsley's killer?'

'No.' Mrs Eglinton spoke firmly.

Eglinton shook his head. 'No.' Visibly controlling himself, he pointed an unsteady finger at Flick. 'I met Hugh Parsley during my first week at Eton, Inspector. We fought then, fists, kicks and hair-pulling. The real thing. Then we made it up and became friends. He was my best man and I his – twice. I persuaded him to leave Goldman Sachs to join Bucephalus, the bank my grandfather founded, and he was very good for us, as we were good for him. We were close, Inspector. When two people know each other well for many years …' He looked away, his shoulders quivering. 'May God forgive whoever is responsible. I never will. I wish we still hanged murderers.' The last sentence was barely audible. Abruptly, he turned to face Flick. Speaking slowly and emphatically he said, 'I don't want his memory, or the reputation of my family's bank, to be dragged through the mud.'

Seeing a passion and depth of feeling she had not expected, Flick said, 'I understand, sir. There is one more thing. The body is not nice to look at, but it will be tidied up after the post mortem. Late this afternoon, Mrs Parsley will be taken to Dundee to formally identify her husband. Would you be good enough to accompany her?'

Eglinton looked startled then apprehensive. 'Of course. I shall do my unhappy duty. Not nice to look at?'

'Some of the blows struck his face, but these things can be disguised,' Flick said.

His wife stood up as if to end the discussion. 'My husband has always put his duty first, Inspector. His directorship of his family's bank is almost a sacred trust to him. If he believed it would be better in Saddlefell's hands, he would support him all the way. I want you to understand that.'

'Thank you both very much,' Flick said. 'Someone will be in touch regarding the identification, sir. Meanwhile, please don't leave the hotel.' She could sense the Eglintons relaxing as she closed the door behind her.

In the foyer she found di Falco busy with departing guests. There had been no problems, but no worthwhile information either. Then she liaised with Wallace who had interviewed two directors, Nicola Walkinshaw and Mark Forbes, and Sheila Anderson, the Client Wealth Manager. Forbes could not recall seeing Parsley at all the previous evening and said he had gone to his room to read when dinner was over. He said he had not left his room. Walkinshaw and Anderson confirmed that after dinner they had talked with Parsley and Eglinton. Saddlefell had organised a big table in the Road Hole Restaurant and afterwards some had gone to the Jigger Inn, just outside the hotel. Walkinshaw and Anderson were in the lobby on their way there when Parsley had invited them into the more comfortable library for a malt whisky. They had stayed for nearly an hour, discussing business. The main topic had been international corporate taxation. Both women had commented that the two men had drunk a good deal, sampling some expensive malts. Walkinshaw and Anderson said they had left at the same time, about quarter past ten, and gone to their rooms and stayed there. They had both made phone calls, using the phones in their rooms, Anderson to her husband, at home with their two small children, and Walkinshaw to her partner, a barrister named Freddy Middleton who was due to arrive later on Friday evening. None of those interviewed had seen anything at all suspicious.

'I didn't find out any more about the bank than Lord Saddlefell told us, ma'am,' Wallace said. 'Do you get the feeling they're clamming up on us?'

'The Eglintons had plenty to say.' Flick summarised what they had told her then paused. Absent-mindedly, she felt her stomach then took her hand away rapidly. She added, 'But I thought Lord Saddlefell seemed to be trying to put a lid on what we learn about the bank. Do you think we should try to squeeze more out of the others before we see him together?'

'Right, ma'am. Oh, I forgot. The waiter who served the Parsleys and the Eglintons last night in the Sands Grill said they came in at eight and left about half past nine. They ate steaks and drank a lot of expensive wine. He heard them talking about golf, and the Parsleys were planning a trip to India. The waiter told them about Mumbai, he said. An odd fellow, pale for an Indian. He speaks with a bit of an Indian accent and, excuse me, ma'am, a bit English like you. He seems to know you. He gave me this.'

Wallace dug into a pocket and produced an envelope. Scrawled across the front was 'INSPECTOR Fortune. Personal'. Flick opened it and found a single sheet of paper torn from a notebook. She recognised the spidery hand which had written, 'I shall be at British Golf Museum near old-fashioned ball maker from 10.30 till 11.30. Must talk. Baggo.'

Flick swore under her breath. Seeing Wallace's quizzical look, she muttered, 'This might change everything. You organise the incident room. I think Cupar would be best. Make more inquiries with the staff, and maybe move on to the other non-director, Knarston-Smith. See what he says about the chairmanship and who did what after dinner but definitely leave Saddlefell till I get back. Oh and get hold of Parsley's laptop. He's sure to have brought it with him.' She got up and headed for her car.

4

Flick needed to Google the British Golf Museum on her i-Phone, but was relieved to learn it was where she thought it was, behind the Royal and Ancient Clubhouse. She drove to the car park beside it, entered the squat, glass-fronted building and paid her entrance money.

Soon she came to a tableau showing a nineteenth century craftsman working at a table. His moulded face was grim, he sported long, black sideburns and was poorly dressed. He appeared to be using an awl to compress white feathers into a leather holder. A larger and more vicious looking awl sat on the table at his elbow, a primitive golf ball beside that. In front of her, four men peered through the protective glass.

'Allan Robertson was the Tiger Woods of his day,' one man explained in a rasping New York accent, loud enough for anyone nearby to hear, 'but I sure can't see Tiger sittin' there just makin' balls.' His companions sniggered agreement and they moved on to another exhibit.

Flick stayed put and pretended to listen to the commentary which came on at the touch of a button. She could hear the New Yorker lecturing his friends on Bobby

Jones and stabbed the commentary button again. She was becoming increasingly impatient when she heard a voice in her ear.

'A perfect murder weapon, that big awl, Inspector ma'am.'

She turned to face Detective Sergeant Bagawath Chandavarkar, known as 'Baggo' from his earliest days in the Met. 'What on earth are you doing here, and why all the cloak and dagger stuff?' she hissed.

Although there was no one nearby, Baggo spoke quietly and urgently. 'I am working undercover. After you left, I joined the SFO at Scotland Yard – your friend Inspector Cummings was instrumental. Now I have been seconded to SOCA.' Born and raised in Mumbai, where English grammar still mattered, he had spent his last three school years in Slough after his father, a consultant urologist, moved to Britain. His natural sing-song voice had been flattened by years in the South of England.

'Yes?' Flick showed her impatience.

'You know, the Serious Organised Crime Agency. We have been investigating the Bucephalus Bank. They nearly went under in 2008, but received money from America to keep afloat. Since then we believe they have been money laundering, but they are very clever. The chairman Sir Paul Monmouth was killed in September, and it may not have been an accident. It looked like a hit and run. When we heard they were coming up here, I persuaded the hotel to let me work as a waiter to observe them. Now this murder … I think we should compare notes.'

She digested the implications of what he had said.

'Come to my house, 52 Kinburn Grove. It's ten minutes from the hotel. Can you be there this afternoon between shifts, say at four?'

'I'll be there. Oh, and congratulations on your promotion. But I too have been bumped up. I'm a detective sergeant now. I shall move on to view the other exhibits. I have taken up golf and find this fascinating.'

'Congratulations to you,' she said as he turned away. She shook her head, and taking the quickest route out, retraced her steps.

* * *

Leaving the museum, Flick could see that the white tent had been removed from the second tee and golfers were walking down the first fairway. The area where the body had lain was still fenced off by police tape. The pin had been put on the other side of the green. Golfing life went on as if nothing had happened.

At the hotel, McKellar waited for Flick. He held a polythene production bag containing a wallet.

'No cash in it, ma'am, but it was Parsley's. You'll want it checked for fingerprints, I take it. We found it in a bush in front of the tee. There was some vomit near it, but Robertson said we shouldn't bother getting a sample. You know what I mean, ma'am?' A smirk creased his dour face.

She felt herself blushing. 'Right. Tell the lab we need a result ASAP.' She turned away from McKellar and strode across the lobby.

Having been informed at reception that Wallace was

seeing Mr and Mrs Knarston-Smith, Flick found their room. Though it overlooked the Old Course, it was not as grand as the Eglintons' and was on the second floor of the spa wing adjacent to the Jigger Inn. Wallace opened the door. The golfer wearing the garish sweater was sitting on the bed, his pale face twitching, his hand gripping his wife's knee. Flick had seen criminals look more relaxed during taped interviews. His wife, who had seemed so out of place in the conference room, was less tense than her husband but looked no happier than she had earlier. Flick sat on a chair facing them, her back to the window. Wallace pulled a second chair beside her.

Earnest looking, with thick, oily, black hair brushed straight back so that it gave him about three extra inches of height before flopping to the side, Gerald Knarston-Smith forced a smile. His wife, Cynthia, fashionably thin with artfully untidy, straw-blonde hair that hinted at a spirit of rebellion, pursed her lips and seemed to find something fascinating about her scuffed trainers.

'Mr Knarston-Smith is the manager of the investment arm of the bank. He and his wife were telling me they went to the Jigger Inn last night. As I say, that's the wee white cottage in the hotel grounds. They came back to their room just after eleven and saw nothing of interest,' Wallace reported.

'Who were you with in the pub?' Flick asked.

'Latterly just the Saddlefells.' Between his rapid-fire delivery and his public school accent Gerald did not speak clearly. His eyes darted to his wife, as if seeking approval. She nodded.

'Did the Saddlefells leave at the same time as you?'

'We left before them, didn't we, darling?'

'Yes. Sandi, sorry, Lady Sandi, was set on trying another of her "superior" Islay malts.' Cynthia's tone was dry.

Flick made a mental note but decided not to pursue the matter. She asked, 'Were you aware of any controversy or ill-feeling during the evening?'

Gerald shook his head. Cynthia showed no reaction.

'And you remember nothing that might help our inquiry?'

'Nothing.' He stroked his nose then added, 'I'm afraid.'

'Did you like Hugh Parsley?' Flick asked, hoping to stir some response.

'Oh, er, yes. Yes.' He managed to make the second 'yes' definite. His wife's curled lip told a different story.

'Simon Eglinton?'

'A great chap.' He smiled. His wife nodded.

'Lord Saddlefell?'

Gerald shrugged. 'I've never had a problem with him.'

'Is there a director you do not care for, sir?'

As he hesitated, his wife raised her eyebrows.

Flick said quietly, 'We are trying to find a murderer, and while we have open minds, it is entirely possible that one of Mr Parsley's work colleagues killed him. The sooner we learn what tensions there are in the bank, personal as well as business, the sooner we'll be able to eliminate people from our inquiry and arrest whoever was responsible. So please be frank with us. We won't disclose what you tell us unless it's necessary.'

Gerald frowned. Cynthia nudged his ribs with her elbow. He took a deep breath. 'Well, in confidence, Inspector, I've never really seen eye to eye with Mark Forbes.'

'Why not?'

'Well … he doesn't go out of his way to be liked. He's respected, good at his job, doesn't suffer fools at all …'

'Those he thinks are fools,' Cynthia cut in. 'You're a lot brighter than he is.'

'Yes, well …' Gerald shrugged.

'Don't be wet, Gerald,' Cynthia hissed then addressed Flick. 'Mark Forbes is a vile man, Inspector. He is rude, mean-spirited and he worships money. He refuses to give to charity because he thinks he pays too much in tax. Eileen Eglinton runs a charity clothing store but Forbes puts his stuff on e-bay. It's people like him who give bankers a bad name.'

Suddenly bold, Gerald cut in. 'This year Cynthia ran in the London Marathon. Her father died of cancer and she ran to raise money for cancer research. Everyone in the office sponsored her, even the cleaners, but when I asked Mark, he just said "Don't be silly". She did it in four hours, fifty-one and raised over four thousand pounds,' he added proudly, patting her knee.

'And Forbes is a total fake.' Cynthia warmed to her character assassination. 'He'll tell you he was at Rugby, but it was the comprehensive, not the real thing. God knows what he based that accent on. He makes The Queen sound common. His mother visited the bank once and he hustled her out of the door before she could speak to anyone. But Jean at reception told you she had a broad

Midlands accent.' She looked to Gerald for confirmation.

He nodded energetically then said, 'He's a terrible bully round the office. I think he enjoys making some of the girls cry.' He paused. 'And I've heard him boast about how he nipped out and pinched a taxi he'd heard a disabled man order in a restaurant.'

'What does Mr Forbes do in the bank?' Flick asked.

Gerald looked disappointed by the change of subject. 'He's in charge of futures, commodities and derivatives.'

'Is there anything at all unusual or, well, dodgy about how he does business?'

Gerald's eyes swivelled round the room. 'I do not believe so.'

Wallace said, 'But you were playing golf with Mr Forbes this morning, sir.'

'That's the way it was arranged. Hugh Parsley and Simon wanted to play the Old with their wives, but they didn't get a time in the ballot. There were four more of us who really wanted to play the Old: Forbes, me, Oliver Davidson and Bruce Thornton. Actually,' he giggled nervously, 'we all wanted to avoid having to play with Lord Saddlefell. I'm not very good but he is dreadful. At our summer golf outing someone called him "the mad axeman". His swing is a sort of chopping movement and he gets incredibly angry at bad shots. So it was worth putting up with Forbes. But I wasn't looking forward to it. He plays unbelievably slowly and he never lets other players pass through. On the first tee, he immediately bagged Bruce as his partner. He's a professional, you know.'

'A professional golfer?' Wallace asked.

'Yes,' Gerald said, pulling a face. 'Oh dear. Well, I suppose you'll find out anyway. There was a bit of a scandal. Oliver Davidson – he's our currencies man - left his wife and children last year and came out as being gay. He's brought his new partner, Bruce, here with him. Bruce is an assistant pro at Haleybourne Golf Club. It's to the west of London. But he comes from St Andrews, I believe. Last night he went off to see some old mates. Either that or he was body-swerving dinner. Gosh.' Gerald stroked his nose. 'You know, I believe Hugh Parsley was a member at Haleybourne. Oh dear.'

'What is it?' Flick asked.

'This could be nothing, Inspector, but Hugh Parsley was really homophobic.'

'You must tell us what you know, Mr Knarston-Smith,' Flick said, her voice severe, wondering if it was just nerves that had made him open up.

'It was so embarrassing. Hugh didn't care what he said. If Oliver had just been an employee and not a director I'm sure he would have taken the bank to the cleaners.'

'What sort of things did Mr Parsley say?'

'Hugh called Oliver "Pinkpound". Last month Oliver announced that he had just made a million pounds by sitting on his bottom doing nothing, and Hugh said loudly, in front of staff too, "It's not often your bottom's doing nothing, Pinkpound". The rest of us didn't know where to look. It was awful.'

'How did Mr Davidson react?' Flick asked.

'He ignored it, or pretended to, but you could see he was mortified.'

'How do you get on with Mr Davidson?' Flick asked.

'Fine,' Gerald said. 'He keeps himself to himself. Some people think he's lost interest in the bank.' He smiled. 'He keeps a jacket in a cupboard and drapes it over the back of his chair as if he's somewhere about the office when all the time he's out for ages.'

'Doing what?'

'I've no idea.'

'What did you think of Mr Parsley?' Flick asked Cynthia.

Gerald bowed his head as she replied, 'He would try it on with anyone. At one bank do he told me it would advance Gerald's career if I had an affair with him. I told him to piss off. And yesterday I could see Sheila Anderson keeping her distance.'

'What about his business ethics?' Flick asked.

'I really could not say.' Gerald went back to stuffy mode while Cynthia looked sceptical.

'But Mr Eglinton and he were great friends, I believe?'

Gerald nodded. 'They'd been at school together. Simon Eglinton is a good man. He saw the best in Hugh.'

'And Mrs Eglinton? Might Mr Parsley have tried it on with her?'

Gerald shook his head. 'If he did, she'd have given him short shrift.'

'She's a real lady,' Cynthia said. 'She speaks the same way to everyone, and she has a great sense of humour. Her father's the Earl of Knapdale, you know. She's actually Lady Eileen Eglinton, but she never rams it down your throat.'

'What about the woman on the board, Nicola Walkinshaw?' Flick asked.

'I don't see much of her,' Gerald said shaking his head emphatically.

'Any reason for that?' Wallace asked.

'No.' He shook his head again. Cynthia frowned.

'How do you get on with Sheila Anderson?' Flick asked, looking at Gerald.

He seemed to relax. 'I don't have a problem with Sheila, honestly. I know why you ask: the vacant seat on the board. Gosh, I suppose there'll be two now.' He put his hand to his mouth. To judge from her raised eyebrows, his wife had realised this already.

'Who do you want to be the next chairman?' Flick asked.

Knarston-Smith gulped. 'Well …'

'My husband has not come out in favour of anyone,' his wife interjected sharply.

'What about lowering the wealth threshold?'

'I … I haven't decided.'

Flick exchanged looks with Wallace. She asked, 'Are you sure there is nothing else you can tell us that might assist?'

They both shook their heads.

Flick thanked the Knarston-Smiths and told them not to hesitate if they thought of anything else. Out in the corridor she realised she was hungry. 'I could do with something to eat. Let's go to the conference room and order a sandwich.'

* * *

After some discussion with Jocelyn, the conference room they had used that morning was given to the police for their inquiry and a Police Only notice was pinned to the door. Flick was handed a key and sandwiches and coffee were promised. To her surprise it was Baggo who brought them, carrying the tray one-handed at shoulder level. As he laid out a tablecloth, plates and knives, Wallace finished a call on his mobile.

'Detective Sergeant Wallace, meet Detective Sergeant Chandavarkar,' Flick said. 'He's undercover, investigating possible money laundering at the Bucephalus Bank. I'll go home this afternoon and he'll brief me there. Don't tell the rest of the squad about him, but you two should know each other.'

The two men shook hands.

'Most people call me Baggo, but the Inspector always seems reluctant.'

The older man looked from Baggo to Flick. 'I'm Lance – to most people,' he said slowly. Both men grinned.

She said, 'Where did you pick up these waiting skills, Chandavarkar? You never showed them off in the Wimbledon canteen.'

'I learned this trade in the Taste of Mumbai on Kensington High Street. A holiday job. And if he had known all that I could do, Inspector No would have had me making him a vindaloo every day. You Christians would call it hiding my light under a bushel, but to me it was no more than common sense.'

'And my common sense is telling me our murderer is part of the bank party,' Wallace said. 'The house to house inquiries have got nowhere, except one old biddy who says she saw a youth with a shaved head running out of Granny Clark's Wynd and onto the golf course waving a hammer. It was two in the morning, she says. She was out looking for her cat. But she can't remember if she had her glasses on, she had most of a bottle of Gordon's inside her, and last month she complained about a witches' coven meeting in the Valley of Sin. That's the dip at the front of the eighteenth green, ma'am.'

Baggo sniggered. 'Where are witches supposed to meet? It must be difficult to find a place to park your broomstick.' He winked at Flick, who glared back. She had forgotten how irritating Chandavarkar could be.

Wallace looked at him then laughed. 'So you're a comedian are you? It was just some drunken students having a picnic so there were no broomsticks with parking tickets.'

Flick sighed. She wished she had a better sense of humour, and was disappointed that Wallace should find Chandavarkar funny. She had never seen him as the frivolous type and dreaded the prospect of the pair of them sparking off each other. 'We'll be duty bound to tell the defence about the old bat so she can muddy the waters at a trial,' she said, trying to be less obviously out on a limb. 'Now off you go,' she said to Baggo. 'You're not getting a tip. I'll see you later.'

'Inspector, ma'am, it will be difficult for me to get off at four, and as we do not know much, it will not take long to brief you. I could do that now and say you were questioning me about the Parsleys and the Eglintons last night.'

Flick saw the sense in that. 'Right, shoot,' she said.

Baggo sat at the table and leaned forward. 'As you know, the SFO have seconded me to SOCA. Under them, the UKFIU deals with proceeds of crime and terrorism, and we rely on SARs from the public.'

'For goodness sake speak English,' Flick said, her mouth full of tomato sandwich.

'So sorry, Inspector ma'am. In the SFO the surest way up the greasy pole is to speak in acronyms. A SAR is a Suspicious Activity Report from the public, and it was through one of them that we learned that the Bucephalus Bank has been buying a lot of euro-bonds. These are unregistered bearer bonds in a denomination not native to the country of issue. For example, you might get a euro-yen bond issued in Britain. The important things are that the owner remains anonymous and they pay out to the bearer, whoever that may be. They are very useful if you want to keep your financial affairs secret. Such bonds have been illegal in the USA for thirty years. We have also been contacted by the Federal Reserve in America who are suspicious about the Sulphur Springs Bank of Atlanta. It has a traditional, blue-chip image but a lot of dodgy clients. It has a close relationship with Bucephalus. In 2008, like so many others, Bucephalus was near to going under. It was saved by a loan from Sulphur Springs. We believe the price may have included assistance in money laundering. The Feds think that drug money is paid by the criminals into Sulphur Springs. It disguises the source by pretending that some of its toxic debt has come good. It then sends the money to Bucephalus in exchange for fictitious invoices for banking or advisory services. Bucephalus then buys euro-bonds which it presumably passes back to the American drug dealers. They can either cash in the bonds and take the money home or simply keep the funds abroad. Of course both banks will have taken hefty cuts as money laundering can mean a lot of jail time.'

He paused, looking hopefully at the last egg sandwich.

'Go on then,' Flick said, pushing the plate towards him.

'Bucephalus,' he said, his mouth full, 'has a lot of PEPs as clients. Sorry, Politically Exposed Persons. Dictators of Third World countries, international football committee men, people like that. They syphon off millions given as international aid or bribes, and euro-bonds suit them down to the ground. All banks are supposed to do money laundering checks, but we have heard that since 2008 Bucephalus barely looks at their PEPs. It used to be a by-word for integrity and class, too. What makes it difficult is that there are "Chinese walls" in the bank, and we have no real idea how many individuals are involved, who they are or how we might prove it. So I am here, eavesdropping, but I haven't learned much, except how to fold a linen napkin in a fancy restaurant. They used cheap paper in the Taste of Mumbai.'

'Right,' Flick said. 'You've given us a lot to think about. These inquiries could well be linked. Do you have anything on Sir Paul Monmouth's death?'

Baggo shook his head. 'Only that he was a creature of habit and careful of himself. He was run over in Camden

High Street going home from work at his usual time. It was a stolen four-by-four and travelling very fast. The vehicle was abandoned nearby. No trace of the driver.'

'Well keep in touch. We'll have to pool what we know.'

'Of course, but please, Inspector ma'am, do not compromise my inquiry. You have very delicate feet, but it would be bad if they were to trample unwisely.'

Flick looked at him coldly. 'I have no intention of doing any trampling, but this is my territory and a murder inquiry takes precedence over money laundering.'

The companionable atmosphere had evaporated. They swapped mobile numbers then Baggo cleared up and took away the tray. Flick thought for a moment. 'I think Messrs Davidson and Thornton should be next on our list,' she said.

* * *

As he made his way back to the serving area Baggo was deep in thought. Fortune had it over him in three ways: this was her territory, murder trumped money laundering, and she out-ranked him. The chances were that the murder or murders were connected to the financial crimes and that the Fife police would ruin things for him by scaring off informants or offering immunity in return for evidence. It had taken a good deal of persuasion before he had been allowed to go undercover and a successful outcome of this inquiry would be a major plus on his CV. Baggo was ambitious and Superintendent Chandavarkar had a good ring to it. There was only one solution: he would have to solve the murder himself. His starting point would be something he had not shared. The anonymous report which had alerted SOCA to the unusual number of bearer bonds bought by Bucephalus had named Hugh Parsley as the director most involved.

5

As a director, Oliver Davidson merited a room overlooking the Old Course on the first floor along the corridor from the Eglintons. He let Flick and Wallace in, then resumed his seat at a table beside the window. A plate of smoked salmon, half-eaten, lay in front of him. Opposite him Bruce Thornton, the young man who in the conference room had appeared nauseous, finished off an American-sized burger. Between them stood an empty bottle of sauvignon blanc. Davidson gestured towards the bed. Wondering if he had deliberately put her lower than him and facing the light, Flick sat down. Wallace remained standing.

There was a world-weary defiance about his tone as Davidson offered no platitudes about the deceased. He claimed to have had an ordinary professional relationship with him. He had dined at Saddlefell's table the previous evening then had gone to the Jigger, staying for only one dram. He had returned to his room about quarter to ten and found Bruce already there. As they had an early time on the Old they had gone to bed. Neither had left the room. A tall man with crinkly fair hair going grey, Flick thought there was a melancholy look to Davidson's prematurely wrinkled face. On the other side of the table,

Thornton alternately stared at his plate and nodded like a puppet. The scene in front of her made Flick think of under-rehearsed amateur actors playing a married couple.

She turned to the younger man. 'It would be helpful to know what you were doing last night,' she said.

A rabbit caught in headlights expression flashed across his face. 'Oh, I went out to meet friends.' His voice was high, the accent Scottish but not broad.

'Yes?'

'I come from St Andrews actually. I arranged to meet some of the guys I played boys' golf with.'

'Where did you go?'

'Ma Bell's. It's on The Scores.'

'A few drinks?'

'A few.' He grinned nervously.

'When did you get back here?'

'About half past nine.'

'Did anyone see you come in?'

Thornton shifted on his chair. 'Can't remember.'

Wallace intervened. 'Excuse me, ma'am.' He moved close to Thornton and peered at the left side of his face. 'That looks very like a black eye, son. How did you get it?'

'Oh, that.' He forced a laugh. 'Wednesday morning in the pro's shop. The other assistant was trying to balance a driver upright on his index finger. It fell and hit me.' He held out his right index finger and balanced an imaginary club on it. He laughed again and shrugged. Flick noted the bulging muscle at the base of his thumb.

'His name?' Wallace asked.

'Tony Longstone.'

'The club where you work?'

After a moment's hesitation he whispered, 'Haleybourne.'

'And if we ask Longstone, he'll back you up?' Wallace's voice oozed scepticism.

Davidson snapped, 'Are these questions necessary?'

'Yes,' Flick replied. 'Will he back you up?'

'Please don't contact Haleybourne.' Thornton looked from one detective to the other. Neither spoke. 'They don't know …'

'That you're gay?' Flick spoke gently.

Thornton nodded unhappily.

'We have no wish to embarrass you or anyone else, but we must know the truth – all of it.' She fixed her eyes on Davidson. 'From both of you. Now,' she turned back to the younger man, 'did you get the black eye from an accident at Haleybourne?'

'Yes.'

'Did you go out last night, meet old friends and return about half past nine?'

'Yes.'

'Your friends' names, please.'

'Archie Turnbull, Linda Hughes, Gregor Mathieson, Tam Auld, Ellie Johnston, Fraser Thompson. And you can talk to them. They're okay about me being gay.' He emphasised 'they're'.

'You come from here, yet you're not staying with your parents?'

Thornton looked at her with respect. 'As you've probably guessed, they can't handle it. Dad especially.'

'Had you planned to see them this weekend?'

'Archie said he'd visit them, but unless they've changed their attitude, no.'

'And you'll give us addresses of your parents and your friends?'

'If you really want them.'

'Please.'

Thornton shrugged, went to the bedside table and wrote some names and addresses on an hotel notepad. He tore out the pages and handed them to Wallace.

'I can't remember all of them,' he said unapologetically.

'Did you see anything at all odd as you came in last night?' Flick asked.

'No.'

'And did you or Mr Davidson leave the room after he had come up to join you?'

'No.'

'Did you like Mr Parsley?' Flick shot in the question she was really interested in.

'Where is this leading, Inspector?' Davidson interjected. 'Are we suspects?'

'We are trying to eliminate persons from our inquiry, sir,' Flick said smoothly. 'If people answer questions truthfully at this stage, it is generally less embarrassing for them in the end. Did you like Mr Parsley?' The question was addressed to Thornton. 'I believe he was a member at Haleybourne.'

The rabbit in headlights look returned. 'Well I …' he stammered, 'I didn't have much to do with him. I believe he played mostly at some other club.'

'Did he see you here yesterday?'

'I don't know. I didn't see him.'

Davidson cut in. 'Bruce came up on the train yesterday evening and went out soon afterwards. He hasn't been around the hotel much.'

'Have you talked about Mr Parsley?' Flick asked.

'Not really,' Davidson replied immediately, before Thornton's shrug became obvious.

'But you didn't like Mr Parsley, did you, sir?' Flick eyeballed Davidson.

He glared back at her.

'He called you "Pinkpound" round the office and subjected you to a lot of homophobic abuse.'

As Thornton buried his head in his hands, Davidson's face became red. 'I don't know who told you that, but he did make the odd comment.'

'It was more than the odd comment, wasn't it? It was persistent verbal bullying.'

Davidson shook his head.

'Did you realise Mr Thornton's employers did not know about his sexuality?'

'I don't want to say anything more,' Davidson said forcibly.

'And before you came to St Andrews, did you know Mr Parsley was a member at Haleybourne?'

Davidson turned to stare out of the window.

'I'll take that as a "no". So when you learned he was a member of the club where Mr Thornton works, you knew that he could make things difficult for him?'

Davidson showed no reaction.

'You wanted to protect your partner, didn't you?'

Davidson clenched his fists and stood up so that he towered over Flick, who remained seated on the bed. Watching carefully, Wallace moved closer. After a moment's tension, Davidson stepped towards the door. With such dignity as he could muster, he said coldly, 'Homophobia takes many forms, Inspector, and is sometimes quite subtle. This interview is at an end, and should you want to question either of us again, we shall have lawyers present. Good afternoon, Inspector.'

Flick remained seated. She said, 'It would help us to eliminate you if we could find someone else with a motive to kill Mr Parsley. Are you sure you can't help us with that?'

Davidson opened the door. 'Good afternoon, Inspector,' he repeated.

Without a word, Flick got up and strode out, Wallace close behind.

* * *

'I'm Lady Sandi Saddlefell. Pleased to meet you.' The heavily made-up Blonde Plastic extended her right hand as if it were to be kissed rather than shaken. 'That's S-a-n-d-i, the superior way of spelling it,' she added with a condescending smile, more twisted than her surgeon would have intended. While the 'Oi'm' was pure Essex, the 'Seddlefail' was evidence of ambitious elocution. Flick glanced at Wallace, who was paying close attention to his notebook. He looked as if he was biting his tongue.

Twenty minutes later Wallace's expression had changed

to one of boredom. Saddlefell was a master of the art of answering questions with apparent frankness while giving away nothing. His unapologetically Northern accent reminded Flick of a cricketer her father had loathed, Yorkshire's Geoffrey Boycott, who had the ability to remain at the crease for hours without scoring many runs. Saddlefell could certainly keep a straight bat. The only new information he had divulged was that he and his wife had finished their drams in the Jigger and had gone to bed at about quarter past eleven. They had seen none of the rest of the party then and had remained in their room until morning. There was no significant personal ill-feeling among the directors, and if he had heard homophobic remarks addressed to Davidson he would have reprimanded the speaker. The bank was making satisfactory profits, though like all others they had experienced some difficult moments in 2008. It had been the inherent strength of the bank that had saved it, not loans from America or anywhere else. At no point did the bullish façade waver.

'Exactly what does your bank do?' Flick asked in exasperation.

The simplicity of this question seemed to surprise Saddlefell. 'What any bank does. We look after clients' money.'

'And make money for yourselves?'

'Of course,' he replied stiffly. 'I'm not sure that I like the tone of that question, Inspector. I have to say I am disappointed by the amount of attention you have devoted to me and my colleagues when it is clear that this murder must have been the work of some unfortunate local with severe mental health issues. You are, if I may say so, quite inexperienced and during the time I have spent waiting for you today I have made contact with your divisional commander. It appears that we have a number of mutual friends. Should it become necessary, I will have no hesitation in making known my views on the investigation.'

The feelings of hurt and anger, so familiar to Flick when she was Inspector No's sergeant, weighed down her stomach like lead, but she was not going to let it show. 'Lord Saddlefell,' she said quietly, 'you can express your views to anyone you like. I shall investigate this death as I think fit, and I can tell you that we are pursuing a number of lines of inquiry. I assume you want to help us as much as you can, so I will ask you: what was Mr Parsley's role in the bank?'

Saddlefell's expression did not change. He would be a good poker player, Flick thought.

The next few seconds felt like minutes. Then Saddlefell spoke. 'There are two arms of our bank, the client wealth management arm and the investment arm. Mr Parsley's area of special responsibility was in the investment arm, overseeing lending, when our money goes out, and gearing, when we borrow from others. All directors have special responsibilities. They have to bring something to the table. For example, I am responsible for our property holdings. I trust that makes it clear.'

'Are you aware of any irregularities in the area for which Mr Parsley was responsible?'

'No. He was extremely good at his job.'

'And did he always obey the rules?'

'Yes. I trust you are not suggesting otherwise or I will telephone your divisional commander.'

Brusquely, Flick thanked the Saddlefells and left, not troubling to ask them to let her know if they learned anything useful.

'The Bucephalus is a superior bank, you know,' Lady Saddlefell trilled as Wallace closed the door.

Flick wondered what the Saddlefells talked about when alone. The intelligence gap was as broad as the Firth of Tay. After wittering about 'superior' Islay malts, Lady Saddlefell had sat at a window, applying a 'superior' shade of pink to her fingernails and ignoring the increasingly tense confrontation. She appeared totally underwhelmed by the magnificent view from her window across the Old Course to the Royal and Ancient Clubhouse, an iconic building due to its situation and the confident confusion of its architecture.

In the lift Flick muttered to Wallace, 'Please God give that woman another word for tomorrow. If I hear "superior" again today, I won't be responsible for my actions.' As she spoke she realised that Sandi fought a battle against feelings of insecurity, just as she did. She just tackled it differently.

'It's undoubtedly a superior sort of mystery, ma'am,' Wallace said innocently, earning one of Flick's killer glares.

* * *

'And if ye try onything, ye'll have ma brither tae answer to. He gets ootae Perth next week.'

'Ootae Perth?' Baggo was mystified. Sharon was the chambermaid who looked after the first floor where the bank directors' rooms were situated. Having negotiated some time off from his boss, he had invited her to have a drink with him that night. Now he wondered if he would understand anything she said.

'The jail, daftie. Whit planet are ye aff?'

'I am from Mars. And you are from Venus. I'll see you at the staff entrance at ten. Must fly.' He blew her a kiss, flapped imaginary wings and rushed back to the service counter.

* * *

'Dr MacGregor! What can you tell me?' Flick spoke from the newly set up incident room in Cupar. The sight of desks, telephones and computers with people working at them had given her a boost. She hoped this call from the pathologist would enable her to put plenty of information on the whiteboard.

'Quite a lot Inspector, from the important to the trivial, but then who knows what small detail is going to snare the killer?'

'Tell me.'

'For a start the late Mr Parsley liked a drink. He had consumed both whisky and red wine before he died. At the time of death he was roughly three times the UK drink driving limit. His last meal was a steak, medium-rare I suspect, with spinach and chips, followed by cheese, probably Stilton. I'll give you all the technical details in writing tomorrow, but I believe that he died about one this morning. I could be out by up to an hour either way.'

'What about the cause of death?'

'Intra-cranial haemorrhage, as I thought. I might be accused of speculating to some degree, and not all of this will appear in my report, but aided by the putter recovered from the burn, I have a pretty clear picture of what happened. The first point of interest is that there are no defensive wounds, nothing on the outer aspect of the arms or hands to suggest Mr Parsley tried to shield his head from any part of this vicious assault. I infer that he was taken by surprise. The heaviest blow was to the right of his skull above his ear. Based on the shape of the wound and the damage to the skin, I believe that blow could have been inflicted by the face of the putter recovered from the burn. It could not have been inflicted by the back of the putter. None of the injuries could have been caused by the ball scoop.

'The injury to the back of the neck could also have been caused by the face of the putter. Marks on the skin would be consistent with that. The injuries to the left temple were caused by repeated striking of that area by two different surfaces, probably the face and then the back of the putter. I estimate that around seven blows in all were landed there.

'Here comes my reconstruction. Mr Parsley has his back to his assailant when he is struck from behind by a right-handed person holding the putter in a conventional grip and using a baseball-type swing. The blow lands just above and in front of his right ear. Had Parsley seen the person swinging the putter he would have almost certainly avoided being hit or deflected the blow. He falls forward and a second blow to the back of his neck is struck probably by the same implement. Face down, he is then attacked by a right-handed person using first the face then the back of the putter, standing in front of Parsley's head and employing a golf-type swing. Had it been a left-hander they would have to have stood very close to his torso. More importantly, the last few swings left an impression on the skin and bone, and I can tell that when the back of the putter was being used the toe of the club pointed down, not up as it would have if swung left-handed. I said I might be accused of speculation, but listening to myself, I would be happy to defend my reasoning in court as deduction. Is all that clear?'

'Thank you, yes. How many attackers do you believe there were?'

'I can't say. It could well have been a single assailant.'

'Can you comment on how strong any of the attackers might be?'

'Some of the blows would have required a degree of strength. A reasonably but not exceptionally strong woman could have managed.'

'You said the heaviest blow was to the right side of the head?'

'I think so. I base that on the damage to the skull. That blow caused significant bony injury. Although the left side of the face appeared to have got the worst of it, the underlying bone was not so severely affected.'

'Should we be looking for blood spatter on trouser legs?'

'There would have been some spatter from the last few swings, and drops of blood might have reached the feet and legs of the assailant.'

'What about the timing?' Flick asked.

'I've based the time of death mainly on body temperature. The slight evidence of post-mortem lividity and rigor mortis would be consistent with my estimate. So would the stomach contents. I am told that he ate between eight-fifteen and nine-thirty. His food had not yet passed out of his stomach into the small intestine. If he was deeply unconscious after the assault his digestive tract might have worked more slowly than usual. I believe that the assault took place at least one and perhaps two hours before death. The blows to each temple fractured the bone which splintered and tore arteries. Blood from the arteries collected inside the skull and formed clots. These continued to grow and compressed both sides of the brain. I cannot be exact, but I estimate that the clots we observed took between one and two hours to form. The clot on the right side was larger than that on the left. Of course, once the heart stopped the clots stopped growing. A similar haemorrhage was found at the base of the skull and that increased the pressure on the brain. After the attack it is likely he lay where he was until he died.'

'Had he been given immediate medical attention, would he have lived?'

'Perhaps. An operation to drill holes in the skull and relieve the pressure on the brain might have saved him. Or it might not. He would probably have suffered permanent brain damage.'

'You believe the attack took place where he was found?'

'Yes. There was a significant quantity of blood, including spatter, on the grass round his head.'

'Thank you, Doctor,' Flick said, genuinely grateful for the fullness of the information. Too many pathologists, in her view, were wary of committing themselves to anything they could not justify with unassailable confidence.

'Not at all Inspector. How are your inquiries proceeding?'

'They're just proceeding so far, but your input has been really helpful.'

'Well good hunting then. And feel free to call me if you think I can help further. And, Inspector Fortune,'

'Yes?'

'You ask some good questions.' The phone clicked.

Trying not to feel too pleased with herself after that unexpected compliment, she picked up her green pen and began to write on the whiteboard.

6

Noel Osborne, formerly the Met's 'Inspector No', swallowed the last bite of his churro and wiped the sugar from his hands onto the leather upholstery of the Mercedes. He felt inside the bag he had bought in Malaga Airport. Two left. Thank goodness for the packs of sugar-roasted almonds he had in his case. When he wasn't drinking he needed them as much as cigarettes. He scratched his crotch then lit up.

'Not in the car please, sir!' The driver had one of these gravelly voices the Sweaties thought made them sound hard. Mustn't call them Sweaties, Osborne reminded himself. He was on their territory. He inhaled deeply and blew the smoke at the driver just to show who was boss. The man was an idiot: hadn't even got his name right. Just as well he had spotted the Old Course Hotel board the fool was carrying, or he'd still be at Edinburgh Airport. He sucked in another satisfying lungful then, unhurriedly, pressed the button to open the window. When he felt the blast of cold, damp air he threw the cigarette out quickly and closed the window.

He looked out over the Fife countryside but in the early evening darkness could make out nothing. A couple of weeks had passed since he had answered the phone in his rented apartment near the beach in Fuengirola and heard a man with a North of England accent who called himself Lord Saddlefell ask if he would investigate a murder. He had thought it was a wind-up but had Googled the names Saddlefell had mentioned and discovered that Sir Paul Monmouth, chairman of the Bucephalus Bank, had been killed in a hit and run incident in London. In subsequent calls Saddlefell had told him that he was sure Monmouth had been murdered but the directors did not want the police prying into their clients' affairs. Osborne was to find out who was responsible without troubling about things that did not concern him. Having realised the man was for real, Osborne had haggled over his fee. He wanted to move out of town, rent a place with a swimming pool up in the hills near Mijas, and that would cost money.

Within an hour of Parsley's body being found Saddlefell had phoned in a panic. There had been another murder. He gave in to all Osborne's demands and told him to get himself to St Andrews as soon as he could. After a lunchtime flight Osborne would reach St Andrews in time for dinner. With some apprehension he asked himself if the bankers would all be wankers.

He closed his eyes. Twenty-four hours earlier he had been in bed, with Maria on top. He visualised her dark nipples brushing his lips, his hands kneading her fat arse … If he moved to Mijas would she move in? Did he want her to move in? Before she came on the scene his life had been given over to internet porn and cheap Rioja. But when a woman got her claws into a man she would take liberties.

That was a law of nature. Already she was bloody touchy and insisted he paid her for housekeeping not sex. It was just as well he was off the batter. He was an all or nothing man and for this job he would need to be sharp …

'Welcome to the Old Course Hotel, Mr van Bilt.' Osborne opened his eyes to find a clown in a kilt holding his door open.

'You mean Osborne,' he muttered as he clambered out. 'Pillock,' he added audibly once in the foyer.

Five minutes later he was in his room, wondering what he should do next. The phone rang. It was Saddlefell, who wanted to see him urgently. Osborne was hungry so they agreed to meet at the Sands Grill on the ground floor.

When Osborne emerged from the lift, Saddlefell was walking up and down outside the restaurant, agitation in every jerky stride and anxious glance. After a peremptory handshake he led Osborne to a table in an alcove where they would not be overheard. Sensing weakness, Osborne's confidence rose.

'You come well recommended,' Saddlefell began.

Osborne tried not to show surprise. His entire career had been a battle against authority.

'You got results,' the banker continued. 'And if the Justice Department didn't like the appeals against contrived confessions, planted evidence and police brutality, many in the Home Office did like the way you put the bad guys behind bars. I believe you know Lord Carr of Trustworth? No? He knows you and was very impressed by your handling of the literary agent murders in London.'

'Called for a delicate touch,' Osborne conceded.

'And that's exactly what we need here. We have clients who are rich, important and sensitive to bad publicity. I am convinced that someone among the senior people in the bank is a murderer. I need you to find out who it is before the police do, and to make sure they get evidence which will sink the guilty party. I think you know what I mean.'

'I've always believed in old-fashioned methods,' Osborne said ambiguously.

Saddlefell smiled. 'Excellent. You've brought your laptop, as I asked? Good. I'll e-mail profiles of all the bank people here and what I know about these two killings. Save it on your computer then delete the e-mail. Have your supper and you can read it all tonight. Oh, and I'd better give you this. The password for the zip file.' He pushed a folded piece of paper across the table. 'Tomorrow you can start interviewing. The other directors have agreed that you should be brought in, for the reasons I've given, and the two senior employees we have with us have been told to cooperate. Let me know if anyone gives you problems, any right to remain silent crap. That includes wives or partners. I'll leave it up to you when you tell the police what you're doing. I don't know whether they'll help or not. They've got an inexperienced woman heading their inquiry so I expect you to have her for breakfast.'

'What's her name?' Osborne asked.

'Inspector Fortune. Quite young. Not bad-looking, either. From her accent I'd say she might come from London. Is anything wrong?'

'We've met,' Osborne said. Inside he was cursing. Flick bloody by-the-book Fortune would suss out what he was up to in no time, and she wouldn't lift a finger to help him.

'Terry! Good to see you at last!' A large American with a Southern drawl sat down at the table and wrung Saddlefell's hand as if he had saved his life.

'Webb!' Saddlefell responded with an enthusiasm Osborne could tell was phony. 'Noel Osborne, meet Webb van Bilt III, a business colleague from Atlanta. He's missing Thanksgiving just to be with us.'

'This trip has gotten me out of a heap of trouble back home. Marlene wanted me to go to Kansas to meet her folks while my mom expected me to be with her in Sacramento. This way both are a little mad at me, but not a lot. And I don't have to eat turkey, which I hate.'

'Well, thank you for coming. Did you have a good journey?'

'Until I reached Edinburgh. There was no car to meet me off the London plane. Eventually I hitched a ride crammed in the back of the hotel mini-bus, but now my suitcase is missing. It must have gotten left behind at the airport in the confusion. But what's this about Hugh? Is it true he's been murdered? It's terrible. I can't believe it.'

''Fraid so,' Saddlefell said. 'I'll tell you about it over a drink. I'm sorry about the car. I told Knarston-Smith to make sure that one should pick you up.'

'Well, best laid schemes, and all that,' van Bilt said. 'Are you eating now? I could sure use a Martini. To drink a toast to Hugh, if nothing else.'

Saddlefell said, 'I could do with a drink too. Noel's

hungry I believe, so we'll see you tomorrow.' He smiled pointedly at Osborne, got up and left.

Long used to rejection, Osborne had a look at the menu but he fancied a curry and the bank was paying.

'Oi, waiter!' he shouted. 'Bring me a prawn vindaloo.'

* * *

'Service!' With a sigh of relief, Baggo put the steaming dish up. 'No, hang on!' he said as the waiter reached for it. He sprinkled some chopped coriander over the brown sauce. 'That's it,' he said.

As soon as he had received the summons to the Sands Grill kitchen he regretted boasting to his new work-mates about his skill in creating hot Indian dishes. Prawn vindaloo was not even on the a la carte menu but Graham Fallon, the chef, had a can-do attitude and Baggo had been astonished at the variety of ingredients available, including garam masala. There had been no ghee, but he had made do with unsalted butter to fry the chilli, garlic, onion, ginger, curry powder, turmeric and vinegar he hoped would burn the roof off the mouth of the awkward guest.

'Who is this man?' he asked.

'I heard he was a private eye,' one of the waiters said. 'I thought Lord Saddlefell was going to eat with him, but they talked for a bit and Saddlefell left with an American.'

Baggo went to the door leading to the dining room and looked out. His heart sank. Redder, fatter and sleazier-looking than he remembered, Inspector No was munching his way through his curry with obvious relish. Baggo's first instinct was to hide as No would ruin his cover. Then he had another thought and approached his old boss.

'Is your prawn vindaloo alright, sir?' he asked.

No did not look up. 'Yeh,' he said, shoving another heaped spoonful into his mouth.

Waiters are invisible, Baggo thought. 'I remembered that this was your favourite, and I am delighted to have satisfied such an esteemed guest.'

No looked up. It took a moment and a glance at the staff nameplate before the penny dropped. 'Baggo!' he said. 'What the hell are you doing here?'

'My career has changed direction, gov. I am now in catering. Eventually I hope to have my own place, but first I must learn my trade.'

'But what about the police?'

'It was one old-fashioned method too many, gov. There was this dirty, rotten scoundrel we were never going to catch. I planted a fingerprint, got found out and was drummed out of the Brownies.'

'That would never have happened in my day.'

Was No re-inventing himself? 'Planting evidence, gov?'

'I mean getting sacked. Unless you got found out in court and had all the do-gooders baying for your blood.'

'May I ask what you are doing here, gov?'

'I'm here to catch the person who's been murdering bankers. The Bucephalus Bank wants it done with discretion.' He paused, scraped his plate, and continued,

'You could help me, Baggo. You could have been a good copper. Let me know, will you, if you hear anything that might help. There'd be something in it for you.' He winked.

'Of course, gov, but mum's the word. They don't know about my past life in the police, so please do not spill the beans. To anyone.'

'Well keep in touch. I'm in room 215. And I've got a lot of homework waiting for me on my laptop, so must go.' He burped ostentatiously.

'I am delighted you enjoyed your meal, sir,' Baggo said loudly. 'It has been an honour to cook for such a discriminating gentleman.'

No thought for a moment, fumbled in his wallet and produced a five euro note. 'The way the euro's going the only thing this will be good for is wiping the ring of fire the morning after a good curry,' he said.

'A most superior guest,' Baggo observed on returning to the kitchen.

* * *

'Are you sure it's not some deranged local?' Fergus Maxwell asked Flick as they cuddled each other on the sofa, disengaged from the film on the TV.

'I just feel there's something very odd about that bank. The people I saw today are like no one I've encountered.'

'You know what they call bankers. But if this is all to do with some great money laundering scheme, would the murder not be pre-meditated? Look, the weapon was found by the murderer or murderers at the scene and left there, and the repeated violent blows are consistent with rage, frenzy even. Don't you think?'

She nodded. 'I see what you mean, and I ask myself how anyone apart from the Eglintons could have known where Parsley was, assuming he was the intended target.'

'In the dark it could have been a case of mistaken identity,' Fergus agreed. 'But from what you say, all the directors might have known where Parsley was. They all have rooms on the first floor overlooking the Old, don't they?'

She nodded.

'Well, when Parsley and Eglinton walked from the sixteenth to the first green they would have passed in front of the hotel. It's a terrific view over to the R and A, which is lit up and looks better than it ever does in daylight. It would have been quite natural for any of the directors to go out on their balcony to soak up the atmosphere. And I bet Parsley and his friend were chatting and making a noise as they went. They could have seen Eglinton return to the hotel, too.'

'Good point, darling. Thanks.' She cursed herself for not thinking of that. In a marriage between two people with the same rank in different divisions, mutually supportive respect was seasoned by unspoken rivalry.

'Would you like me to check on all the recent releases to see if there is someone out there who might have done this? I've a better chance of recognising the names of local criminals than you have. I'm not interfering in your case,' he added, feeling her stiffen.

'Yes, please,' she said after biting her lip. 'It's been a tough day,' she whispered. 'I was sick at the crime scene. Made me feel so pathetic. Then at the end, the sheriff refused a warrant to search the bankers' rooms or even the clothes they sent to the laundry. "Lack of probable cause," he said, despite what MacGregor told me about blood spatters. How am I supposed to catch whoever did this?'

Fergus patted her stomach as if it were delicate porcelain. 'It's such a difficult time for you. And this case would come along now. How's your team?'

'Oh, McKellar's surly. The rest are fine. Wallace is dependable. How did he come to be called Lance? It's not Scottish.'

'I've heard he was conceived after his parents had watched *Camelot*. I'm glad you've got him. And don't under-estimate McKellar. He's been a bobby in St Andrews for nearly thirty years. He knows all the problem families, keeps his ear close to the ground. You should ask him tomorrow if he's heard anything interesting and I bet his attitude will improve.'

'I doubt it. His resentment of me seeps out of his pores.'

'Darling, it was once said of Maggie Thatcher that she was unpopular in Scotland because she was bossy, English and a woman. She'd have got off with being any two of these, but all three and she was finished up here.' He grinned.

She didn't find it funny. 'So I mustn't be bossy in case I upset the Scots?' Her voice caught.

'It's your job to give orders, but if you make men like McKellar think that you rate them, even if you don't, they're far more likely to come on-side. And if they don't, they will make themselves seem bigoted.'

'I'll try. But I can tell he's the type to bend the rules to get a result and justify himself by saying he's old-fashioned. Not as bad as Inspector No, of course.'

'At least you don't have him to deal with any more. How did you find MacGregor?'

'At first I didn't like him. He's chauvinist and patronising. But he was really helpful on the phone. Prepared to stick his neck out.'

'He can be brilliant in court.' He chuckled. 'There was a murder case in which the deceased had been stabbed by one man then run over by another. Counsel for the man with the knife suggested MacGregor was wrong to say that the stab wound had been fatal. There was a moment's silence. Then MacGregor picked up the knife, which was on the shelf in front of the witness box, and pointed it at the lawyer. "Mr Laverty, if I were to come across the court and stab you in the identical way, within five seconds you would be very, very dead." It's not often Craig Laverty's stuck for words but his mouth opened and closed like a goldfish. And his client went down for murder.'

'Well let's hope we get someone in court for this,' she said grimly. Then the phone rang. 'It's a bit late,' she muttered as she reached for it.

'Jamieson here.' It was the divisional commander's clipped voice. 'That's Inspector Fortune, I take it? I've had

Lord Saddlefell bending my ear this evening so we'd better have a word. Nine am tomorrow. My office.'

Her heart sank. 'Glenrothes?' she asked, knowing she sounded stupid.

'That's where my office is, Divisional Headquarters. Goodnight, Inspector.'

'And I thought today was bad. I bet he thinks I've been drinking,' Flick said, then burst into tears.

* * *

'Ma brains are in ma bum. It wis Hearts that put Celtic ootae the Cup.'

Baggo sipped his second pint of IPA beer as Sharon neared the end of her third vodka and coke. Half an hour earlier he had started the conversation on football, without reckoning on her encyclopedic knowledge of the history of East Fife FC, a team he had been only vaguely aware of. She had moved on to bigger and better teams, and required to be diverted.

'Do you enjoy working in the Old Course?' he asked as she drained the glass.

'It's alright.'

'Do you get to do the rooms on the first floor facing the Old?'

'Aye.'

'The views must be wonderful.'

'Aye.'

'Did you do the room for the guy who was murdered?'

'Aye.'

'What are these bankers like?'

'Like anyone else, I suppose. No' perfect, ken whit I mean?'

'No. How?'

'Well there are these two poofs who share a bed, and they leave their mark, like.'

'Yes. Tell me more.'

Sharon banged the table as she set her glass down. 'Time for another?'

'Same again?' he hoped he was not wasting time and money.

'And that Mrs Parsley,' she whispered when he returned, 'she's no' the devoted wife she's made oot tae be.'

'Really?' He tried to sound casual.

'There's a man called Forbes along the passage from her. He's supposed to be on his own, but this morning I found marks, ken, on his sheet. There wis a long hair, kinda gingery-blonde, on his pillow, and the pillow smelled of perfume – her perfume. Guilty, they call it. I notice these things, ken. I'd seen it in her room yesterday and had a wee fly sniff. It's sort of flowery. And I liked the way they wrote the Gs of Gucci Guilty on the bottle. Do ye think she did awa' wi' her man?'

'I don't know. Someone did. Exactly when did you see this hair?'

'Ho, you're as bad as thae polis wi' yer questions.'

'Sorry, but it's interesting. Did you tell the police this?'

'Naw. Take me for a grass or something?'

It was time to move on. After a brief re-cap of East Fife's problems over the last decade, the drinks were finished. Sharon lived at home in the town. Baggo offered to walk her back.

'Naw. I dinnae need that. Ye may be a Paki, but ye'r a right fucking gentleman,' she added. He took it as a compliment.

Chilled to the bone by a bitter wind off the North Sea, Baggo walked briskly back to the staff quarters. Cold, damp weather always made him miss the heat of Mumbai. Images of happy years spent there warmed him. He remembered his first girlfriend, a year older and the most beautiful person he had ever seen. They had done it only once, the evening before the Chandavarkar family moved to Britain. He had written to her but had received no reply. Suspecting that her father had found out, he waited with a mixture of dread and hope for his own father to ask him about her, but the silence had been deafening. After some months he felt relief, and was ashamed of that.

Then he imagined making love to Sharon and found the notion surprisingly appealing. She was not pretty, but there was a sexy provocativeness about her. A few months earlier his only long-term relationship had ended. The girl could not escape from her own difficult history and his working hours did not make for an easy home life. More upset than he had at first been prepared to acknowledge, Baggo had immersed himself in his cases, in particular the Bucephalus inquiry. As far as sex was concerned, it had been a while … As he tried to get to sleep, the duvet in his narrow bed wrapped round him, he felt uneasy and root-less.

7

'It's three minutes past nine.' Jamieson's opening remark dismayed Flick. Allowing for slippery roads, she had left plenty of time for the journey, but traffic had been unexpectedly heavy for a Saturday, probably due to Christmas shopping, she thought. There had also been an unscheduled stop to bring up her breakfast.

'Sorry, sir,' she said meekly.

'How's this banker murder progressing? Sit down for God's sake.'

That was more promising. She looked at him, bald and red-faced, across his vast, empty desk. She could almost feel his bloodshot eyes assessing her. 'It's difficult, sir. We're following every reasonable line of inquiry. We have to look at the bankers staying in the hotel, and already we've found one who might have been driven to murder by the deceased, who was very homophobic. There's a lot going on in the bank: electing a new chairman, lowering the wealth threshold for clients …'

'Right. As I said last night, I've had Lord Saddlefell on the phone and he's not happy. Now, this is your first real test up here and I want you to understand a few things.'

'Sir?'

'When I decide whether I want someone from another

force, I take the formal references with a pinch of salt. Too many people give glowing references to duffers just to get rid of them. I look at who they've learned from, and I see that Noel Osborne was your boss in Wimbledon. He was a great copper in his day. I know he went off a bit, but he got results. And he didn't get them by sticking to the bloody rule book. I don't expect you to stick by the rule book, and I'll back you up as long as I can. If I'd thought you were a girl guide I wouldn't have let you into my force, but you are going to have to be very careful with Saddlefell. He is capable of making a lot of trouble. As long as you're investigating this bank you'd better do everything by the book – or not get caught. It's your inquiry and I want you to get on with it, but though I'd like to, I won't be able to back you if the shit really hits the fan. Do you understand?'

'Yes, sir,' she stammered, astonished and appalled.

'Is there anything I should know at this stage?'

'Well, sir, there's an officer from London, SOCA, who's investigating a big money laundering case involving the same bank. He's undercover as a waiter in the hotel, and I'm afraid we might get in each other's way. I told him that our murder takes precedence.'

'So it does, Inspector, and thank you for telling me. Forewarned is forearmed, but don't piss off SOCA unless you have to. Mind you, they might have had the courtesy to inform me. Now I have other things to do. So good luck and remember: don't get caught!'

As Flick got up she saw that while the divisional commander was wearing his black uniform jacket, his trousers were brown tweed. In the car park she sat digesting what had been said and spotted him emerging from the main door, his jacket now matching his trousers. He drove away at speed.

* * *

'Mr Osborne?'

'Yes. Who's that?' Osborne sounded cross and sleepy and didn't care. In his dream he had been skinny-dipping with Maria in a private pool, swimming like a dolphin and inflating her breasts by blowing into her nipples. The phone had spoiled his fun.

'My name's Mark Forbes, and I know you'll want to see me. The earlier the better as far as I'm concerned and I'd like to fix a time.' The voice was grand, with drawn-out vowels. It reminded Osborne of judges, of whom he had learned to be very wary. He checked his watch.

'Quarter to ten,' he said firmly. He had sat up till after midnight, poring over the dossier Saddlefell had sent him, and had no qualms about sleeping late.

'Could you not manage a bit earlier? You'll have a lot of people to interview.'

'Quarter to ten. Your room.' Osborne's instinct to have the upper hand asserted itself.

'Well if …' Osborne ended the call then realised he did not know Forbes's room number. He dressed and shaved quickly. He was not going to talk to all these bankers without a full cooked breakfast. He'd get the room numbers from Saddlefell later.

In the Sands Grill, his plate heaped with fried eggs, bacon, mushrooms, black pudding and sausages, Osborne was in heaven. Not as greasy as a good greasy spoon meal, but what it lacked in quality it made up for in quantity. As he mopped up the last of the yoke with a forkful of black pudding, his stomach gurgled loudly. A spasm gripped him. He knew what was happening. His prawn vindaloo was on the move. He rushed out in acute discomfort.

* * *

Baggo had been unable to decide whether No's indolence would overcome his greed. Would it be room service or restaurant breakfast? If he went down for breakfast, Baggo could access his computer and see what 'homework' was on it. He had promised the hotel manager that he would not exceed his powers and would respect guests' privacy, but this had to be done. Feeling conspicuous, he had hung about the corridor, making sure the CCTV camera would not pick him up until No had left the room.

His staff access card got him in and the laptop was in plain view on the table. Baggo had called a colleague in London who had given him the words and figures No was most likely to use as a password, but after several attempts the computer remained locked. Baggo sat back and thought. There was a sergeant No had learned most of his tricks from, whose exploits he had described in tedious and repetitive detail. Thumper, he was called. Thumper, Thumper ... Binks! Baggo typed in 'thumperbinks' and the computer welcomed him. Soon he was in the documents. A zip file named 'BB' looked promising, but contained an album of big breasts. Baggo smiled and told himself to get on with the job. All the files were named ambiguously so Baggo decided to put them all on his USB memory stick and sort them out later.

He had only just started this process when there was a frantic scrabbling at the door. Baggo seized the laptop and rushed into the bathroom. The shower curtain in the bath was closed so he went behind it and stood still, hoping that the computer would not make a noise. The light came on and Baggo heard the unmistakable sounds of a man who needed the lavatory very badly. Standing silently behind the curtain, barely daring to breathe, he hoped No had got there in time and would not need a shower afterwards.

* * *

Flick looked round the incident room. There were eight men and three women. Half of the men were older than she was; all were bigger. Some had faces hewn from stern granite. Whisky and harsh East winds had polished others to an angry red. Moncrieff and Robertson finished handing out mugs of coffee then leaned against the wall. The tight-lipped Scottish mutterings sounded to Flick like a distant gravel-grinder. She wished she could run away.

'Alright! Attention!' she shouted, conscious of her English accent. The faces didn't alter but the gravel-grinding stopped. 'I hope you're all familiar with the information on the whiteboard. Is there anything new in this morning?'

Wallace stood up. 'Yesterday evening I accompanied Mrs Parsley and Mr Eglinton to Dundee where they identified the body. Mrs Parsley was very tearful, and while Mr Eglinton's a stiff upper lip type, I could tell he found it distressing.'

Flick said, 'He had known Parsley since schooldays. Did either of them say anything interesting?'

'No, ma'am. Almost nothing was said during the whole business.'

She was not surprised. 'Is there anything from the lab?' she asked.

Wallace replied, 'Yes, but nothing surprising. There are no prints other than the deceased's on the i-phone, the wallet, the ball or the putter. There are traces of human blood in the grooves of the putter face and in the manufacturer's name at the back. The local inquiries have brought in nothing useful. There's been little in the press, just the basic facts, no name yet. I asked them to put in the usual "any member of the public who knows anything" bit, but there's been nothing so far.'

Flick cursed herself for not thinking about the press. Murders attracted more interest here than in London. She asked, 'Have we got anything interesting off the deceased's computer or mobile?'

'Spider' Gilsland stood, his appearance transformed. Hair combed, the feeble beard shaved off, he wore a clean shirt and cord trousers. With his big head and long, flapping arms, Flick could see how he got his nickname.

His bony hands waved about jerkily as he talked. 'I have his i-phone call records, ma'am, but they don't mean much at the moment. He used a lot of initials and nicknames in his address book. It was on voicemail on Thursday night. There are four messages. Do you want to hear them?' He held up the i-phone.

'Yes,' Flick said, hoping for something helpful.

The first was timed at Thursday at 21.12. The voice was female, slurred and could have come out of *Eastenders*, 'Hugh, my darling, Tricia here. When are we going to have that drinky-winky you promised me?'

The next two had come in on Friday morning. At 07.31 a man with an accent from the Deep South called, 'Webb speaking. I'm at Heathrow, just gotten off the red-eye and have a bunch of meetings in London. I'll be in Saint Andrews this evening. We need to talk.' Like all Americans he gave 'Saint' full emphasis.

At 08.12, 'Good morning, Sauce! I don't care about your hangover. Stir your stumps so you and Belinda can join me and Simon on the Eden. I've just booked a time at ten past eleven.' Flick immediately recognised the plummy voice.

'That was Mrs Eglinton,' she said. She turned to McKellar. 'Please check that she did make that booking and when she made it. Is there another one?'

Gilsland replied, 'Yes, ma'am.' Timed at 16.18 on Friday, a rich, deep, male voice with African intonation said, 'Mr Parsley. I want to talk about my bonds. Phone me, on this number as usual, tomorrow afternoon. I'm hunting in the morning.'

'Do you have the number?' Flick asked.

'Yes, ma'am. I had to get it from the provider. In the address book that's the number of "XPB". I haven't got any further yet.'

Flick wondered if Baggo might know who that was. 'What about the computer?' she asked.

Gilsland shrugged, his bony shoulders nearly touching his ears. 'It's full of business stuff. I couldn't make anything of it. Oh, he had a Twitter account, too. His tweets were usually about TV programmes or sport.'

She shook her head. She could not understand intelligent adults who bothered with Twitter or Facebook. She asked, 'Has di Falco anything useful to report this morning?'

Wallace replied, 'When I spoke to him he was busy as a party of Japanese was checking out, but he had nothing for us.'

Flick said, 'Has anyone heard any gossip, even if it's only old wives' tales? McKellar, can you help us?'

McKellar, whose eyes had been almost shut, started. 'Well, ma'am, the murder's the talk of the steamie, as we say in Scotland, but I haven't heard anything interesting.'

'Well keep your ear to the ground,' she said. 'Anyone else?'

Some shook their heads but most didn't react.

Flick was determined to sound upbeat. 'In the absence of something better to go on, I'm working on the assumption that the killer is someone connected with the bank, so I want to know what they were all doing late on Thursday night and into the early hours of Friday. I've prepared a list of the times each one claims he or she went to their room and stayed there for the night, and I want all of you to have a copy. This morning I want you to question hotel staff to see if they can support or contradict these accounts. I'm thinking particularly of porters, receptionists, waiters, including staff at the Jigger Inn. McKellar, will you organise that please?'

A twitch of his nose showed his surprise. 'Yes, ma'am,' he said, not disrespectfully, then added, 'And I could check the CCTV in the corridors too. Sergeant Wallace told them yesterday that we'd need it.'

Flick winced inwardly but ignored the implied rebuke. 'Thank you, but I think that's a job for Gilsland. Wallace and I shall re-interview the bankers. I want to find out how that bank works, and what's been going on in it. If any of the hotel staff can tell you things they overheard, take a note, however trivial it may seem. I've asked the Met to let us know if any of our bankers have form, and I expect to hear from them today. Any questions?'

There were none. As the briefing ended her sullen team filed out, giving her an inkling of what Maggie Thatcher had been up against. She saw Wallace take McKellar's arm as if he intended to say something to him.

Gilsland was one of the last to go. She called him over. 'You're looking smart today. Well done,' she said.

He grinned. 'Between you and my mum I didn't have any option, ma'am.'

'I'm sorry about the wedding,' she said.

'I'm not really that bothered, ma'am. My mum is more upset than I am, but she can go round telling everyone I'm working on an important murder inquiry.'

'Well let's hope the CCTV cameras will help us,' she said, wishing that the uniformed officers were more like Gilsland and di Falco.

* * *

'Good morning, Mr Osborne, thank you for seeing me.'

Osborne nodded. He was surprised that Forbes, who had come across in the file as a complete bastard, did not complain about his lateness. By the time he had pacified his gut, sprayed himself with after-shave and obtained a list of room numbers from Saddlefell he was quarter of an hour late for his appointment. Forbes had to want something from him, simple as that.

In truth, Osborne was uneasy about his assignment. He could sense there was something funny going on in the bank. What that was he could only guess at, but it looked as if Parsley had been involved. Monmouth's murder was a complete mystery, if murder it was, and as far as Parsley's death was concerned, he was reduced to suspecting the spouse and as Thumper Binks always had, the last person to see the deceased alive.

Osborne sat at the table near the window, opposite Forbes. The man had cold, calculating eyes, like lawyers and serious criminals. 'Well?' Osborne said.

Forbes got up and went to the door. 'We don't want to be disturbed,' he said. He walked slowly back to his seat, but did not sit down and leaned across the table so he was close to Osborne's face. Speaking quietly, he said, 'You are not here because you're a brilliant detective. And you're not a brilliant detective.' He let that sink in. Osborne raised his eyebrows. Forbes sat down then continued, 'You're here because you want money.' Osborne said nothing, thinking that Forbes's mouth looked like a talking belly-button.

'Are you wired?' Forbes asked languidly. With his plummy accent he sounded as if he was asking if Osborne had slept well.

'No.'

'Prove it.'

'Why should I?'

Forbes gave a condescending smile. 'Because you are desperate to know what I'm about to say, and I need to be satisfied I'm not being recorded.'

Osborne shrugged and unbuttoned his shirt.

The smile disappeared. 'I'm not an idiot. Some devices are tiny. Strip to your boxers.' Seeing Osborne's frown he added, 'I don't fancy you, so don't worry about that.'

Slowly, Osborne undressed and passed each garment to Forbes who, despite handling them with obvious distaste, subjected them to a meticulous examination. Then with Osborne standing self-consciously in the middle of the room wearing nothing but his grubby boxers, Forbes inspected him as a sergeant-major would a new recruit.

'Good. Sorry about that,' Forbes said eventually.

Osborne dressed quickly and took his seat again. 'This had better be worth it,' he said. 'Now you.'

'Touché,' Forbes said. Without demur or embarrassment he peeled off his clothes and handed them over. Osborne noted nothing about them except that they were clean, smart and expensive. When Forbes stood in his boxers, white-skinned and puny-looking, his pot belly sticking out, Osborne made him lift both arms as if he might have hidden a bug under an armpit. Apparently unconscious of how absurd he looked, Forbes's expression did not change, but Osborne felt he had at least done something to level the score.

'Well?' Osborne repeated after Forbes had dressed.

'I did not murder Sir Paul Monmouth and I did not murder Hugh Parsley.' Forbes paused for effect. 'I do not know who did, and here I am assuming that Monmouth was murdered. He may not have been. You and I are two of a kind, out for number one.' He paused again. 'I see you don't deny it. I want to pay you a large sum of money, more money than you will ever have had a chance of getting your hands on. I want to pay ten thousand pounds, or equivalent in any currency you name, into your bank account and I want to do it now. Then, on Monday morning, I want to pay you one hundred thousand pounds. Again in a currency of your choice.'

'I'm not stopping you.' Osborne's heart raced. This was the sort of arrogant bastard he usually enjoyed being dismissively rude to, but not today. He tried not to show his surprise and excitement.

'But you have to do something.'

'There's a surprise.'

'You will plant this on Lord Saddlefell.' He opened a drawer and brought out a small item wrapped in a handkerchief. Unfolding the linen, he revealed a gold money clip. Osborne peered at it. On the clip was an engraving of a bull sinking his horns into a man's bottom. On the other side SHAFTED BY HP was inscribed.

'You don't need to know how or where I got this,' Forbes said smoothly, 'but it will focus police attention on Lord Saddlefell when they search his room, following information you will give them. You will also tell them that Lord Saddlefell did not go straight to his room after drinking in the Jigger on Thursday night. He stood beside the seventeenth fairway and smoked one of these naff little cigars he seems to like. I know because I went out on my balcony and smelled it. The porter will be sure to remember that idiot wife of his coming in ahead of him and needing her room card. For some reason she always leaves it with the porter.'

'But …' Osborne was lost for words.

'Come on, you've planted evidence before. Lots of times.'

'Yes, but on people who were guilty of something.'

'I'd better explain. The directors of the bank are split into two factions. There are two issues: one, whether we lower the threshold to allow less wealthy people to become clients, and two, who will be the next chairman. The faction of which I am a member will prevail. Lord Saddlefell is presently its leader and will be elected chairman – unless he's arrested for murder, in which case I will be chairman. Once the decision to appoint me has been taken, the flaws in the police case will become apparent and, assuming he's not the killer, he will be released. So no substantial harm will have been done.

Arguably, the arrest of Saddlefell will make the real murderer relax and make a mistake, and without that you and the police will struggle? No?'

Osborne did not know what to say. He did not like the sound of Forbes's proposal. But there was the money …

'What's the number of your bank account?' Forbes opened his laptop and pressed some buttons. 'I'm ready to pay the ten thousand now.'

8

'Fresh orange juice for Room 130. Ms Walkinshaw.'

'I'll get it!' Baggo, his memory stick safe in his trouser pocket, had returned to the service area after refreshing himself in his room. He had not yet encountered the sole female director who had a formidable reputation in financial circles.

His knock answered by an imperious 'come', Baggo entered and placed the juice in front of Nicola Walkinshaw, who sat at the table beside the window, a sheaf of papers in front of her. As she ran her eye over him, he took in the artificiality of her black hair and young face on an old neck, but it was her nightdress that caught his attention. Ruby-red silk edged with lace, it brushed the tops of her thighs and plunged almost to her navel. She leaned forward for the juice and watched his reaction as her white breasts and pointed nipples were exposed.

'I have an itch between my shoulder blades,' she said in a matter of fact voice. 'My idiot friend missed his flight yesterday so I have no one to scratch it. Would you?' Without waiting for a reply she turned her back.

If he was going to flee, this would be the time to do it.

Generally he was attracted to women with flesh on their bones, and she was much thinner than he liked, but there was something sensuous about her and he had missed sex. What was more, he might learn something useful. Words were redundant. Baggo stood behind her and massaged the gap between her shoulder blades with his thumbs. At the same time he read the top sheet of paper. It was a photo-copy of a handwritten letter from Saddlefell addressed to all directors. It called two meetings, one that day at noon, the second on the following day at eleven am. The business of the first meeting was to be the composition of the board. The business of the second was unspecified, but Webb van Bilt was to be present for part of it.

'A bit to the right ... firmer ... lower,' Walkinshaw purred as Baggo kneaded tight muscle.

Suddenly she stood, faced him and kissed him passionately. Surprised by the brazenness, if not by the approach, he responded, pushing his tongue between her spongy lips and putting his arms round her. Soon his hands were feeling her surprisingly firm, bare bottom. Without warning she broke away from him. 'Do not disturb,' she said, pointing to the door. By the time he had fixed the card she was naked on her back on the unmade bed, legs apart, knees bent. On the bedside table lay some twenty pound notes and a pack of Durex Pleasuremax condoms. 'Strip,' she commanded then added, 'slowly ... everything ... turn round.'

Baggo did not see himself as being prudish but he disliked parading himself unclothed for the pleasure of this strange woman, who played with herself as her gimlet eyes strayed over his body. The large mirror behind the bed made him extra self-conscious but 'in for a penny, in for a pound,' as the odd English saying went. He adopted a legs-astride, arms-folded pose he hoped looked masterful then knelt on the bed between her knees.

'Tongue first,' she commanded.

A quarter of an hour later he lay on his back, exhausted. It had been an unforgettable experience, devoid of emotion and more like school PE with erotic sensations than love-making. At times what he saw in the mirror made him feel very foolish. He looked at Walkinshaw, also on her back, gazing at the ceiling.

'So who killed your colleague, Mr Parsley?' he asked, hoping to surprise her.

Apart from a flicker of her eyebrows she did not react. 'What business is it of yours?'

'Everyone is talking about it. It's not every day a guest gets bumped off.'

'Well I can't help you. It wasn't me, anyway. I enjoyed our occasional over-the-desk sessions too much to want to "bump him off" as you put it.'

'Is it true Mr Osborne has been brought here to do a Hercule Poirot and solve the case before the police?'

'You ask a lot of questions, young man. What is your name?'

'Baggo, Ms Walkinshaw. Sorry, I did not mean to cause offence.'

'Well, Baggo, get your tight little bottom out of my bed and into its trousers. I have work to do.'

He had hoped she would go into the bathroom, giving him a chance to look at her papers. Before he put his clothes on he said, 'Excuse me, but I need the toilet.' He did not wait for her permission.

Apart from enough cosmetics to stock a small chemist's shop, he saw nothing strange about the contents. He ran the tap and rinsed his mouth, applying some of her toothpaste with a finger. Then he quickly wiped himself with a facecloth and pulled the plug.

When he emerged, Walkinshaw, wearing a white toweling dressing gown, was sitting at the table, sipping her orange juice and reading. Baggo dressed, positioning himself behind her. He could see columns of notes and figures with headings in capitals. From the left these read: ACCOUNT; DATE OF OPENING; INVESTMENT; EURO-BONDS HELD; EURO-BONDS PASSED. Once dressed, he tidied his hair in the mirror and hovered about beside the table. 'Can I take your glass when you are finished?' he asked.

'No,' she said without looking up, frowning at the data in front of her and drumming her purple nails on the table. He could feel where these nails had scratched him.

'Wait,' she said as he made to leave. 'Come here.' She pushed some notes into the waistband of his trousers and patted his crotch. 'Five,' she added with a smile.

'Five?'

'Out of ten. A good score for a waiter. Had you been rich and powerful, it would have been eight or nine. I may need some more fresh orange juice before I go, so be prepared.'

He nodded and left, feeling like an insect after a bruising encounter with a Venus Fly-trap. He nearly bumped into a woman emerging from a room on the opposite side of the corridor. It was Inspector Fortune. She gave him a quizzical smile but said nothing.

* * *

Flick had driven to St Andrews silently resenting male police officers and bankers. She decided to question the two female bankers, partly to see how they coped in the man's world they occupied. When she arrived at the hotel preparations for the annual Christmas Fayre were under way. A full month before the day which she privately called 'Cashmas', and with a murder to solve Flick had seldom felt less festive. The hotel staff did not share her feelings. Many wearing silly hats, they were busy hanging glitzy decorations and creating red and silver arrangements. *Ding Dong Merrily on High* was playing in the background. In a corner beside the main door what looked like an open shed was taking shape, a sign advertising Santa's Grotto beside it.

After checking at reception that both Walkinshaw and Anderson had made the phone calls they had claimed on Thursday night, Flick and Wallace went to Nicola Walkinshaw's room to find a Do Not Disturb card outside. Sheila Anderson's room was almost across the corridor and she was available.

Flick remembered her as the woman with wet hair who had come to the conference room from the spa. Her hair was now wavy and honey-coloured and she wore neat black trousers and a frilly pink shirt. She sat in a chair by the window, her laptop open on her knee. Apparently unfazed by the police, she gave them a business-like smile as if inviting questions.

Flick started by asking about her family. Her husband, Donald, was at home looking after their two children, Alan, three and Dotty, two. Donald was a self-employed surveyor whose career had stalled in the recession and he was the one who stayed at home if the children needed attention. She explained this freely, a hint of the West Country in her soft voice. With no hesitation she agreed with Flick that this was an important weekend for her career. 'They will be taking a vote on new directors today at noon,' she added, smiling nervously.

'How did you get on with Mr Parsley?' Flick asked.

'I didn't see much of him.'

'Had he ever made sexual advances towards you?'

Anderson blinked then scowled. The directness of the question had surprised her, as Flick had intended. 'I can't see how that's relevant.'

'I'm afraid it may be but we will not betray confidences unless we have to.'

Anderson looked down at her computer as if the appropriate response was there. 'Yes,' she said slowly, 'but I have nothing to be ashamed of, so I'll tell you.'

'Thank you,' Flick murmured.

'You obviously know that there is a vacancy, two now of course, on the board. Last week I was working late and Hugh Parsley came to my room. He sat close to me, fondled my knee and all but said that he would vote for me only if I had sex with him. He showed me he had some condoms in his pocket. I told him to go fuck himself, Inspector. You may find that hard to believe, but it's true.'

'Why should I find it hard to believe?'

'Because from your face in the conference room yesterday, you despise bankers, just like everyone else.'

It was Flick's turn to be surprised. She felt herself warming to Anderson. 'Was that the only occasion?'

'Well he made a suggestive remark on Wednesday night, but I didn't react so he gave up.'

Wallace cut in, 'Did you not tell me you had a drink with him after dinner on Thursday?'

'Yes, I did, but Simon Eglinton and Nicola Walkinshaw were there too. If I were to be elected to the board I'd have had to work more closely with Hugh. I wasn't going to give anyone a reason for not voting for me.'

Flick asked, 'Did you tell anyone? That was sexual harassment.'

'No. I don't know what it's like in your world, Inspector, but in mine a complaint would be a sign that I couldn't take a joke.' She looked directly at Flick, who knew exactly what she meant but kept a poker face.

'Ah well,' Flick said noncommittally.

Wallace cleared his throat.

Flick moved on. 'Do you know if Mr Parsley made advances to other women connected to the bank?'

'As I said, Inspector, I didn't see much of him at work and that suited me fine.'

'What about office gossip?' Wallace asked.

'I don't know if I should be saying this, as it may be untrue, but a cleaner told me she had come across him having sex in his office. Of course it could have been another man using his desk. Or an over-active imagination.' She shrugged.

Flick asked, 'Did he have any enemies in the bank?'

'Enemies? If so they kept it well hidden. He was really mean to Oliver Davidson. Do you know about him?'

'Yes. We've been told about his ... change in direction,' Flick said.

'I feel sorry for his poor wife Violet, and the children.' A flash of anger showed in her eyes.

'Can you think of anyone apart from Davidson who might have wanted to kill him?'

'I really can't help you there, Inspector.'

'It would help if you told us how the bank works. I understand you are the Client Wealth Manager?'

'Yes. Pretentious, isn't it? The bank has two arms, one of which is wealth management, which is really just looking after our clients, handling their investments and financial affairs generally. I am an international tax lawyer and pensions expert, so my skills come into play. The other arm is the investment arm and deals with the bank's assets. Gerald Knarston-Smith manages it.'

'Is he good at his job?' Flick had put him down as a chinless wonder.

'Oh yes. He is very organised. Seriously bright, too. He's an actuary and can make numbers sing. He does the most amazing sums in his head. He's not got a lot of common sense, and that goofy public school act drives most of us demented, but his job is all about margins and percentages and, as I say, making the numbers sing for the bank profits.'

'What do the other directors do?'

'Each one has a different expertise, and their skills are available to both branches of the bank. Davidson deals with currencies, Eglinton UK corporate, Walkinshaw international corporate, Saddlefell property and Forbes futures, derivitives and commodities. Parsley was in over-all charge of the investment arm and Gerald was effectively his assistant.'

'What about Sir Paul Monmouth?'

'He handled blue-chip companies. So-called. He assured us that Royal Bank of Scotland was "sound as a bell" less than a week before it crashed. Actually that's a bit unfair. Lots of others who should have known better were fooled. He was a really nice old man, a complete gentleman. Integrity was everything to him. After 2008 he took what he called a supervisory role, in other words he got in the way a bit, but as he had built the bank up in the past and a lot of clients looked to him, the directors let him carry on.'

'Do you think his death was an accident or murder?'

'He was quite old, seventy-five I think, but he was careful of himself. You could tell the time by when he arrived in the morning and when he left at night. I don't know. It's horrid to think someone killed him.' Anderson shuddered.

'How do you get clients?' Flick asked.

'We can all introduce clients, provided they pass the wealth threshold. The person doing the introducing puts the client through all the preliminary stuff, money laundering regulations and so on, then each client gets a number. Their name is known only to the introducer and others on a need to know basis. That keeps things confidential. The client deposits some money, at least half a million, with the investment arm, earning them an excellent rate of interest. My arm handles the rest of the money and assets they give us to manage on their behalf.'

'Are you aware of any irregularity in the way the bank is run?' Flick carefully watched Anderson's reaction.

She looked her straight in the eye. 'No, Inspector. I should tell you that I have had a number of approaches from head-hunters representing other financial institutions, and I have turned them down. I enjoy working for Bucephalus. I like to be in control of my area, as I can in a relatively small organisation. I guarantee that there is nothing wrong with my arm of the bank, and if I thought there was something crooked about the other arm, I would not want to become a director. That would be like flushing my career down the toilet.'

'Do you trust your colleagues?'

Anderson thought before she answered. 'I have to. Once trust goes we might as well shut up shop.'

'How did the bank recover from the turmoil of 2008?'

'Hugh Parsley was a real rain-maker. He went round the world attracting clients who showed faith in us. So we pulled through. Simon and Eileen Eglinton were good, too. She's very well-connected. Her father was a big noise in the Tory Party during Thatcher's time. He seems to know anyone who's anyone anywhere.'

'Have you noticed any change in atmosphere in the bank recently?'

'Yes. We were all shocked by Sir Paul's death. And the bank seems like less of a family now that he's gone. You may think that's an odd thing to say, but we were quite close-knit, with mutual respect and quite a bit of banter. That's changed. When Oliver Davidson decided he was gay people took sides. Then this business of lowering the wealth threshold has divided the directors. It wasn't a live issue when Sir Paul was around. There's been a bit of tension about that.'

'Where do you stand?'

Anderson smiled. 'A few people have tried to find that out. I have attempted to be Delphic, and I'm not going to tell you now.'

Flick nodded. 'And you still want to be a director of this bank?'

'Absolutely. Why ever not? We'll get through this difficult time, I'm sure. It would help if you could catch this murderer,' she added.

'Do you want to ask something?' Flick asked Wallace, who had been scribbling furiously.

'No ma'am. I think that covers everything.'

Meaning it this time, Flick thanked Sheila Anderson. She stopped herself from wishing her good luck in the election. If Chandavarkar's suspicions were right, a seat on the Bucephalus board would be a poisoned chalice.

In the corridor she nearly collided with a waiter. It was Chandavarkar. He looked harassed and as he hurried away Flick saw that his shirt-tail was hanging out. There was still a Do Not Disturb sign on Walkinshaw's door.

9

With increasing desperation, Baggo typed in another variation on the theme – alexanderthegr8. He pressed the confirm button and said a silent prayer to Ganesh that at last he had hit on the password for file 123. The god with the elephant's head, revered for removing obstacles, listened. The file opened and Saddlefell's briefing for No appeared on the screen. It had taken half an hour going through files bursting with bums, tits and unspeakably obscene clips then a guessing game ended by Googling Bucephalus, but this was what Baggo needed to see.

Carefully, the brief described each director in turn: Forbes was a mean bastard; Davidson temporarily mixed-up; Walkinshaw a shagger; Eglinton a toff. All were clever, good at their jobs and very rich. Saddlefell himself came over as conceited but perceptive. He had viewed Parsley as a risk-taker and a charmer. His comments about the dead man and Eglinton hinted at a lingering resentment at their privileged backgrounds.

The brief dealt shortly with the boardroom argument over lowering the wealth threshold and identified Forbes and Walkinshaw as supporting Saddlefell's position. On the chairmanship, the same two directors were identified as backing Saddlefell, while Davidson seemed likely to vote for Eglinton, should he throw his hat into the ring. The passage ended with a cryptic comment that Parsley had been loyal to Eglinton, who had recruited him to the bank.

The description of Gerald Knarston-Smith, the manager of the investment arm, was interesting. Baggo had scarcely noticed him around the hotel. His wife, thin but attractive in an off-beat way, appeared to be the dominant character, but according to the brief he was a mathematical genius, just the sort of person you'd need to keep track of a multitude of financial transactions, hiding rogue ones among the rest.

Sheila Anderson on the other hand, was portrayed as a rose among thorns; professional, very clever, hard-working, with skills that saved the bank's clients millions of pounds without putting a foot outside the law. Saddlefell fancied her, Baggo was sure.

It was from the break-down of responsibilities within the bank that he learned most. If Sheila Anderson had half the integrity and intelligence Saddlefell credited her with, there was no way that any large-scale dishonesty was being practised in the wealth management arm for which she was responsible. That was consistent with the anonymous information linking Parsley and the investment arm with the purchases of bearer bonds. Generally, it had been the investment arms of banks that had made piles of money then caused the shit to hit the fan. The niche Bucephalus Bank was probably no exception.

The passage on Sir Paul Monmouth stressed his

integrity, his predictability and his carefulness. Saddlefell reported that before his death he had been making enquiries about loans from the Sulphur Springs Bank, and had been anxious that Bucephalus might have been guilty of mis-reporting rates for LIBOR. The London Inter-Bank Offered Rate was an important barometer of interest rates world-wide and during the financial crisis of 2008 a number of banks had claimed they could borrow at rates significantly lower than those they were paying. This deception was designed to camouflage the parlous state of their finances. The thought that Bucephalus might have departed from long-established standards of honesty had clearly worried Sir Paul. Baggo wondered how much Saddlefell himself had known. The brief hinted at no dishonesty beyond mis-reporting for LIBOR yet the page dealing with euro-bonds he had seen in her room had appeared uncomfortable reading for Walkinshaw. Was it possible that Parsley, aided by Knarston-Smith, had been behind a series of illegal activities that had first saved the bank then swelled its profits while keeping the other directors in ignorance?

As he lay back on his narrow bed and tried to put his thoughts in order, someone thumped his door. 'Baggo, you there, mate?' It was Jimmy, a cheery Scottish waiter who had showed him the ropes.

Hurriedly Baggo closed the file, shut his computer and put it to one side. 'Come in,' he shouted, trying to sound drowsy. 'I didn't sleep last night and I'm knackered,' he explained to Jimmy.

'Well ye'd better shift yer arse aff yer bed and get along

to room 215. Yon private eye wants tae speak to ye aboot yon prawn vindaloo ye gave him last night.'

'I know all about that,' Baggo muttered. Remembering how Walkinshaw had told him to get out of bed, he smiled wryly. To come to think of it, he was knackered.

* * *

'Ah, Baggo, come in!' No was in expansive mood. 'Have a seat. Funny place, St Andrews. I've just been for a walk. Had enough fresh air to last a lifetime but it's the only way to smoke an honest fag round here.'

In the Wimbledon CID room, where he ignored the no smoking rule, it had always been obvious when No was about to bore his team with one of his Thumper Binks stories. Baggo sensed something similar was coming.

No held out a clear tubular bag of brown, candied nuts. 'Have some of these. Almonds roasted in sugar. Got them in Fuengirola. Next best thing to a fag.' After Baggo had taken a few, No tipped half the packet into his own hand and started to crunch them. 'They call this the Home of Golf, Baggo, and that odd grey building you can see from the front of the hotel is The Royal and Ancient Clubhouse, the headquarters of the game world-wide. It's not impressive, Baggo. Dunno about being royal, but it's certainly fucking ancient.' He paused to put more nuts in his mouth. 'I looked in that big window and there were just a few old farts in leather armchairs. Half-dead, most of them. And this is Saturday, Baggo. I waved at one and he glared at me as if I was a fucking undertaker come to take him away before his time. It needs a membership drive, Baggo. Should be obvious to anyone. So I went round the side to the main door and asked the geezer in a blue uniform if I could take out temporary membership – the bank would pay, and the clubs in Spain do it – but he looked at me as if the cat had dragged me in. Wouldn't even let me have a gander round the place. I can't see it lasting, Baggo. You can't run a sport as big as golf like that. Here, have some more.' He emptied the nuts into Baggo's hand.

Baggo looked at the un-ironed green shirt, open at the neck with a missing button, the beige linen jacket carrying evidence of many meals, the creased trousers and the worn and discoloured suede shoes and was reminded of Groucho Marx's line about not wanting to join any club that would have him as a member. His heart sinking, he could tell that No wanted something big.

'Golf is a very challenging game, gov, if I may call you that. I have taken it up recently and it is conspicuous for its ethics. It is not the done thing to cheat at golf. Do you play?'

No raised his eyebrows. 'No time, Baggo, no time. But one day … Now, there's something I need you to do for me, Baggo, and I'll see you all right, know what I mean? I've cracked it, Baggo. I know who murdered Parsley. And Monmouth too, I'm sure. But you remember the old problem, Baggo, fucking proving it. And I need to move things along so the case stands up and no smart-arse lawyer can get the guilty man off. And that's what will happen, Baggo, unless you help me.' He paused. 'Another fucking guilty man will walk. I don't want that to happen, and I know you don't either.'

He can't possibly have solved the case already, Baggo thought, but said nothing.

'See this.' No took a linen handkerchief from an inside pocket, laid it on the table beside him and unwrapped it, revealing a gold money clip. 'Watch for prints,' he said as Baggo bent forward to examine it.

'What is it?'

'It's a money clip. You fold your cash and this holds it together. It's for people who are loaded. This has to be found in the killer's possession. And that's where you come in.'

'You want me to plant it.' A statement, not a question.

'Old-fashioned methods work, Baggo. You know that. It's how I got my results in the East End. And I only went for villains, Baggo. Whatever bleeding-heart liberals say, innocent men did not go to jail. I'm not that sort of guy. And I'll make it worth your while.' He rubbed thumb and forefinger together.

'Who's the murderer then?'

No looked round the room as if the walls had ears and whispered, 'Saddlefell.'

'Saddlefell? If I plant something on him I could lose my job and spend years in jail.'

'But you won't, Baggo. You can easily get into his room. If you're picked up on CCTV you can say it's room service. And they'll assume if anyone's planted evidence it'll have been a policeman.' He wrapped the clip and put it in Baggo's hand. 'In with his underwear would be best. Soon as you can. Must be by mid-afternoon.'

'How do you know it's Saddlefell?'

'Because I've had an anonymous tip I know I can rely on. And he's been telling porky pies about his bed-time on Thursday night. His wife went up to their room half an hour before he did. The porter will say that. He was outside, near the scene of the murder. The stupid bastard smoked one of his poncy little cigars after drinking in the Jigger Inn, yet he's telling people he went to bed with his wife. Circumstantial of course, but he had a financial motive as well. I've seen a lot of bank papers, you know.'

So have I, Baggo thought. 'How much?' he asked quickly.

'What do you mean?'

'How much? For me?'

'Two K.'

'It's a big risk.'

'Three.'

'Four. Cash. By Monday lunchtime. Plus five hundred now.'

No glared at him. 'Don't know if I can do that.'

'You always carried cash. Just in case, you said. You'll have five hundred here "for emergencies" and this is an emergency.'

'You drive a hard bargain, Baggo. All right.' He reached inside his jacket and produced a wad of notes. He counted out six fifties and ten twenties and handed them over. 'Let me know as soon as you've done it. I'll stay here till you contact me. You mustn't let me down, and if anyone asks, we've been talking about that vindaloo you made. It's got a helluva kick, you know.'

'I hope it didn't upset you,' Baggo said innocently as he left the room.

* * *

Along the corridor was a room Baggo knew was unoccupied. He used his staff key to get in. He needed thinking time. He carefully unwrapped the money clip and smiled at the engraving. After a moment's thought he put it back into his pocket. He didn't want to risk anything happening to it and he would work out later what to do with it.

He counted the cash again. Six hundred quid in tips for a morning! Pity he would have to declare it all. Or might he stay silent about having sex with Walkinshaw? That would make him the butt of a lot of jokes. He wondered who was paying No to frame Saddlefell. There was no way the ex-inspector would have agreed to pay so much if it had been his own money.

He checked his watch. It was just after twelve. The board meeting would have started. If ever there was a time to plant something, this was it, but that would not be a good idea.

On the other hand, a search of all the bankers' rooms would reveal a lot of documents which would help his money laundering case. If the inspector were to legally search for a clue in the murder, the officers could look for evidence about what had been going on in the bank. He thought carefully then took a decision.

* * *

'Sharon!' Baggo hissed and looked into the room she was cleaning.

'Whit do you want?'

'Can you tell me something?' He moved closer to her and gave her his best smile.

She put her nose to his collar and sniffed. 'Ye dirty beast. You've been shagging yon Walkinshaw. David Beckham after-shave and your curly black hairs all over her sheets. No' just on the pillow.'

He felt himself blushing. Her eyes blazed and her small but lethal ski-jump nose twitched. Denial was futile. 'She was very persuasive,' he said lamely.

'Aye, right. Can ye no' do better than that?'

He grinned. 'That's a hell of a nose you have.'

'I'm no' going to spend all my days cleaning other folks' rooms. One day ye'll find me working at the perfume counter of fucking Harvey Nicks.'

'You should be there already. But I do need to know something.'

She stepped back and looked him up and down. 'Whit are you doing here? And dinnae tell me ye'r a fucking waiter 'cos I willnae believe you.'

Remembering she didn't like the police he said, 'I'm a journalist. There's a big story about the Bucephalus Bank and I'm trying to get it before the authorities do. And I really need your help.'

She nodded. 'That makes sense. How much do ye need my help?'

'I'll make it worth your while.'

'If I'm tae get intae fucking Harvey Nicks, I'm going tae need whit they call eeloc-ution lessons. Three hunner pounds.'

One look told Baggo that haggling would be pointless. He produced the cash but held on to it. 'I have to know you can help me. There's a fat, slobby man with a red face who's a private detective working for the bank. I need to know where he was between ten and ten-thirty this morning.'

A smile spread across her face and she held her hand out. 'He wis right where you're standing, here in yon Forbes's room. I dinnae ken whit they were talking aboot, but they had the Do Not Disturb sign up for a good half hour.'

He felt like kissing her but stopped himself. He handed over the money.

She sniffed it, wrinkled her nose and stuffed it into her bra. 'I'm done here, so I'll leave ye. I dinnae want tae see whit ye do.'

'Thank you, Sharon, and this conversation hasn't happened.'

'Weel, I'm no' a fucking grass anyway. And I dinnae want tae see my face in any fucking paper.' She gathered her dusters and left, shutting the door behind her.

Baggo had searched many rooms in his time, but seldom one as meticulously tidy as this. For all Forbes was said to be tight with his money, he knew how to spend on himself. Everything was of the highest quality, neatly arranged and in immaculate condition, but there was nothing of interest. Forbes must have taken all relevant documents and his laptop to the meeting.

Baggo wanted to be able to pretend to No that he had planted the clip, so moved along the corridor to Saddlefell's room and knocked. There was no reply and he let himself in. From the bathroom he heard splashing and a tuneless female voice singing *I'm Gonna Wash That Man Right out of my Hair.* Was Lady Saddlefell another in the group who had enjoyed guilty pleasures, or did she just like old musicals? Smiling, Baggo checked for incriminating documents, found nothing and left without Lady Saddlefell becoming aware that she had entertained someone.

He went back to the unoccupied room and dialed room 215. 'Done,' he said and hung up, the gold money clip still safely in his pocket. Then he worked out what he should say to Inspector Fortune.

10

'So could Saddlefell be our murderer?' Wallace asked.

Flick looked round the conference room the hotel had made available to them and nodded. 'If he's not, why should he lie about the time he went to bed? He had motive. With Parsley out of the way, he'll probably get his way on lowering the wealth threshold and become chairman, and it's because of Monmouth's death he's acting chairman in the first place.'

Wallace nodded. It had been a productive morning. Joe Marshall, the porter who had been on duty on Thursday night, remembered Lady Saddlefell coming in without her husband at about eleven-fifteen. Bizarrely, she had left her room key-card with him rather than at reception, sweetening this minor inconvenience with a five pound note on her return. He could not remember seeing Lord Saddlefell return, but with people coming and going all the time this was hardly surprising. He remembered Mrs Eglinton going out shortly after eleven-thirty. She had held up her cigarette packet and told Joe not to dare to report her to the Health Police. A smoker himself, they had similar views on the smoking ban. When he had pretended to write laboriously in a notebook, she had given one of her horsey laughs. He did not remember her coming back in.

To Gilsland's disappointment, the CCTV camera covering the first-floor corridor where all the directors' rooms were situated had been misaligned. Twisted towards the rooms facing the back of the hotel, it showed only part of that side of the corridor and traffic in and out of the lift. It did not show any doors of rooms facing the Old Course, and it would have been possible for someone to use the stairs in the spa wing, approach from behind the camera and enter any of these rooms unseen. Sheila Anderson was the only banker with a rear-facing room. The camera captured her going there at 22.18 and remaining inside until long after the murder.

Belinda Parsley, Forbes, Walkinshaw, Davidson and Thornton all used the lift then went out of camera-shot, presumably into a room, at about the times they had given. Sandi Saddlefell came up alone in the lift at 23.21 and was followed at 23.33 by Simon Eglinton, who carried something that looked like a golf club. Eileen Eglinton entered the lift at 23.41 and returned, again using the lift, at 00.04. None of the pictures showed facial expressions. There was no footage of Lord Saddlefell returning to his room. The one camera in the spa wing which would have picked up Knarston-Smith's movements had not been working.

A potentially important witness had been found. Olive Brodie, a housekeeper, had been going home just after quarter past eleven when she heard raised voices, one 'posh', the other 'ordinary English'. She had been on the rough road beside the seventeenth hole leading to town and the voices had come from the course. She had not seen the speakers. The posh voice had said, 'I've got everything from the start ...' then something about a stick. The other man had a lower voice and he sounded angry. He'd said, 'As long as you've done it'. Uneasy about overhearing something she shouldn't, Ms Brodie had coughed and the men had fallen silent. She had smelled a cigar, but not distinctly.

'Did she say any more about the "ordinary English" accent?' Flick asked.

Wallace screwed up his face. 'I think she said he pronounced "done" as "doon".'

'Well that's North of England, not South. So it's almost certainly Saddlefell. I'd love to search his room,' she added. 'Is there any point in going back to the sheriff?'

When she had been told that local judges in Scotland are called sheriffs, Flick had thought of Wyatt Earp in a kilt. This image had vanished when she had met Sheriff Humphrey Logan, the sheriff for her part of Fife. A cheery little man with a twinkle in his eye, he persisted in seeing the best in people, giving criminals chance after chance to the despair of the police. He was also acutely conscious of human rights and regarded the liberal pronouncements from the Court of Human Rights as modern Holy Writ.

'Hopeless Humphrey would still block us, I think,' Wallace said. 'Any other sheriff would have been happy for us to search for bloodstained clothes yesterday. If only the hotel manager had let us search without a warrant.'

Flick shook her head. 'You can't blame him for looking

after his guests' interests. He has to watch his back, just like the rest of us.'

Wallace said, 'As today's Saturday, I think we can by-pass the sheriff.'

'How …'

Without waiting for his knock to be answered, Baggo burst into the room. 'Inspector, ma'am, I have got to the bottom of what has been going on in this bank,' he said. 'We must get a search warrant to recover papers that will be destroyed. Computers too.' Without asking, he took a seat and explained. 'My undercover work has proved fruitful. The deceased Mr Parsley was the head of the investment arm of the bank, and Mr Knarston-Smith does the sums. He is a geek. Around 2008 the bank struggled and had to resort to illegal means to survive. Since then Parsley and Knarston-Smith have been money laundering, using bearer bonds to camouflage what has been going on. Sir Paul Monmouth was concerned about illegal activity before he died. Now Parsley is dead. The money laundering and the murders must be linked and to find out more we need to search all the bankers' rooms. At the moment the directors are meeting and they have papers showing the crooked transactions. I've seen them, but they are sure to destroy them after the meeting. Could we go in and seize them now or do we need a warrant?'

Flick said, 'We definitely need a warrant. We couldn't risk the evidence being inadmissible.'

Baggo said, 'I have electronic surveillance equipment with me, and I'd like to use it. "Bug the buggers," as Inspector No would say.'

'We've made some progress too,' Flick said. 'Saddlefell may be our man.'

Wallace checked his watch. 'I think we should ring the duty fiscal now. She'll be able to draft an application we can present in half an hour. If we wait till quarter to one, the sheriff will have left for the golf club and we can go to Mr Murray, one of the JPs. He's usually obliging, and he lives in St Andrews.'

'Will the warrant be effective if we deliberately avoid the sheriff?' Flick asked.

'It's never been a problem before,' Wallace said as Baggo looked heavenwards.

'Right,' Flick said. 'Do it.'

'Is a JP a jolly person?' Baggo asked flippantly.

Wallace smiled. 'No, especially if you get one out of their bed to sign a warrant. Mr Murray's a justice of the peace, roughly equivalent to a magistrate in England.'

As Wallace talked to the fiscal, there was a tentative knock on the door. After Flick shouted 'Come in,' PC Robertson stuck his head in. 'I have some urgent information,' he said.

Standing awkwardly and shifting from foot to foot, he explained that he was having a cigarette outside the hotel when a man came up to him and started to talk about the murder. He was an ex-detective and so Robertson had said more than he would otherwise have done. The man had spoken to a chambermaid who had seen a gold money clip with the dead man's initials on it in Lord Saddlefell's room, and he thought that the person leading the inquiry should know this immediately.

Robertson had not thought to ask any questions, and

the man had left without giving his name. He was English, not exactly old, a bit fat and had a red face.

Baggo looked at Flick. She doesn't realise No's here, he thought.

'You should have taken his name, at least,' she snapped at Robertson. 'This strengthens our case for a warrant,' she said to Wallace, who was still on the phone. She turned to Baggo. 'Is there any chance of some coffee and sandwiches, or is waiting beneath you now?'

* * *

The bagpipe music audible from the front path of Hamish Murray's house made Flick imagine strangled haggises. It reminded Baggo of home in Mumbai, where Indian pipe bands continued to play Scottish tunes long after the British Empire had retreated.

'I'll tell him you're here,' the homely woman in a tartan skirt shouted as she opened the front door. 'He's practising his pibrochs,' she added by way of explanation.

The mournful strains continued for another two or three minutes as the detectives stood uneasily in the hall with Joy Hollis, the duty fiscal. Suddenly the noise stopped, and Mrs Murray ushered them into the front room where a short, bald man in a kilt was wrapping his pipes in a cloth and fitting them into a wooden box.

Flick looked round the room, astonished. Everything screamed Scotland, from the clan map, Highland landscapes and portrait of Bruce on the walls to the red tartan carpet which was worn and stained.

'You can keep your heather flowering till Christmas by sticking the ends in a raw tattie,' Hamish Murray said. Flick had been staring at a huge china bowl overflowing with stalks of purple heather, still blooming unseasonally. 'There's not been a drop of water in that bowl. We got these beauties in August. Glen Muick, the Queen's estate, but she willnae mind, or is that whit you're here for?' Chuckling at his own joke, the justice of the peace sat at the table and inspected his visitors.

'Are you a polisman or a waiter?' he asked Baggo, having noted the hotel livery.

'I am both today, but mainly a policeman, sir. I am working undercover.' Murray raised an eyebrow. 'I enjoyed your piping,' Baggo continued. 'It is one of the things about Mumbai I miss now I am based in London.' He hoped he had not over-done it.

The little man's smile told him he had said the right thing. 'Some fine pipers have come out of India. But you're not here to listen to me blawing my pipes.'

Joy Hollis took her cue and, producing three applications, one for money laundering, one for murder and one for electronic surveillance, explained why the police should be allowed to search the bankers' rooms and possessions and eavesdrop on their communications. Pressed by Baggo, she had also sought power to seize all their laptops. Murray listened intently then put Flick on oath. He asked a few pertinent questions and seemed satisfied with what she told him. Next, he put Baggo on oath and his eyes widened as the suspected financial wrongdoings were described. Before

Baggo had finished Murray had signed all three warrants.

'Where will they be tried, here or in England?' he asked.

'I can't say, sir, but I expect the murder trial will be here,' Joy said.

'Hm,' the little man snorted. 'Anyway, always happy to help out the English.'

Not sure how to take this last remark but grateful for his common-sense approach, they thanked Murray and left, Flick happy to be planning the search operation.

* * *

'So that's all we've got to show for it?' Flick pointed at the black plastic bin bag in the corner of the conference room. 'We wouldn't have needed a warrant for stuff they've shredded. I hope Gilsland finds something on these laptops or we'll be in trouble.' Beside the bin bag seven laptops had been piled one on top of the other.

Wallace shook his head. 'No bloodstains, no money clip. Do you think we'll be able to put these papers back together? The bankers wouldn't have destroyed them as soon as their meeting was over if they hadn't been up to something.'

The directors' meeting had broken up shortly before Flick and Baggo had returned with the warrants. A shredder had been ordered for the conference room where the meeting had been held and the police found it full. Against a background of indignant protest, mostly from Saddlefell, the eight bankers' rooms had been thoroughly searched with no result. As Baggo had joined in, his cover was blown and he had gone to change out of his waiter's uniform and pack his things.

'Do you think we should formally question Saddlefell, ma'am?' Wallace asked. 'He's our main suspect.'

'He'll make a fuss, call a lawyer then say nothing,' Flick replied, her head in her hands. She had not told anyone what the divisional commander had said to her. Might she become Fife's shortest-serving inspector? Suddenly life as a housewife and mother seemed very appealing. 'Where is Chandavarkar?' she asked petulantly. 'How long does it take to change out of a waiter's uniform?'

* * *

As Flick divided up the rooms to be searched among the officers available, Baggo had attached himself to McKellar and a bovine youth with huge red hands and a uniform straining against well-fed flesh. They had been assigned to the dead man's room. As McKellar explained to a passive Belinda Parsley what the search would involve, Baggo busied himself looking in places he thought Hugh Parsley might have concealed incriminating documents.

'I am an undercover policeman and will soon get rid of these waiter's clothes,' he told the widow when she looked at him with mild curiosity.

As McKellar checked the bathroom and the bovine officer examined the shoes at the bottom of the wardrobe, Baggo saw at the back of the wardrobe the black case for the computer already in the hands of the police. He leaned past his new colleague and pulled it out. In one of the many pockets he found an envelope folded in half. He felt the envelope but could not tell if there was anything inside. It was a plain, white envelope, slightly scuffed. Seeing he was unobserved, he put it in his trouser pocket.

There was nothing else of interest in the room. Baggo returned to the unoccupied room and broke the envelope's seal. Inside was a photograph, probably taken by a mobile phone. Two people were having sex on an office desk. One of them was Walkinshaw. The other was Gerald Knarston-Smith. While she held her head back, her mouth open, he stared wide-eyed at the camera, his trousers round his knees and alarm all over his face.

This photograph might explain a great deal, Baggo thought. He slid it back into the envelope and put it beside the clip in his pocket.

* * *

'Mr Knarston-Smith, I need a word.' Still dressed as a waiter, Baggo used his pass key to open the door. He had not knocked.

'Excuse me!' Cynthia Knarston-Smith sounded indignant. She stood, facing her husband, who sat slumped on the edge of the bed.

'I apologise for disturbing you, ma'am, but I am a policeman, not a waiter, and if you want to save your husband many years in jail, you will leave us for ten minutes or so.' He put on his most authoritative voice and produced his warrant card.

Cynthia glared at him but did not seem shocked by what he had said. With a snort of disgust she left.

Baggo waited until the door had swung shut then opened it to check she had not stayed to listen. He pushed it shut then said quietly, 'I know.'

Not raising his eyes and sounding almost disinterested, Knarston-Smith asked, 'What?'

'Sulphur Springs, Politically Exposed Persons, bearer bonds. And the photograph.'

'The photograph?' he squeaked.

'You know the one I am talking about. Why do you think I asked your wife to leave?'

'Do you have it?' Desperation in his voice, he turned towards Baggo.

'It is evidence.' He let that sink in then pulled a chair up close. 'You are, as they say, deep in the shit, my friend. Now that we know what has been going on we will gather a case. It may take time, as documents have been shredded, and we will want to see what is on the computers, but we will do it. You will not look at all good because you activated the bad transactions. I know you did what Parsley said, but it will be far too easy for the surviving directors to paint you as a rogue trader, solely responsible for a great deal of money laundering. You will have to spend several years in jail.'

Knarston-Smith ran his hands through his hair, making it stick out comically. 'Sorry, I'm so sorry,' he said tearfully, his shoulders shaking.

Poor drip, Baggo thought, letting silence ramp up the tension. 'Tell me everything,' he said quietly, 'then I will help you.'

For a moment Knarston-Smith sat immobile then began to speak quickly, words tumbling over each other. 'I joined the bank in 2007. My father knew Simon Eglinton. At first everything was great. Cynthia and I had been married the previous year, I was earning good money and she was able to spend time writing her book – a family saga thing, not my cup of tea but people say it's quite "evocative".' He blew his nose into a linen handkerchief. 'Have you met Nicola Walkinshaw?' he sniffed.

'I have, briefly,' Baggo lied.

'Well, she's a man-eater. She took a fancy to me and, well, she seduced me – a lot of talk about fast-tracking me to a directorship, that sort of thing. I'd heard that the guy doing my job before me had turned her down and she'd made his life hell. I love Cynthia, Mr ... what's your name?'

'Chandavarkar, Detective Sergeant Chandavarkar.' He produced his warrant for a second time.

'Oh, right. Well, I do love her, really I do.' He looked pleadingly at Baggo. 'She doesn't know about Nicola, or the photograph.'

'I will do my best to keep it that way, if you tell me everything. Now, please.'

'The first time, I thought it would be a one-off, but it wasn't. I couldn't say no to her. Tuesday evenings after work, sometimes her place, sometimes a quickie across the desk. She helped me with my work, kept promising me a directorship. I stopped enjoying it – I was terrified Cynthia might find out. Then there was the evening she wanted to stay in the office and we did it on her desk. Right in the middle, Hugh Parsley came in and took some photos. Looking back, there were two things that were odd. She had gone to lock the door herself – she usually told me to do that – and I swear Hugh Parsley had his phone out and ready to take the pictures as soon as he came in.

'The next day, Hugh came to me and told me to conceal a series of payments from Sulphur Springs. It was late September 2008, and the whole financial system looked as if it was going to go belly-up. He waved the phone at me as he spoke, so I knew I had to do it or Cynthia would know. The sex with Nicola stopped a few months later but the money laundering has been going on until very recently. But you obviously know that.'

'I have to prove it, and someone has been doing a good job with the shredder. Has the money laundering stopped?'

'There's been nothing new for the last month and we haven't been paying out. I don't know why.'

Baggo raised his eyebrows. 'Who produced the documents for this morning's meeting?'

Knarston-Smith tensed but said nothing.

'It was you, was it not?'

Knarston-Smith nodded unhappily.

'Did you print them off a memory stick?'

'Yes,' he whispered.

'Did the searchers find it?'

He shook his head.

'Where did you hide it?'

Knarston-Smith's face twitched and he ran his fingers through his hair.

Baggo smiled. 'I think I can guess. You're going to hand it over. Now, please.' He moved close enough to lick the tears from the other man's cheek, invading his space, intimidating him.

'No.'

Baggo moved away, shaking his head. 'No? Can you not take a little embarrassment? Do you not mind if Cynthia finds out? Do you want to spend a lot of years in jail? There will be men in prison who will make mincemeat of you. In more ways than one, I am afraid.'

Knarston-Smith gulped audibly. 'All right, but please don't tell Cynthia.'

Baggo raised an eyebrow. 'Now, please,' he repeated.

'It's very embarrassing. I'll need to go to the bathroom. I panicked when I knew they were going to search the room. I'd seen them stick things up there, you know, on TV.'

'I'll come with you.' Seeing the stricken look on Knarston-Smith's face, he added, 'It was my unhappy duty to search a lot of back passages in the drugs squad. I won't hurt you.'

Moving awkwardly, Knarston-Smith went to the bathroom, lowered his trousers and boxers and bent over the basin. Baggo had a rubber glove left over from the search. Ignoring the squeaks of discomfort and an agonised facial expression in the mirror, he inserted two fingers and pulled out a memory stick wrapped in one of the hotel's clear plastic shower caps. He unwrapped it, wiped it and put it in his pocket.

'Please may I have the password too.'

'homeofGOLF18#1.'

Baggo noted it on his waiter's pad. 'Next, I need to know which directors knew about the money laundering,' he said as Knarston-Smith, blushing furiously, tidied himself and the detritus.

'I don't know.' He wrapped Baggo's discarded glove in toilet paper and put it in the waste bucket.

Baggo grabbed his shoulder and turned him so they were face to face. 'That is not the correct answer. Walkinshaw?'

'I think so, maybe.'

'You can do better than that. Please do so.'

'All right then, I'm sure she did. She enabled Parsley to take the photo.'

'Saddlefell?'

'Yes,' a whisper. 'Certainly recently, but maybe not till after Sir Paul died.'

'Forbes?'

'Yes. He definitely has known for some time.'

'Why do you say that?'

'A couple of years ago I was working late and he came into my room. He made it clear he knew what was happening, hinted he'd check I wasn't creaming some off the top for myself, and warned I'd be in trouble if I didn't keep him in the loop. So I gave him a confidential update every few months.'

'Without telling Parsley?'

'Absolutely. Hugh was obsessive about secrecy. So is Forbes.'

'Has there been much talk about it in the office over the last few weeks?'

'No. They all pretend it hasn't happened. To hear Saddlefell sometimes, you'd have thought he'd invented integrity.'

'What about Davidson?'

'I don't know about him. Genuinely.'

'Eglinton?'

'I'm sure he didn't know about it. Till very recently anyway, if at all.'

'Who told you to make the memory stick?'

'Saddlefell.'

'When did he tell you?'

'About two weeks ago.'

'Did he say why?'

'Just that he'd need it for this weekend.'

'Does Cynthia know about the money laundering?'

'She suspects something is far wrong. She was asking me about it when you came in.'

'Oh, and after this morning's meeting, are you now on the board?'

He shook his head. 'They didn't appoint anyone.'

Baggo took him by the shoulders once more and looked him in the eye. 'They would not have appointed Sheila Anderson because she knows nothing and has too much integrity, and they would not appoint you because they're getting ready to hang you out to dry for the money laundering and probably for the murders.'

'Murders? I didn't, I wouldn't. God knows, I couldn't.'

'Actually, I think I believe you. I am not in charge of

the murder investigation, but I am involved, so keep in with me. Keep nothing from me, nothing. Do you understand?'

Knarston-Smith, pale and trembling, nodded energetically.

'Do you know anything at all about the murders, Parsley's or Sir Paul's?'

'Nothing, nothing. I promise.'

'Well keep thinking and tell me anything you can. Right?' He handed him a card. 'My mobile's on that, so no excuses, please.'

'I promise. I promise.'

Baggo gave him a final glare then left. He passed an unhappy-looking Cynthia in the corridor. He wished her a good afternoon but she ignored him.

* * *

'Inspector, ma'am, Lance, you must see this.' Baggo struggled in the doorway of the conference room, a heavy bag over one shoulder and his laptop on the other. He threw the bag into a corner, booted up the laptop and held up the memory stick.

'Before I packed I visited Mr Knarston-Smith and persuaded him to surrender this. He had hidden it, wrapped in a shower cap, where the sun doesn't shine, but now sees that the best policy is cooperation and the sun shines on it. It has been well and hygienically wiped,' he added.

He typed in the password for the one file on the stick.

It contained many pages with columns of figures, some of which were highlighted. After some minutes' study, Baggo knew he had struck gold.

'This details the transactions with Sulphur Springs. Some are genuine and some are false. See, the false transactions are highlighted, otherwise it would take a team of accountants to detect them. Then we move on to individuals who come to the bank because they want money laundered.' He scrolled down. 'Parsley introduced them, they made the usual deposit with the investment arm plus the dirty money then sent the rest to the client wealth management arm. There are some famous names here.'

'Thank goodness for that,' Flick said. 'At least we can show something bad was going on. But it doesn't help that much in the murder.'

Baggo said, 'We need to prove which directors knew about this and when. It is going to be easy for them to pin the blame on Parsley, who's dead, and Knarston-Smith, who can easily be made the fall guy. Knarston-Smith says Forbes, Walkinshaw and maybe Saddlefell have known about this for some time and I want to nail them all.'

'I think the three of us should formally question Saddlefell now,' Flick said. 'He won't expect us to know about this and it'll be a good time to catch him off-guard.'

A loud knock on the door interrupted the discussion. McKellar rushed in. His voice panicky he blurted out, 'There's been another murder. Santa bloody Claus. Actually, Mr Davidson.'

11

'Mild He lays His glory by,
   Born that man no more may die …'
In the foyer the singers were belting out the old
Wesleyan carol for the enjoyment of the happy crowd and
a queue of parents with small children snaked back from
the grotto, from which Santa was noticeably absent.
Collecting her thoughts, Flick made her way to the lifts.
The body was in Davidson's room.

'Felicity! Nice to see you!'

There was only one person since school days who had
called her Felicity. Flick turned, horrified, to see No
pushing towards her through the Christmas Fayre crowd.

'What are you doing here?' she blurted.

Elbowing a lady looking at Christmas cards, No stood
in front of her, invading her space. 'Helping you, that's
what I'm doing. I assume that young lad gave you the tip
about the money clip?'

'It was you, was it? What are you doing here?' she
repeated.

'What I'm good at. Catching villains.'

'Who's paying you? You are retired, aren't you?' Flick
had a vision of No and a couple of other dinosaurs being
recruited to form a *New Tricks* team from hell.

No waved a finger at her. 'That's confidential, Felicity,' he said reprovingly. 'But I'm on the side of justice.'

'Well don't impede my investigation,' she snapped. 'Now, I'm busy.' She strode past him, trying to conceal her shock.

In the lift she found herself behind a tall man with crinkly fair hair going grey. When they reached the first floor he turned sideways.

'You're supposed to be dead,' Flick gasped before she could stop herself.

Oliver Davidson's exclamation was cut off. When the door slid open it was clear that something extraordinary had happened. A group of people had gathered round one door on the Old Course side of the corridor. PC Robertson stood in front of it, a roll of crime scene tape in his hand. When Flick approached, the manager, whom she had met briefly, explained that one of the under-managers had found a body in the room about five minutes earlier. Further along the corridor, Jocelyn stood shaking, her hands to her face. Di Falco stood beside her, his hand on her shoulder.

Addressing the manager, Flick asked him to open the door. She turned to Robertson and told him not to allow entry to anyone other than herself, Sergeant Wallace and Sergeant Chandavarkar.

As they went in there was a scuffle in the corridor. Robertson and McKellar managed to restrain Davidson, who was nearly hysterical.

Daylight was fading fast. In the subdued light one thing stood out. Beside the table at the window a figure in a red-hooded Santa Claus costume lay face down.

Flick knelt beside it, put on plastic gloves and gently pushed the head to one side. Underneath the white beard and moustache she recognised Bruce Thornton, his face contorted, his eyes wide open. Blood, still wet, had trickled forward from the back of his neck, matting the beard and staining the carpet.

Wallace was already checking the bathroom while Baggo looked round the room, in wardrobes and under the bed.

'Everything seems normal in here,' Wallace said.

'He's still warm,' Flick noted.

Baggo pointed to a lofted iron club on the bed. 'Is that the murder weapon?' he asked.

Flick got up and took command, ordering Wallace to call scenes of crime officers and Dr MacGregor. That took little time. In the corridor Davidson was loudly demanding to be allowed in.

'We'd better break the news to him,' Flick said. 'Sergeant Wallace, would you help escort him to our room downstairs? Sergeant Chandavarkar, would you remain in this room to preserve the crime scene?'

* * *

'Someone said he was murdered. Is that true?' a distraught Oliver Davidson asked Flick and Wallace.

'We believe so,' Flick said.

'Did he suffer much?'

'We can't tell yet, I'm afraid.'

'I want to see him.'

'That'll have to be later, sir. But rest assured, we respect your relationship.'

Flick sensed that Davidson might talk more freely if she were alone with him. She sent Wallace to organise statements, wait for the SOCOs and arrange for the hotel to make another bedroom available for Davidson. She added, 'You have Mr and Mrs Thornton's address. I'll inform them after I've talked with Mr Davidson.'

'I'm truly sorry,' she said after Wallace had gone. She sat silently and, she hoped, exuded sympathy. Davidson gave her a puzzled, helpless look then nodded. She had seen many people whose lives had suddenly been thrown into grief-stricken turmoil and his empty, forlorn expression, made more pathetic by his wrinkles, showed that Davidson was another, the aggression of their previous meeting in the past.

'It was just supposed to be a bit of fun,' he said wistfully. 'They have this Christmas Fayre in the hotel and Santa had fallen ill. I overheard them wondering who could replace him and I volunteered. I've never played Santa Claus,' he added. 'Then things got very fraught at our noon meeting and I needed to think and talk to some other directors this afternoon. So Bruce said he would do it. The costume arrived after lunch and I went for a walk to clear my head. He was putting on the costume as I left.' Shoulders shaking, he buried his face in a handful of tissues. Different people react differently to sudden bereavement. Some clam up, others need to talk. Flick's instinct told her Davidson was a talker.

'I called him Ambrose, you know,' he continued in a shaky voice. 'We haven't been together long, you know. My previous partner had left me, too much baggage with the divorce, he said. One night I went to a gay bar and found myself beside this good-looking boy. "I'm Olly," I said. "Ah'm Bruce," he replied. With the background noise and his Scottish accent I thought he said "Ambrose". It became my pet name for him. And we had golf in common. Our relationship was really coming on. He had been so unsure of himself. We didn't live together, you know. I wanted to, but he said he needed more time.' He blew his nose. Flick put a hand on his arm and squeezed gently.

'He was nervous about this weekend, more because of his parents than anything else. They couldn't cope with him being gay and that upset him. His friends had known for a while. Ironically, young people are much more mature about it these days.'

'Very often,' Flick said.

'I heard someone say something about a golf club. Was he killed with one?'

'He may have been. There was a heavy-looking iron club in the room. Do you know anything about it?' Flick wished she knew more about golf.

'That would have been his lob wedge. He had been practising chipping on to the bed and getting the ball to stop on the sheet.'

'Where did he keep it when he wasn't using it?'

'Just in the corner as you open the door.'

'Who knew you were planning to act as Santa, sir?'

'I told the rest of the board at the start of the meeting. Before it got difficult.'

'Why did it get difficult?'

The spell was broken. Davidson sniffed and shook his head. 'I'm sure it has nothing to do with Bruce's murder.'

'You should let us be the judge of that, sir. It's possible the killer may have thought he was attacking you, not Mr Thornton. And if so, he or she may try again.'

'Then I'll be careful, Inspector.'

'Who knew about your change of plan, that Mr Thornton would be playing Santa?'

'I can't think of anyone. We only decided after your search. When the meeting broke up I went to the room then Bruce and I went to the Fourth Floor Bar for a light lunch. Everyone else was there. Then we heard you were going to search our rooms and we all went down so we would be present when ours was being searched. We returned to the Fourth Floor to finish our sandwiches and I knew I needed time to think. Bruce was bored and he said he'd always wanted to play Santa, too. So we agreed he should. I left him in the room, putting on the suit. I went straight out and walked to the turn.'

'The turn?'

'You don't play golf? The bit of the Old Course near the Eden Estuary.'

'What time did you go out, sir?'

'Just after half past two, I think. I told Bruce he had half an hour to practise his ho-ho-hos. He was due at the grotto at three o' clock.'

'And did anyone connected with the bank see you leave?'

'I noticed Cynthia Knarston-Smith in the foyer. She was at the Christmas pudding stall. I think she pretended not to see me.'

'Why might she do that?'

Davidson clamped his lips then said slowly, 'We decided not to appoint any new directors. It would have been a big disappointment for her.'

'Was she the only bank person who could have known about the switch?'

'Oh no. I forgot. On our way out of the Fourth Floor we stopped to talk to the Eglintons. Simon and I arranged to meet for a chat at half past three. There were business matters we needed to discuss. I told them Bruce would be Santa.'

'Might other people have overheard?'

Davidson frowned with concentration. 'Nicola and Mark were a couple of tables away, I think. But Simon and I weren't speaking loudly. Belinda Parsley was with Simon and Eileen. Like us they'd watched their rooms being searched then came back to finish their lunch.'

'What about Lord Saddlefell?'

'He arrived at the Fourth Floor with Sandi as we left. He was in a terrible temper over your search, especially having our computers seized. He had been on the phone to all sorts of people, he said.'

'Did you speak to him then?'

'No.'

'Is there anyone you can think of who had any reason to want either you or Mr Thornton dead?'

Davidson shook his head. 'Honestly, no, Inspector. At

least not anyone here in St Andrews. My ex-wife …'

'But she's not here,' Flick said quickly. 'Look, Mr Davidson, I am genuinely very, very sorry about your loss, but I need to catch a murderer and I need to know what has been going on in your bank. I believe there is a lot you haven't told me. I will find out and if I find you've been holding out on me, I won't hesitate to prosecute. Please understand that. I assume you really do want your lover's killer brought to justice. Give yourself time to think and I'll speak to you later.'

Her last words brought tears to his eyes. She called Wallace on her radio and asked him to escort Davidson to the room that had been made available for him. After some thought she decided to take McKellar with her to inform the dead man's parents.

* * *

Osborne's plans were coming unstuck and he hadn't a clue what was going on. He had gone to the first floor where he heard talk of Santa Claus being killed with a golf club. Saddlefell, who had not been arrested after the search, had glared at him and Forbes had hissed 'We must speak'. Ominously, behind Fortune as she went through the foyer, Baggo, no longer dressed as a waiter, had been with the experienced-looking man who Osborne guessed was her number two. He needed time for things to settle down. Meanwhile he should stay out of the way. He drifted to the concierge in the hope of hearing something useful.

'What'll we do about the bairns wanting to see Santa?' one porter said to another.

'There's a spare costume in the store. You could put it on.'

'No' me. With this crowd we both need to be on.'

'Are you looking for a Santa?' Osborne heard himself ask.

'Aye, we are. The bairns are getting desperate, no' to mention their parents.'

Five minutes later, with the choir singing *Jingle Bells*, Osborne took his seat in the grotto duly attired as Santa with instructions to give out one present to each child, boys' toys on the right, girls' on the left. He had played Santa once before, in his drinking days when he was cleaning up the East End of London in his own, irregular way. He'd had one drink too many and told his chief superintendent's granddaughter to fuck off when she didn't like the doll he had given her. No danger of anything like that this time, he thought. He wouldn't give the little buggers time to unwrap their presents before heaving them off his knee. He hoped none of them would pee on him.

The first few children were easy. If they knew what they wanted he nodded and went 'ho, ho, ho'. If they were overawed and tongue-tied he just went 'ho, ho, ho'.

Beside him, on a low table, a plate of mince pies had been left. He ate one then another and wanted something to wash them down. Fortunately there was a glass of lemonade beside the pies. He gulped down a big mouthful as a little girl with pigtails, wearing a spotless pink dress with red circles and trimmed with lace, perched on his knee.

But it wasn't lemonade. It was a very strong gin and tonic. Osborne coughed some over the little girl, whose father demanded the hotel should pay for cleaning the frock. The girl began to cry. Osborne shoved her off his knee and gave her a second gift, not caring that it came from the boys' sack. He had not drunk alcohol for months and the gin pressed all the wrong buttons. He didn't just want more. He needed more. Ignoring the little girl's father, who was shaking his fist at him, Osborne drained the tumbler and, with a blast like a trombone solo, emitted a room-clearing fart.

* * *

As Flick made her way through the foyer with McKellar she was aware of a noisy altercation in the grotto between Santa and two porters. Although it drew the crowd's attention she ignored it, rehearsing what she might say to Bruce Thornton's parents. It was one of the worst tasks a police officer had to undertake and she was not about to delegate this one to a subordinate.

The house was situated in the village of Strathkinness, a couple of miles west of St Andrews. As the streetlights came on Flick could make out its red pantiled roof and a neatly-kept front garden with a bed of brutally pruned roses prepared to take whatever winter would throw at them. Paving that was no longer quite level went up to the front door of a bungalow typical of 1960s architecture. A nice, middle-class home, Flick thought. The chiming bell was answered, with obvious reluctance, by a stressed-looking woman of about fifty with pure white hair cut unflatteringly short who grudgingly conceded that her name was Grace Thornton. She wore an apron bearing traces of flour and cocoa powder. Her eyes were red as if she had been crying. Flick could see in her the same sharp, regular features that had made Bruce handsome. She did not react when Flick explained that they were police, but led them into the sitting room where a thin, bald man in a home-knitted jumper was watching a rugby match on the television, the volume up high. Walter Thornton's expression was as unwelcoming as his wife's.

After they had agreed that they were Bruce's parents and, with ill grace, Mr Thornton had turned down the sound, Flick said her piece, 'You may know that your son has been staying in the Old Course Hotel for the last two nights. I'm very sorry to tell you that he was found dead in his hotel room earlier this afternoon. We believe he was murdered, but will have more details later. I'm …' she looked at McKellar, 'we're terribly sorry.'

Mrs Thornton said nothing but burst into tears. As she rocked to and fro in an armchair, wailing, her husband sat with his mouth open, as if unable to take in the news.

'I'm afraid there's no doubt,' Flick said.

'How?' the man asked.

'We don't know yet, but he may have been struck on the head with a golf club.'

'Did he suffer much?' Mrs Thornton asked.

'Probably not,' Flick said.

Mrs Thornton rushed from the room and the house echoed with the sound of retching. Unmanly tears ran down her husband's face. He stared vacantly at the television as the commentator described a seemingly endless scrum. Opposite the set, a glass-fronted cabinet contained a variety of silver cups and spoons, all highly polished, with hand-written cards detailing each triumph. On the wall above, framed photographs tracked Bruce's golfing development from toddler with a plastic club to professional beside an enormous bag with his name on it.

Flick remained silent while Mrs Thornton was out of the room. When she returned she asked, 'When did either of you last see your son?'

'Three months ago,' Mrs Thornton said quickly.

Her husband nodded. 'Have you arrested Davidson?' he asked.

'No, sir.'

'Inspector, my son was not gay.' He spat out the last word. 'He was a bit confused and that … man took advantage of him. And now he's killed him. Well, who else would do such a thing?' His voice rose to a shout when he saw doubt on Flick's face.

'I assure you that we are looking at all possibilities, sir.'

'Well I'm telling you now. It was him, and if I see him …'

'Hey, Walter, enough.' McKellar spoke for the first time. 'I'd think the exact same in your shoes, but he's no' worth it. Ye cannae bring yer boy back.'

Thornton turned away and pretended to concentrate on the television.

Flick told them they would be assigned a family liaison officer and that someone would be in touch regarding a formal identification of the body. They saw themselves out.

In the car, McKellar said, 'I remember when Bruce was a boy golfer. Some people said he would go far, but I had my doubts. His faither was tough on him, pushed him all the way. As far as he was concerned the sun shone oot o' the boy's arse.'

12

Left with Robertson and the corpse, the contrast between Christmas and Diwali had never seemed so glaring to Baggo. A few weeks earlier, as a lax but family-conscious Hindu, he had been in Bedford with his parents celebrating what was still a spiritual festival during which Hindus welcomed the goddess of wealth, Lakshmi, with small lamps and religious ritual. Today in Britain Christmas was little more than an orgy of hedonism, with retail therapy and alcohol used to mark the birth of Christ. A young man battered to death in a Santa suit emphasised the distance the festival had drifted from its origins.

His musings were interrupted by the arrival of SOCOs followed by Dr MacGregor. Baggo told Robertson to look after the crime scene. He wanted to pursue his own inquiries and decided to start with Belinda Parsley.

She opened her bedroom door after a short delay. There was a film on the TV, an indentation in the bedcover. 'Yes?' she asked in a flat voice, then looked inquiringly at Baggo. 'You served us dinner on Thursday night, didn't you?'

He produced his warrant. 'As I told you when your

room was searched, I'm Detective Sergeant Chandavarkar. I have been undercover.'

Not registering any emotion, she asked, 'Well, what do you want?'

'May I come in, please?'

She shrugged and walked slowly to the bed, turned down the TV volume then sat in the chair beside the window. She brushed her hair back from her face.

Baggo stood in front of her. 'You may know there has been another murder, Mr Bruce Thornton. What were your movements between two and quarter past three this afternoon?'

'Am I a suspect?' she asked, suddenly alert.

'We are asking everyone this question,' he assured her.

'Well, after my room had been searched, I went to the bar upstairs to finish my sandwiches. I sat with Eileen and Simon, the Eglintons, you know.'

'Did you see Mr Thornton or Mr Davidson?'

'Oliver's boyfriend's name was Thornton? I just knew him as Bruce. They left as we were having coffee.'

'When was that?'

'I wasn't watching the time.'

'Well, how long was it before you left the bar?'

'Not long. I really don't know. Five, ten minutes.'

'Did the Eglintons leave with you?'

'Yes. I went to my room and turned on the TV.'

'Is it a good film?' The screen was filled by a car chase through city streets.

She looked at him blankly. 'I have no idea. I'm just numb.'

'Did you know Bruce Thornton at all?'

'No, but he seemed a friendly boy, told me he was sorry about Hugh.'

'Was anything said about playing Santa Claus?'

'Yes. Oliver had wanted to do it, but wasn't going to be able to. Bruce seemed quite keen on standing in. He didn't look a likely Santa to me, too young and with a funny way of looking at you.'

'What do you mean?'

'Well, he didn't. Look at you when he was talking to you, you know?'

'Do you remember anything else that was said?'

'Simon and Oliver arranged to meet later in the afternoon. Business. Simon looked dreadful and he hardly touched his food. He had a couple of large G and Ts, though. Oliver said something about needing fresh air before they met.' She looked out of the window into the late afternoon gloom of a Scottish winter. 'When will I be able to leave? Can you tell me?'

'That's up to Inspector Fortune. I can have a word with her if you want.'

She looked imploringly at him. 'Please do. I'm so … miserable.'

'But there are things I need to know. Please tell me about your relationship with Mr Forbes.'

Her eyes opened wide and her mouth opened and shut like a fish. 'What … no!'

'There's no point in denying it, ma'am, but the sooner we know all the facts the sooner people can leave.'

'But the cameras …'

Baggo raised his eyebrows. 'What about the cameras, ma'am?'

'The CCTV. I didn't think they covered our doors.'

'Did Mr Forbes tell you that?'

She nodded then put her head on to the table in front of her. Her shoulders heaved with silent sobs. Baggo sat opposite her and put a hand on her arm.

'Please tell me everything you know. It really would be in your best interests.'

She lifted her face and wiped it with a tissue. Seeming to cave in on herself, she spoke deliberately, her voice sad and soft. 'I loved Hugh, but we were growing apart. He'd always been a womaniser and wasn't going to change. And I discovered I wanted children. He has two by his first marriage but he never sees them and he had a vasectomy. It was part of the deal when we married, no kids. Recently all my friends, my sisters … I discovered that Mark Forbes wanted children. We had got chatting at a business do. So … you can guess. We were talking about me leaving Hugh, marrying Mark, but Mark insisted on doing nothing till some business problems had been sorted.'

'And on Thursday night?' Baggo prompted.

'Mark and I both made our excuses after dinner. I knew Hugh would be ages till he came to bed. I went to Mark's room, but you probably know that already.'

'When did you return to your own room? Just to confirm what we have,' he added.

'About quarter to eleven. I'm sure Hugh didn't know about us – he was too busy hiding his own affairs from me – but Mark didn't want him to find out till the business problems were over.'

'Did you know anything about these business problems?'

'No.' She answered too quickly, Baggo thought.

'Mrs Parsley, you would be surprised how much we know about what was going on in the bank. Look, we can tell when someone is being cooperative and telling us what they know, and when they're not. We can prove that your husband was very involved in transactions that broke the law. There's no point in you trying to protect his memory or anything like that, and if you help us we would not want to prosecute you. On the other hand, should you be obstructive, you might find yourself in very hot water, widow or not.'

'I knew my husband had business problems because for the last couple of months he was nervous and short-tempered. He kept on checking his phone for messages. He'd never been like that before. At least not for any length of time. I asked him what was wrong and he just said it was business and clammed up. I know he took risks, Mr Cha …'

'Chandavarkar.'

'He has always taken risks, sailed close to the wind, but recently he was really spooked.'

'Did you not ask Mr Forbes?'

'Yes, but he said something about "expanding the client base" and "proactively pursuing new options". I knew he wasn't telling me everything.'

'So Mr Forbes knew what was really troubling your husband?'

She shook her head. 'I can't say that.'

'Who were the other people at work he spoke to most often?'

'Simon. They've always been friends. Nicola sometimes. Terry, too. And Gerald, of course.'

Changing tack, Baggo asked, 'Of the other bank people, who thought the CCTV didn't cover their rooms?'

'I've no idea. Just me and Mark, I think.'

'Was it Mr Forbes who twisted the camera round?'

She nodded. 'He said he found a chair in the corridor behind the camera and stood on it. Certainly the Eglintons didn't know. Eileen was saying at lunch how surprised she was that they hadn't spotted the murderer on CCTV. I told them I'd overheard someone say the camera didn't cover our doors. Well, I couldn't tell them about Mark twisting it round. I know they hate him.'

Baggo searched her face and decided she was probably telling him about as much as she knew. 'Thank you, Mrs Parsley. I'm sorry to have troubled you. And you have my sympathy for your loss.'

'How much could you see on the CCTV?' she asked.

He did not respond, just nodded towards her and left.

* * *

Simon Eglinton did look dreadful, as Belinda Parsley had said. He lay on the bed and scowled at Baggo while his wife sat at the table by the window doing the crossword, her left hand clawed round awkwardly as she filled in the squares.

'I am sorry to interrupt …' he began.

'No you're not,' Mrs Eglinton corrected him. 'But at least you're showing your true colours today. I should have known you were a phoney. Your silver service was not up to scratch for an hotel like this.'

Baggo knew that the best way of coping with someone like her was to stand up to her. 'I learned my waiting in the Taste of Mumbai in Kensington. If you have ever dined there you will know they don't do silver service.'

She glared at him then suddenly made a noise like a startled horse. He stopped himself from stepping back and noted a twinkle in her eye. As a child he had been regaled with stories of the memsahibs, formidable English women who ruled their husbands who, in turn, ruled India. He had found these women awe-inspiring and he had little doubt that this lady was out of the same mould: haughty, outspoken and, within her sphere of influence, a despot.

'I regret that it is necessary that I speak with Mr Simon Eglinton,' he said, holding up his warrant.

'My husband is very tired. He will speak to you later,' his wife said grandly.

'Later will be too late, ma'am. There are things we have to know urgently. And I do believe it would be in your husband's best interests to cooperate with us as far as he can.'

'All right, all right. We can't put it off for ever.' Simon Eglinton sat up on the bed and wiped his eyes. 'What do you want to know?' he asked impatiently.

'Simon!' his wife said, glaring at him. 'Tomorrow

morning would be far better. You've had a very stressful time today.'

As Eglinton swung his legs round to the side of the bed facing him, Baggo caught a waft of gin.

'I don't care,' Eglinton said. 'They can go to hell as far as I'm concerned.'

'Do you mean your fellow directors?' Baggo asked.

Eglinton nodded. 'Bastards,' he muttered.

'Simon!' his wife said again. He caught her eye and bowed his head.

'I know about the money laundering,' Baggo said, trying to keep momentum in his favour. 'When did you learn about it?'

'Today, dammit. Today. Oliver Davidson was waffling on about being Santa Claus. Saddlefell interrupted him to announce that the bank has a major problem, and that we've been breaking the law for years. Apparently most of our recent profits have come from money laundering. I thought that Hugh was doing a great job in the investment arm, but he was making criminals of us. Saddlefell then circulated papers setting it all out. I couldn't believe what I was reading, but it's real enough. Oliver Davidson was as appalled as I was, but the rest … We have "Chinese walls" in the bank, so we don't know each other's business, and the whole enterprise is based on trust. Trust …' he shook his head.

'Simon …' his wife said for a third time, pulling at her left ear.

'We do know about the bearer bonds, the Politically Exposed Persons and LIBOR,' Baggo cut in. 'For anyone not involved, the best course is complete frankness.'

'So you say,' Mrs Eglinton said forcefully. Baggo wondered if she was about to ram her newspaper into her husband's mouth.

'God!' Eglinton exclaimed, looking away. 'I can't believe this is happening.'

'It is, sir,' Baggo said gently. 'Please tell me as much as you know.'

'Well, my conscience is clear, officer. Saddlefell claimed it was all down to Hugh and Gerald and he'd known nothing about it. So did Nicola and Forbes, but they weren't shocked, like I was shocked and Oliver was shocked. Saddlefell said you, the police, had started poking round and we were in for a tricky time. He assured us that the bad practices had been stopped as soon as he learned about them, which was about a month ago. That was why it was essential that we lowered the threshold for our clients. If our profits suddenly nose-dived it would look suspicious without some big change in the way we did business. He said the transactions were well hidden. They'd got past our auditors and there was no reason why they should not get past the police, so we should just sit tight and hope the storm passed. It could all be blamed on Hugh and Gerald if necessary. Oliver said he was sick of banking anyway. He was appalled by this and he was going to tell Inspector Fortune everything. We all asked him to wait and think things through. Yes, I wanted him to wait, too. This bank is my birthright, officer. I don't want to see it going down in scandal. Anyway, he agreed to think about it.'

'But was there not concern about Sir Paul Monmouth's

death being a murder? Was he not concerned about possible criminality in the bank?' Baggo asked.

'Yes, but I thought that was just mis-reporting inter-bank lending rates for LIBOR. All the banks were doing that in 2008, just to keep confidence up. I didn't see that as a major problem for us, though Sir Paul was a man of total integrity and would definitely have seen it as quite unacceptable. Saddlefell wanted to get to the bottom of what happened to Sir Paul without involving you, and I backed him, as did the rest.'

'Was that why you hired ex-Inspector Osborne?'

'You know about that?'

'We know a lot. But did you really not suspect anything about the money laundering sir?'

'Honestly, no. I trusted my colleagues. We're all individuals, with separate skills, but we all know the difference between right and wrong, at least I thought we did. My area is UK corporate, and I can tell you, I'm a damned good stock-picker. I go for companies without much debt, that pay dividends, that are well-run. If one goes sour on me, I don't hesitate to exit quickly. I've out-performed our bench-mark for each of the last five years, and my advice is available to both the investment arm of the bank and the client wealth management arm. I assume that my colleagues are equally skillful so when I saw good profits I was confident they came from honest banking practice, and I didn't put the accounts under a microscope. The auditors were quite happy, so I was too.' He glared at Baggo, defying him to disbelieve him.

'I see,' Baggo said. 'But apart from their reaction this

morning, what makes you believe your fellow-directors knew what was really going on?'

'I just knew this morning that they had known. I can't say any more.' He clenched his fist. 'I'm so angry with Sauce, so disappointed in him. I thought he'd learned. And Gerald, I could strangle him. What on earth was he thinking of?'

'Officer, my husband is very tired and he has told you all he can. Please leave us now.' Mrs Eglinton got up and stood between her husband and Baggo.

'I am just going, ma'am, and I am very grateful for your time. I have just a couple of questions. After you finished your lunch upstairs in the Fourth Floor where did you go?'

She spoke, 'We came straight back here and didn't move till we heard the noise in the corridor when that boy's body was found.'

'Have either of you any idea who might have killed Mr Thornton or Mr Parsley?'

'No,' she said. He shook his head.

'Did you hear any bangs, thumps or voices at or around three o' clock?'

'No,' they said in unison.

'When did you learn that the CCTV in the corridor does not cover the rooms on this side?'

Mrs Eglinton snorted. 'That's four questions, but Belinda Parsley told us today at lunch. Goodbye, officer.' She put an arm out and shepherded Baggo towards the door.

'Thank you, ma'am, sir. You have been most helpful,' he said as the door slammed.

13

As she drove through the cold, damp blackness towards the lights of St Andrews Flick felt depressed and helpless. Bruce's untimely death had robbed him and his parents of the opportunity to mend their estrangement. They had parted for ever on bad terms and his parents would never get over that. Bigotry had a lot to answer for, she thought, then asked herself how she and Fergus would cope should they find themselves in a similar situation. Her hand went to her stomach and she wondered what the future might bring.

'It's a damn shame, ma'am,' McKellar said as they neared the Old Course Hotel.

'It is, and we're going to find out who did it and make them pay,' Flick said, warming to the man.

'Keep driving, ma'am,' McKellar said sharply as she pulled into the car park. 'Press,' he added.

A dozen or more individuals, well muffled against the cold, milled round the front entrance. Out of the corner of her eye Flick glimpsed long-lensed cameras, tripods and clipboards. A figure in a padded anorak carried one of the long, furry microphones used by TV crews. If the unnamed corpse on the second tee had failed to attract much interest, the fact that it was a London banker who had been bludgeoned to death made it very newsworthy, particularly with another violent killing in the nearby five-star hotel.

'I don't know what to say to them,' Flick blurted, driving out of the car park without slowing down.

'Go back in the far entrance and park beside the Jigger Inn. We can get in that way,' McKellar ordered.

'Thanks,' she replied meekly and did as she was told. She fumbled as she turned off her lights, got out and remembered to click the car lock as McKellar ushered her towards the side door.

'Quick, in here,' he said, pushing her into the well-stocked Pro's Shop where an athletic-looking young man in golfing clothes smiled expectantly at her. She half smiled at him as McKellar left through another door and came back quickly. 'The *Courier* man is waiting for us,' he said then turned to the bemused-looking golf steward. 'Laurie, the inspector needs to see the club store. Show her there in one minute's time and wait. I'll come for you when the coast is clear, ma'am,' he added to Flick then left again. She heard him speaking firmly to someone.

Catching on, Laurie showed her into a room next to the shop. It was packed with golf bags, neatly arranged in rows. 'Was there anything you wanted to see?' he asked.

Flick looked round the room. The golf clubs were like ranks of soldiers, the ridged faces of the irons all similar yet subtly different. One bag contained clubs which faced the other way, showing their backs.

'Why are these clubs not pointing the same way as the rest?' she asked.

'They're Mr Thompson's clubs,' the young man said. 'He's left-handed.'

'Of course,' she said, feeling vaguely foolish and remembering what Dr MacGregor had said about Parsley's injuries. Thinking about the likely murder weapon in the second killing she asked, 'Could you show me something called a lob wedge, please?'

The young man picked a club out of a bag and showed it to her. 'This is one. It's the most lofted club in the bag, sixty degrees. You use it to cut the legs from under the ball and lob it over a bunker so it lands and stops.' He executed some practice swings, deftly clipping the floor with the sole of the short-shafted club. He handed it to Flick, who examined the big face and the leading edge of the sole. 'Was that what …?' he asked.

'I can't say,' she said, aware of sounding abrupt, then added, 'I mean we have to wait for the pathologist to tell us. Thank you for your help.' She handed the club back to him and he replaced it in its bag.

'Is there anything else?' he asked.

'I don't suppose you were working late on Thursday night when Mr Parsley and Mr Eglinton collected some things from here?'

'Yes I was, actually. I gave a statement yesterday.' From his tone, Flick guessed that he expected her to have read it.

'Oh yes,' she said. 'But I'd like to hear how you would describe their mood.'

He looked at her for a moment, weighing up how to say it.

She smiled encouragingly. 'You don't need to be polite.'

'They were pissed. Totally pissed. Mr Parsley told me: "Eggers is the luckiest fucking golfer on the fucking planet." Mr Eglinton said: "And I'm going to teach him another lesson." Then they had a pretend sword fight with their putters. I wondered if I should have tried to stop them, but if I had they'd have made more noise. So I just let them get on with it. Now I wish I'd done something.' His face creased with worry.

'You weren't to know what would happen,' she said. 'Don't beat yourself up. And you've been most helpful.'

The door opened and McKellar signaled Flick to come with him. 'Quick and we'll miss him,' he said, then added, 'Thanks, Laurie.'

Half-running along a corridor displaying the names and images of generations of Open Champions, Flick and McKellar reached the sanctuary of the conference room used by the police. Baggo and Wallace stood waiting for them and Dr MacGregor sat at the table, drumming his fingers.

'We should give them something soon, ma'am, or they'll never stop pestering us,' Wallace said.

'Right,' she said. 'Oh and thank you very much, McKellar.'

'Cannae have the boss looking daft in public,' he replied, a crooked smile on his face. 'Shall I stay or go?'

The realisation that all the time he had been helping her he had been laughing at her made her want to slap him. Pretending her skin was thicker than it was, she smiled and said, 'Stay, please. I'd value your input.'

Eyebrows raised but not looking displeased, McKellar leaned against a wall.

'My part in this is thankfully brief, Inspector,' MacGregor said, 'and you should know how Mr Thornton died. The murder weapon was almost certainly the lob wedge found in the room. I believe that this killing was not dissimilar to Mr Parsley's demise. The attacker approached Mr Thornton from the rear and struck him first on the back of the head with a right-handed, downwards, chopping blow, the wedge being swung above the attacker's head. This blow probably rendered him unconscious and he went face down on the floor. The killer stood to the left of his head and hit him repeatedly, four or five times, on the back of the neck, swinging the lob wedge right-handed as if trying to hack a ball out of thick rough. For non-golfers that means violent downward blows. All blows were struck through the Santa outfit. They caused gross damage to the brain and death took place rapidly. I believe you already know the time. There is nothing more I can tell you at the present. I'll do the PM tomorrow morning, but this evening I was hoping to spend time in the company of people who are still alive.'

'Of course, thank you, Doctor,' Flick said, her mind on the press. As the pathologist left the room she sat down and began to draft a brief, factual statement.

'There's been another development, ma'am,' Wallace said. 'Di Falco and I questioned the Saddlefells, Forbes and Walkinshaw about their movements between half past two and quarter past three, and they all say they were in their rooms. But Forbes, whose room is next to Thornton's, said he heard a voice in the corridor saying, "It's me, Terry." He said it could have been Saddlefell, but he couldn't swear it was. He was vague about the time. I think we have enough to bring Saddlefell in for questioning.'

'I am very suspicious of Forbes,' Baggo cut in. 'He plays games with people's lives and he has been having an affair with Belinda Parsley.'

Wallace whistled softly and McKellar shook his head.

Flick was astonished. 'How did you find that out?' she asked.

'She admitted it to me. I haven't spoken to him yet.'

'But does that change anything?' Wallace asked.

Baggo said, 'I don't know, but I do know that I wouldn't trust Forbes not to try to frame Saddlefell.'

'Why do you say that?' Flick asked, sensing he could say more.

Baggo did not want to reveal his part in No's scheme to plant the money clip, which was still burning a hole in his pocket. 'I will explain it all later, Inspector ma'am.'

She said, 'Saddlefell had the opportunity to commit both murders, and he lied to us about when he went in on Thursday night. Killing Parsley would make it easier to blame all the money laundering on him and Knarston-Smith. But why kill Thornton?'

Baggo said, 'I have just spoken with Eglinton and his formidable memsahib. He told me that at the meeting this morning, when Davidson heard what had been going on, he threatened to spill all the beans to you. Eglinton said the rest of the directors, but particularly Saddlefell, wanted to keep a lid on things. If Thornton was killed wearing the Santa outfit, it was probably mistaken identity. Davidson had told everyone he would be dressed as Santa this afternoon.'

Wallace said, 'Thornton's alone in the room, wearing the Santa costume. There's a knock on the door. He either looks out the spy-hole or the killer identifies himself. Thornton knows him and is not afraid of him so opens the door and turns to walk back into the room. The lob wedge was beside the door so the killer comes in and hits him from behind, believing he is attacking Davidson.'

'That is as good a theory as any,' Baggo said.

'Saddlefell had a motive for both killings,' Flick whispered. 'It's just a pity there's been no sign of that money clip.'

'I had a quick word with Mrs Parsley,' Wallace said. 'She said her husband would either have carried the clip in his pocket or left it in the room. I checked and it wasn't on the body and Mrs Parsley couldn't find it in the room. We didn't find it either. The killer probably took it.'

Baggo shook his head. 'Is Saddlefell the sort of person who would want to take a trophy after killing Parsley? He's not the only one who did not want Davidson to spill the beans. If we take him in, he'll call a lawyer and say nothing.'

'If he's rattled he might make a mistake,' Flick said dismissively. 'But I'd better say something to the press first. I think I'll confirm the identities of the victims and the times and places of death. I'll say we're treating both cases as murder. We're pursuing a number of lines of inquiry and if any member of the public has information about either killing they should contact us. I have the incident room number. Will that do?'

'They'll want to be told something they don't already know, but we should give them as little as possible,' Wallace said.

'There will be questions,' Baggo said, 'such as whether we hope to make an early arrest. It would probably be best to reply "No comment" to all questions.'

'You'd be surprised how much these reporters can find out when they put their minds to it,' McKellar warned. 'They're fly beggars,' he added.

'Should I say that both victims appear to have been beaten to death by golf clubs?' Flick asked.

'I'd say no,' Wallace said. 'We want to keep plenty of details up our sleeves so we can sort out the attention-seekers when they come to confess.'

'And spot when a suspect tells us something only the killer would know,' Baggo added.

Flick read through her notes, took a deep breath and got up.

'Do you want me there, ma'am?' Wallace asked.

Flick smiled at him. 'No, but thank you,' she said.

Hoping she appeared more confident than she felt, she strode through the lobby as the Christmas Fayre shut down. The news of the second murder had cast a pall of fear mixed with excitement round the hotel but a few determined shoppers continued to seek late bargains.

In a non-speaking role Flick had attended a number

of press conferences in London. They had all been well-planned, held in an appropriate room with microphones. This was virgin territory for her, but she was determined not to let the situation overwhelm her.

'It's her, the inspector,' she heard as she moved clear of the hotel entrance and positioned herself facing the journalists and under a light. Slowly, loudly and clearly, she read out her prepared text, a confusion of flashlights, cameras, microphones, notepads and people a few feet in front of her. When she came to the end she smiled, nodded and made to return to the hotel.

'Were both men killed with golf clubs?'

'Was the second victim in a gay relationship with a banker?'

'Is anyone else in danger?'

'Are you investigating the Bucephalus Bank for money laundering?'

'Do you have a prime suspect?'

All these questions were fired at once. 'No comment,' she said firmly.

'Can we expect an early arrest?'

'No comment.'

'Do you mean that there will be no early arrest as this murderer is too clever for you?'

Flick rounded on the weasel-like man in a dirty raincoat who had asked the last two questions. 'I don't mean that at all. Of course I hope for an early arrest. We are following some promising lines of inquiry.'

More questions were shouted but Flick ignored them and walked quickly back into the lobby.

'How did it go, ma'am?' Wallace asked.

'Okay, I think,' she replied, wondering if she should have risen to the reporter's irritating challenge. 'Now, what do we do about Saddlefell?'

As she spoke, there was a knock on the door and Gilsland rushed in, hair now wild, shirt front out of his trousers, arms making strange semaphore signals. He had been checking the CCTV covering the corridor where the directors' rooms were. 'You have to see this, ma'am,' he blurted.

In the CCTV room a number of grainy screens were active. Gilsland pointed to one which was frozen and showed a lift, a couple of doors and a lot of wall and ceiling. No one had thought to twist the camera back to where it should have pointed. Gilsland pressed a button and at 14.20 Sheila Anderson went from the lift to her room. 'She stayed there till the alarm was raised,' Gilsland commented. He hit fast forward until 14.43 when a woman came from the lift. She was middle-aged, with white hair cut short. As she looked round her sharp features were clearly shown.

'That's his mum,' Flick gasped.

After looking left and right the woman went out of the picture but reappeared at 14.51. Head down, a hand to her face, she waited for the lift then went in. Nothing happened until 14.59, when Jocelyn came out of the lift. At 15.02 unidentifiable heads bobbed about as the alarm was raised. Di Falco emerged from the lift and appeared to be the first police officer to get there.

Flick said, 'We have to see his mother again

immediately.' She looked at Gilsland, half blaming him for not using his initiative. 'I know we're bolting the stable door after the horse has bolted, but please make sure the CCTV in that corridor is properly set.'

Wallace said, 'No one could have foreseen that there would be a second murder, ma'am.'

Baggo said, 'Lance is right. What has happened was not on the cards.'

McKellar smiled wryly and shook his head. Flick sensed he blamed her and feelings of insecurity crowded in on her again.

Taking Wallace to Strathkinness, in ten minutes she was back at the Thornton's home. The chiming bell was answered quickly, the door opening a fraction.

'What do you want?' It was the voice of a woman.

'Police. We're here to see Mrs Thornton.'

The door opened fully, revealing Grace Thornton, her face grim, still wearing her apron and clutching a sodden handkerchief.

'We have to see you, I'm afraid,' Flick said. 'We don't need to bother your husband.' From the sitting room the voice of a Scottish football pundit boomed.

The unhappy woman sighed. 'You'd better come into the kitchen, then.' She led the way through the hall to the back of the house where there was a rich aroma of baking. A chocolate cake fresh out of the oven lay on the table, a bowl of icing beside it. 'Bruce loved a chocolate cake,' she said. Then tears ran down her cheeks and she began to weep.

Flick and Wallace stood awkwardly for a time, then

Flick said, 'We know you went to see him this afternoon.'

She nodded and stopped crying. 'I thought you'd be back. Don't tell Walter, please.'

'Tell us what happened,' Flick said.

She took a couple of deep breaths and sat on an unsteady wooden chair. 'I was in town this morning and I ran into Archie Turnbull. He's one of Bruce's friends, and he told me Bruce was here, staying with that man in the Old Course. He even had the room number.' She paused then continued, speaking slowly and carefully, her eyes never leaving the cake in front of her. 'He'd seen Bruce on Thursday night and he wanted things to be better between us. Archie's been coming round the house since he was a wee boy. Anyway, I met my friend for lunch, as arranged, and we spoke about it. It was the first time I'd mentioned it outside the family, and Walter won't talk about it. I decided to go round and see Bruce, and beg him to give up that dreadful man and come and see us.' Her whole body shook, she lifted her gaze as if for strength and stared at the wall ahead.

'He was dressed as Santa,' she continued. 'And he said he would have to go in five minutes. I said my piece, and he just stood there. He said, "Why can't you see this is how I am? I've fought it for years, but this is me. If it wasn't Oliver it would be another man. And he's good to me. You'd like him, if you gave him a chance."'

'Then?' Flick prompted.

Her eyes darted round the room then she said, 'I left. As I went he said, "I love you, Mum."'

'Did you see anyone, suspicious or not, in the corridor, ma'am?' Wallace asked.

She shook her head. 'No.'

Flick did not know what to do. Her instinct told her she had been given only part of the truth and the time of the visit meant there was a very narrow window in which anyone else could have committed the murder. Yet there was no mistaking the woman's genuine grief, and to bring in a traumatised mother for questioning was a serious step, not to be done unless she was pretty sure.

'Why didn't you tell us earlier?' Wallace asked.

'Walter can't cope with the whole business.' She looked at him pleadingly. 'When I got home I told him about meeting Archie and he started raging. I couldn't tell him I'd seen Bruce. I would have told him, but much later. Please, does he have to know now?'

'Not immediately,' Flick said. 'But whom did you meet for lunch when you talked about Bruce?'

'Ina Campbell.' She opened a drawer in the table and brought out a notepad and pencil. She wrote quickly and tore a sheet off the pad. 'There's her address and phone number,' she said, pushing the paper towards Flick.

Flick took it and stood up. 'That will be all for now, Mrs Thornton,' she said formally. 'We'll see ourselves out.'

In the car she said to Wallace, 'She won't go anywhere. If it was her we'll be able to find her when we need to.'

Wallace said nothing for a while then muttered, 'I just can't see her doing it, but if he said something really hurtful to her, you never know.'

Some journalists had remained beside the front entrance so they used the Pro's Shop door again. In the conference room she found McKellar with a grin cracking his face. Beside him, Baggo was in a state of excitement.

'Mr Parsley had some very rich clients,' Baggo said after Flick had reported on their visit. 'I called the man who left a message on his phone and who wanted to speak this afternoon about his bonds. I said, "The President, please." I had guessed that XPB might stand for ex-president something, and I was right, but not ex-President Bush. "Bathalloppo speaking," he said. He wanted to speak to Parsley and would not say what his business was, but I can guess that he wants cash. I said Mr Parsley was not available but had asked me to call. Bathalloppo was not impressed.'

'Who is Bathalloppo?' Flick asked.

'The ex-president of Congango, a tiny African state with lots of starving people and two huge diamond mines. He was ousted three years ago in a coup that was bloodless only because he escaped before anyone could catch him. It was said he took millions of dollars' worth of diamonds with him.'

'That doesn't help us catch our murderer,' she snapped.

'But this might,' McKellar said. 'While he was Googling Bathalloppo one of your pals in London phoned. He said that none of the bank people have a record, but Saddlefell nearly had one. As a student he was charged with grievous bodily harm as you call it in England. He got off claiming it was self-defence. The victim was badly injured. The fight was over a girl. The trial was in Leeds Crown Court in 1982.'

'Good,' Flick exclaimed. 'It's not evidence, but it shows

he can be violent. We're on the right lines with him. Who phoned?' she asked.

McKellar shook his head. 'Tom something, maybe. I can't remember. He was disappointed not to speak to you, but he was going off duty as soon as he finished the call.'

Flick tried not to show her irritation. She sat down and thought.

'We're going to detain Saddlefell for questioning. Now,' she said.

14

When Flick told him that she was detaining him Saddlefell was incandescent. Secretly enjoying the display of impotent bluster that he put on, she knew she had rattled him, as she had planned. She did not want to attract attention from the press and, with Wallace and two constables, she led him down the spa stairway to exit by the Pro's Shop door. As they approached the door one of the constables hissed that there was a cameraman outside. Quickly, Flick took off her coat and threw it over Saddlefell's head before leading him out. A muffled 'How dare you?' could be heard as a series of flashlights went off.

In the interview room of Cupar Police Office Flick sensed pure, controlled aggression from her detainee as he glared across the table at her, mouth shut. His fists were clenched, resting as if in a boxing pose on the grubby formica. He demanded a phone call to his solicitor, which she was bound to permit.

The arrangements, made through Saddlefell's London solicitor, took some time to put in place but she was told to expect Murdo Munro QC, a solicitor-advocate from Edinburgh, who would be with them in an hour. This pleased her. She had six hours in which to question her man, and waiting alone before starting might jangle his nerves.

Wallace was less pleased. 'In the good old days we wouldn't have to wait for a lawyer,' he complained. 'English courts mucking up Scots law,' he added.

'I basically agree with you, actually,' Flick said. 'I've always thought that lawyers in police interviews help the guilty and do no good for the innocent. But there were two very senior Scottish judges in the Supreme Court when they made that ruling.'

'Aye, maybe,' Wallace said. 'Do you want a coffee, ma'am?'

They drank their coffees in silence then Wallace began to pace about the room. Flick hoped the delay might have the same effect on Saddlefell's nerves.

'I think this is him!' Wallace exclaimed later, looking out of the window. They saw a shabby-looking Mazda draw up in front of the building. A small man with crinkly hair and wearing a puffa jacket got out of the passenger seat. Flick met him as he came in the front door. He smiled pleasantly and shook her hand.

'I'm Murdo Munro, here to see Lord Saddlefell.' He emphasised the 'Lord' and Flick thought she spotted a quirky smile flash across his face. 'Thank you for waiting for me but I had to bribe my son to drive me here. Can't be too careful with the drink, no?'

Flick sniffed but detected no whiff of alcohol. This was not the sort of lawyer she loved to hate. Under his jacket he wore an open-necked shirt and a stained jumper. He produced a small notebook and a biro from a pocket and asked what the case was about. As she told him he listened attentively and made notes. He gave no indication of what he thought of the evidence she had gathered. He thanked her again and stated very firmly he would need ten minutes with his client.

'Seems a nice chap,' she observed to Wallace. 'I wonder how he can bear to represent the people he does.'

'He's deadly,' Wallace replied. 'He is incredibly polite and hardly ever raises his voice, but he knows the law backwards and wins over juries just by being reasonable.'

After Munro and Saddlefell had been together for ten minutes Flick and Baggo entered the room. She switched on the recording equipment and read out a full caution. As she adjusted the papers in front of her Munro spoke.

'I have had a necessarily brief discussion with Lord Saddlefell in relation to these matters, which are very complex. It appears to me that you have no hard evidence against Lord Saddlefell on any charge, and that this is a sort of fishing expedition in which you hope he might say something that might be used against him later. While normally he would wish to assist police inquiries, on this occasion I have advised him to refuse to answer any question apart from giving such personal details as he is obliged to give. You have the power to keep him here for nearly five more hours, but in the circumstances I hope you will release him now as this interview is pointless. He tells me that he is already late for an important board meeting scheduled for seven pm and, as a courtesy, I shall inform you that I have instructions to make a formal complaint regarding his treatment this evening which has caused him embarrassment and distress.'

Flick did not know what to say. A strong sense of foreboding gripped her, numbing her brain and squeezing her stomach. Pretending to ignore what Munro had said she asked, 'Did you not lie to us about when you went to bed on Thursday night, claiming you went in earlier than was in fact the case?'

Saddlefell sat back, arms folded in front of him, lips clamped shut and with a gleam of triumph in his eyes.

After a full minute of silence that felt like five she asked, 'Did you visit the room occupied by Davidson and Thornton shortly before Thornton's body was found?'

Another silence.

'Did you kill Thornton by mistake, believing him to be Davidson?'

Another silence. Saddlefell began to smile. Munro kept a poker face but wrote in his notebook.

Baggo nudged Flick's knee and shook his head at her.

'Interview terminated. You're free to go,' she spat, switched off the recorder and swept out of the room.

Saddlefell shook his head in mock sadness and got up.

'Do you want a lift to St Andrews?' Munro asked. 'I'm afraid it's just an old Mazda and I can't vouch for some of the things my son leaves in it.'

'Yes, that would be all right,' Saddlefell said, a hint of doubt in his voice.

'Before you go,' Baggo said, 'we are amassing evidence regarding illegal activity in your bank. Those who were not involved in that activity and who learned of it only recently should consider helping us. That's all I will say now.' He looked pointedly at Munro, who raised an eyebrow.

'Let's get to St Andrews. I need to be at that meeting,' Saddlefell said and they left.

* * *

Still in Cupar, Baggo found Flick at her desk, head in hands.

'We have to think,' he said.

Holding back tears, she looked up at him.

He said, 'We must put our heads together or neither of us will get anywhere. Come on, Inspector ma'am, let us go through all the evidence now and see what we know.'

And so they did. Baggo started by giving a detailed account of his discussions with Gerald and Cynthia Knarston-Smith. Testing the water as far as tricky topics went, he told her about the photograph and pulled it out of his pocket.

'Wow!' she said as she examined it. 'But it hasn't been properly logged,' she protested.

'Knarston-Smith would not have told me all that he did without this,' he replied. 'And as soon as it becomes official it will cease to be effective leverage. If necessary I can add it to the log later.'

'Not on my watch,' she said. 'One bit of planted evidence can destroy the whole case, and if you add it later, who will believe you found it when and where you said you did? Did you seize the computer case?'

'No, but I can tomorrow.' Her promotion had not made her more flexible. He made a mental note to take care if he wanted to use the photograph as evidence. There was no way he would tell her the truth about his sex with Walkinshaw or the saga of the money clip.

They talked about Belinda Parsley and her affair with Forbes then went on to Lord Saddlefell, Sandi Saddlefell, Simon Eglinton, Eileen Eglinton, Nicola Walkinshaw and Oliver Davidson.

They agreed that for Thornton's murder his mother Grace could not be ruled out. They discounted Sheila Anderson as the CCTV gave her an alibi for both murders and she seemed most unlikely anyway. Sandi Saddlefell, Eileen Eglinton and Cynthia Knarston-Smith ended up at the bottom of the list of suspects.

Baggo repeated that taking a trophy from Parsley was a strange thing for a frenzied, non-sexual killer to do. He did not want Flick to give the money clip too much importance.

'I've asked the constables to track down the chambermaid who told Osborne about the clip,' she said. 'But what on earth was he really doing here anyway?'

'I spoke to him briefly to tell him I had been kicked out of the police so he would not blow my cover. He said he was here, paid by the bank, to find out who murdered Sir Paul and Parsley while being discreet. In other words, the bank hoped the killer would be caught quickly without the sort of investigation which might uncover the money laundering.'

'It would be just like him to plant something like a money clip on his prime suspect,' Flick mused.

Baggo felt the small metal object warm against his thigh and changed the subject. 'I wonder why they are having that board meeting,' he said.

The phone on Flick's desk rang. It was McKellar, who had been left at the hotel to keep his ear to the ground. She listened intently, astonished at what she heard.

'We'd better get back to the hotel. McKellar's arrested Saddlefell. He's assaulted Forbes.'

* * *

'I'd do it again. The bastard stitched me up.' Saddlefell thumped the table in what was now known as the police room and glared at Flick, then at Baggo and Wallace. 'And you lot helped him.'

There seemed to be no dispute about what had happened. Saddlefell had got back to the hotel to find that the meeting was over. After a brief word with Eglinton he had gone looking for Forbes and found him drinking champagne in the Fourth Floor Bar with Walkinshaw. Forbes had stood up and Saddlefell had punched him twice, once to the solar plexus and once to the face. Although groggy, Forbes insisted he was fine, but the bar manager had summoned McKellar.

'How do you think we helped him?' Flick asked indignantly.

'You got me out of the way at the time of that meeting.'

'I didn't know about the meeting till you told us. What happened at it?'

Saddlefell breathed deeply and shook his head. 'You must know about the chairmanship.'

Baggo interjected, 'Lord Saddlefell, we do not know what you are talking about. Honestly.'

'Honestly, we don't,' Wallace added.

Saddlefell looked from Baggo to Flick and shrugged. 'In view of recent events, I considered it essential that we should have a properly appointed chairman immediately and I called a meeting for seven o' clock this evening to elect one, hopefully myself. As I was with you in Cupar, only Forbes, Nicola, Simon and Oliver attended. Forbes insisted the meeting should go ahead and produced a proxy I had given him months ago for a different meeting and a different issue. But the proxy was so widely phrased that it enabled him to count me as voting with him on any issue if I was not there. So he steamrollered it through. Nicola proposed him, Oliver proposed Simon. It was three against two and now he's chairman of the bank. I'll check with my lawyers, but I suspect there's not a damn thing I can do about it.'

Baggo and Flick exchanged glances. It had been Forbes who had heard 'It's Terry' in the corridor before Thornton was killed. He had used the police to become chairman. Baggo was not surprised but Flick was furious.

She said, 'This assault will be reported to the procurator fiscal, who will decide what to do. You're free to go, Lord Saddlefell, but I advise you to keep out of Mr Forbes's way. If you were to assault him again we'd have to take much stronger action.'

Wearily, Saddlefell rose and left the room. 'You know, a bit of me feels quite sorry for him,' Baggo said.

'But we're no closer to finding our murderer,' Flick replied.

As the three detectives sat thinking, Baggo's mobile rang. He listened then said, 'Stay where you are. I'll be with you in five.' After ending the call he explained, 'Forbes, the new chairman, has summoned Knarston-Smith to a meeting in his room at nine-fifteen. I'm going to see him before he goes there.'

'We'd better interview Forbes about that assault,' Flick said to Wallace. 'It won't take long.'

* * *

Baggo found Gerald and Cynthia in their room, the atmosphere thick with conflict. She was looking daggers at her husband while he sat on the bed twitching and running his hands through his hair. She turned to Baggo, her expression full of anger and despair, but said nothing.

'Thank you for calling me,' Baggo said to Gerald.

Gerald shrugged.

'I will need to know what is said at this meeting,' Baggo continued, 'and this is where you can do yourself a lot of good.'

Cynthia snorted with disgust.

'You can dig yourself out of the hole you dug for yourself,' Baggo said.

'Or into your grave,' Cynthia turned on her husband, her fists clenched. 'Remember, two people have been killed. I could kill you myself,' she added, her voice catching.

'I'll tell you what's said,' Gerald said meekly.

'But you could do more,' Baggo told him. 'I would like you to wear a bug so we can hear and record everything. That would provide terrific evidence if Forbes said anything incriminating.'

'You'd incriminate yourself as well,' Cynthia said sharply.

'We've already got plenty evidence against him, Mrs Knarston-Smith,' Baggo said. 'If he helps us he helps himself.'

'So he might not go to jail?'

'That would not be up to me, but that would be possible.'

Cynthia searched Baggo's face then turned to her husband. 'You fool, you total bloody idiot,' she hissed.

Gerald recoiled as if he had been slapped. Baggo reckoned he had spent most of the day as a verbal punch-bag. 'Forbes is paranoid about secrecy. He's been known to check people for bugs in the office,' Gerald said, his voice rising in alarm.

Baggo was glad he had brought his computer with him from Cupar. He opened the case and from one of its many pockets produced a flat metal chip about half an inch square, some wires and a small plastic box. Trying to lighten the atmosphere, he held up the chip and said, 'Imagine I am Q in a James Bond film. This is what I would like you to wear. It will be very difficult to find.'

'Not if he checks my clothes. As I say, he's paranoid and very careful.'

Baggo looked at him. He was entirely unsuited to the sort of role he was needed for. He was an inoffensive, timid guy, brilliant at maths but otherwise, as his wife said, an idiot. Although his hair had reminded Baggo of the new Q in *Skyfall*, he was no 007. It would have to be Plan B.

'You have a mobile phone,' Baggo said, smiling encouragingly. 'I want you to switch it on, ring this number, put it in your trouser pocket then go into the bathroom and say something.'

'What?'

'Quote something. You must know a poem.'

Gerald did as instructed and closed the bathroom door behind him. Baggo pressed some buttons on his own mobile then flicked a switch on the black plastic box from which Gerald's muffled voice could be heard. He was reciting numbers.

'Prime numbers. He can go on for ages,' Cynthia said.

'It's not as clear as I would like, but it will have to do,' Baggo observed. He knocked on the bathroom door. 'Right, you can come out now.'

'211, 223, 227,' Gerald said very quickly as he opened the door.

Baggo shook his head. He dimly remembered a king, perhaps James I, had been called 'the wisest fool in Christendom'. Here was his twenty-first century equivalent. 'Go to meet Forbes as you are,' he said once Gerald had emerged. 'If he wants to search you, or there's any problem, you can put your hand in your pocket and turn the phone off before you bring it out. Forbes will not recognise my number and this box has sent a message to your phone so it will look as if the call to me is already over, though it is not. We might be dealing with dangerous people and your safety is paramount. You are to take no risks. If the conversation is not incriminating, so be it. Do not try to trap Forbes into admitting something. I, with other policemen, will be in the hotel, ready to come to your rescue should that be necessary. What will you say if you are asked what you have told the police?'

Gerald ran his hand through his hair. 'I'll say I told you nothing.'

'Forbes is too smart to swallow that, I suspect. I think you might get away with saying that you helped with the LIBOR mis-reporting but know nothing about any other criminal behaviour. You can say you told us that Parsley handled a lot of deals himself.'

'He did, actually.'

'All the better. Keep as near to the truth as you can. First rule of lying.'

'And the second is don't get caught,' Cynthia said. Baggo found her lively eyes and forceful personality attractive. How she had been snared by a wet fish like Gerald was hard to understand.

'And the third is lie with confidence,' Baggo added. While Gerald nodded sagely, Cynthia raised her eyes to the ceiling.

Wishing Gerald good luck, Baggo put his eavesdropping equipment in the computer case and left. He switched up the receiver's volume in the police room. Cynthia was still giving her husband an ear-bashing.

* * *

Mark Forbes did not pretend he was pleased to see Flick

and Wallace when he answered the door of his room. She had to stop herself from smiling when she saw how his full lips had swollen until, bulbous and red, they looked as if they were being squeezed like toothpaste out of his tiny mouth. He did not invite them to sit down and remained standing while she explained why they were there.

'Lord Saddlefell was over-wrought, Inspector, and I have no wish to take the matter further. I regard it as an internal matter for our bank and I will not be pressing charges. Thank you for coming to see me, however.' He appeared to be making an effort to form his words clearly.

'It doesn't work that way in Scotland, sir,' Wallace said. 'Once a crime has been committed and can be proved it's up to the procurator fiscal to decide if it would be in the public interest to prosecute, whatever the victim says he wants.'

Momentarily taken aback, Forbes addressed Flick as if Wallace was not there. 'I do hope you feel you have enough on your plate at the moment, Inspector. With people being murdered almost daily, I trust you won't feel the need to get a conviction for petty assault which the victim is happy to forget.'

Ignoring the implied criticism, she smoothly got Forbes to agree the facts of the assault, which he did with ill-natured grunts. She took a picture of his injured face on her mobile phone then asked if there had been a motive for the attack.

'I am now the chairman of the Bucephalus Bank, Inspector, and it is possible that Lord Saddlefell felt envious. I shall say no more.'

'Did you really hear a voice in the corridor this afternoon saying "It's Terry"?' she asked.

Forbes raised his eyebrows as if shocked. 'I believe I did, Inspector. I trust that you have no criticism of a member of the public helping the police, especially when they appear to be struggling in an inquiry that may be too complex for them.'

Flick stared into his cold, unblinking eyes and said, 'You have no idea how our inquiry is progressing Mr Forbes. And genuine assistance from members of the public is always appreciated. ' Then she turned on her heel and left the room.

'Arrogant bastard,' Wallace muttered in a stage whisper before the door had closed behind him.

15

Flick, Baggo, Wallace and McKellar sat round the table in the police room, listening to the black box. '3259, 3271, 3299, 3301 ...' Gerald was making his way to Forbes's room reciting prime numbers, presumably to keep calm.

They could hear a knock then, 'Hello, Mark'. Gerald said this loudly, with forced jollity. 'Ah, Nicola,' he continued with less enthusiasm. The listeners strained to hear Forbes's plummy tones but could make out, 'Gerald, meet Webb van Bilt III, of Sulphur Springs'.

'This could be interesting,' Baggo whispered.

'In view of the situation,' Forbes said, 'we have to be particularly careful about the security of our discussions, so I'm going to have to ask you to submit to a search, as the rest of us have already done ...' The sound went dead.

'We've got to hear this,' Baggo said.

'Is there someone you can rely on among the staff?' Flick asked.

'To do what?' Baggo asked.

'To deliver something to that room. We've got a warrant to bug them.'

He thought for a moment. 'Jimmy might help us. He's a waiter and they'll maybe have seen him round the hotel.'

'Get him here, quick.'

Baggo dialed a number, asked for Jimmy and then spoke to him for a minute. 'He's coming, but what's your idea?' he asked Flick.

'I've noticed that the best rooms have orchids in them. They're grown in pots filled with little bits of bark that are dry at the top. I think Mr Forbes could do with a fresh orchid.' She looked at the others. She was gratified by Chandavarkar's smile, but the nods of approval from the two Scots felt like a victory.

Jimmy needed no persuasion. As Baggo launched into an explanation, Jimmy interrupted, 'It's cool, mate. I dinnae like these stuck-up shits. Forbes never says please or thank you and he's aye complaining about something. I'll happily plant a bug for you.'

Ten minutes later he was on his way, a fine purple orchid in his hand. A couple of inches under the surface of the bark chips, the electronic chip nestled.

The officers gathered round the black box, hoping that the ruse would work. Jimmy's knock came across clearly.

'Fresh orchid, Mr Forbes.'

'I don't need it. Go away.'

'But all the rooms get one today, sir. That one on your table looks guy peely-wally.'

'What did you say – peely-wally? What does that mean?' – van Bilt.

'It means needing a drink, sir. I'm usually peely-wally at the end of my shift.'

'Hurry up then. We have business to discuss.' – Forbes.

After some clicks and rustles, 'As we were saying,' – Forbes.

'Yes, Gerald, how much do we have to pay to Webb's people?' – Walkinshaw.

'Thirty-one million, eight hundred and sixty-five thousand pounds, to the nearest thousand.' – Gerald.

'And that money is available now in bearer bonds?' – van Bilt.

'Correct.' – Gerald.

'Why would it be risky to give it to those entitled now?' – van Bilt.

'Because as long as the bonds stay as they are we can attribute them on paper to anyone we like, even someone fictitious. If we're being closely monitored, a transfer to, say, a drug baron might be very damaging evidence.' – Forbes.

'Gerald, can you think of any way we can pay Webb's clients safely?' – Walkinshaw.

'No, not if we're being watched by someone who understands what's happening.' – Gerald.

'Right, you can go now.' – Forbes.

A door clicked.

'The Federal Reserve are very suspicious of both banks and they mean trouble. You Americans lock up far more white-collar people than we do here, and the extradition laws mean you can just reach over the Atlantic and pick up anyone you want if there's an American angle. That's why we have to be ultra-careful, at least till the danger's past.' – Forbes.

'But as Gerald has told us, there's nearly thirty-two million pounds owing to clients of my bank. And they haven't gotten to be where they are by waiting patiently.' – van Bilt.

'They have a lot to lose too if the Federal Reserve comes down hard on us. They may have to learn patience.' – Forbes.

'That's just not the way they do business, and they're ruthless, as Sir Paul found out.' – van Bilt.

'Killing him was a mistake. I hope you don't think either of us had anything to do with it.' – Walkinshaw.

'I don't know what to think, lady. I just know some real mean guys are looking for their money, and when I tell them you have it, they're gonna come over the pond and kick your asses real good.' – van Bilt.

'We could sweeten the pill with a bit of interest when we do pay out.' – Forbes.

'Not gonna save your ass.' – van Bilt.

'Webb, they trust you. You can make them see reason.' – Walkinshaw put on her seductive tone.

'They see their own reason, which is: you owe them money, you pay them money.' – van Bilt.

'How long are we going to have to be careful?' – Forbes.

'The Feds don't quit easy. They've been known to spend five years investigating something.' – van Bilt.

'Sorry, Webb, but you're going to have to tell your clients that they'll have to wait for their money. When we do pay, we'll add interest. And if we go down, they'll finish up with nothing.' – Forbes.

'I guess we've taken this as far as it's gonna go. Please get your numbers guy to work out a way to give my clients their money, even if the Feds are looking over his shoulder.' – van Bilt.

The officers heard a door click then two deep sighs.

'Mark, we're between a rock and a hard place. Thank goodness for Venezuela.' – Walkinshaw.

'I wonder who did order Sir Paul's hit. It wasn't you, was it?' – Forbes.

'Of course not. You maybe? If in doubt, blame Terry Saddlefell.' – Walkinshaw.

The door clicked again. Silence reigned.

Baggo said, 'That was interesting, but no admission of having been involved in whatever was going on from the start.'

Wallace asked, 'Will that box record everything the bug picks up?'

'Yes.' Baggo grinned. 'We will know tomorrow if Mr Forbes snores, and perhaps if Mrs Parsley does too. And it should all be admissible evidence.'

'I wonder what Walkinshaw meant by her reference to Venezuela,' Flick said, 'apart from their extradition policy.'

Baggo said, 'Or non-policy. It is the current destination of choice for sleazeballs who want to go off the radar. But it is not a place I would go to get away from gangsters. Personally, I'd take my chances with the Feds. Right now I'd better go and get a statement from Knarston-Smith. There may have been something important said before the orchid was delivered.'

* * *

Walkinshaw and van Bilt had been in Forbes's room when

Gerald arrived. Forbes had got straight down to business and interrogated him on the transactions between Bucephalus and Sulphur Springs. Gerald's powerful photographic memory had enabled him to quote dates and figures, complete with percentage profits on selected deals.

'There was nothing beyond what was on that memory stick I gave you,' he said. 'Forbes didn't want anything on paper with you about, and none of them took notes.'

'Did you get the impression that they realised we know as much as we do about the financial crimes?' Baggo asked.

Gerald ran his hands through his hair. 'I'm pretty sure they don't. They think that if they act legally they should be alright.'

'Did anyone say something that showed they had been involved from the start?'

Gerald scratched his chin, ignoring or not seeing Cynthia who was nodding her head furiously. ''Fraid not,' he said gloomily. 'I hope I've been helpful?' he added.

Baggo didn't have the heart to further dent his confidence. 'Yes,' he said, 'you have.'

Out in the corridor he could hear Cynthia. 'Idiot!' she shouted.

16

'Where are you going to stay tonight?' Wallace asked Baggo as they packed up for the day.

'I haven't thought,' Baggo said. 'I suppose there will be plenty B and Bs happy for off-season trade.'

'You can stay with us,' Wallace said. 'Jeannie is always happy to meet new people and we can chat about the case over a dram. I have an eighteen-year-old Glenmorangie that will help you think.'

Baggo was delighted. He had taken to Lance Wallace and he wanted to bounce ideas off someone intelligent. He had wondered if the inspector might have made the offer, for the sake of old Wimbledon days if nothing else, but it had always been difficult to get close to her.

'Let's check on Forbes before we go,' Baggo said, pressing a button on the black box. They heard male and female grunting then Belinda Parsley said, 'Kissing's horrible with your mouth like that.' 'Saddlefell will regret this,' was Forbes's muffled reply.

'Shall I leave it on?' Baggo asked the constable left to guard the police room and maintain a presence in the hotel.

'No thanks, Sarge.' The young man blushed.

'It might be a hit on YouTube one day, particularly if

someone takes some pictures to go with the soundtrack,' Baggo said, pretending to be serious as he switched off the speaker and checked the machine was still recording.

'Come on or that Glenmorangie will evaporate,' Wallace said, leading Baggo to his car. He added, 'Don't underestimate the gullibility of a young copper. If he goes out snapping …'

'I'll blame you as you are his sergeant,' Baggo retorted.

They both laughed.

* * *

Inspector Fergus Maxwell was sitting with his feet up, a third glass of sauvignon blanc at his elbow, when Flick arrived home. He turned down the volume on the television, which was showing an American golf tournament, and rushed to the kitchen to heat up the lasagne he had prepared hours earlier. He asked if she wanted a drink.

'Yes but I can't,' she said, tears in her eyes.

He took her in his arms. 'You obviously need a glass of wine and there's no reason why you shouldn't have one,' Fergus whispered. 'I told you, that professor of toxicology insisted there's nothing wrong with pregnant women in good health having the occasional small glass. Remember, I played with him in last month's medal? He kept on going on about the nonsense talked about babies these days. I sometimes wonder how the human race evolved to where it is without all these gurus. Sorry. How was your day? Not good?'

'Midway between that and bloody awful. And I feel as if I'm going to cry whenever anything goes wrong.' She didn't add that, as someone who did things by the book, on this particular evening she found her husband's Jurassic Park views particularly irksome. 'And I just want water, thanks,' she added.

He hugged her close then said, 'You go and get comfortable then come back here. I've done lasagne with avocado salad. And I've opened a nice chianti so I'll pour you a little, as well as your water of course. After we've eaten we can talk. Oh, and your dad phoned. You were on the national news and he's chuffed to bits. So am I, by the way.'

A wan smile lit her face slightly. 'I'll ring him now,' she said.

Her father answered on the second ring. His familiar, cheerful South of England vowels immediately lifted her spirits. Her press conference had impressed him, at least. Gently, she explained that real life was quite different to detective novels. She was not about to put a hand to her brow, tell everyone she had been an imbecile, gather the suspects in the parlour and unmask the murderer. 'I just go where the evidence leads me, Dad,' she said more than once. She checked that he was looking after himself. A widower in his late sixties, he was increasingly content with his own company. Flick worried that he might become isolated, even living in a suburb of Maidenhead. His account of visits to Waitrose sounded too glib for her liking but before she could press him she was on the back foot, telling him that she was managing to keep warm and well as the Scottish winter approached. Putting the phone down, she wished she could break the news about his first grandchild due in the summer, but she and Fergus had agreed to keep that secret until twelve weeks had passed.

Fergus brought in the food and they sat together on the sofa in the warm sitting room, the golf tournament playing silently in the background as they ate, plates on their laps. Flick felt better with every mouthful. 'Delicious, darling,' she commented as she devoured the savory mince and *al dente* pasta.

He beamed. As a bachelor, canteen food and carry-outs had been his staple diet. After marriage, encouraged by the various cookery programmes on the television, he liked to prepare the meal, except in summer when evening golf exercised a stronger pull. He wished Flick was more relaxed about cooking. She could produce some excellent dishes but lacked confidence. It was his mission to build up that confidence, and not just in the kitchen.

'He's a real gentleman,' Fergus commented, his mouth full, nodding at the screen.

'Who?'

'Phil Mickelson. Look, he's signing autographs while waiting on the tee. He really knows it's the public who ultimately pay his wages.'

She glanced at the screen. She knew she must overcome her instinctive coolness about golf if she was to live happily in St Andrews, particularly married to a man whose passion for rugby, which she shared, was being replaced by a growing addiction to golf. 'He's the one who's left-handed, isn't he?' she asked.

'Quite right, darling.' Fergus hoped to make his wife a golfer one day. 'If you're not going to, I might as well have this.' He reached for her wine glass and set it beside his. He took the dirty plates through to the kitchen and returned carrying mugs of tea.

'Do you want to talk about it?' he asked gently.

'Yes, I think I do.'

'Well let's have everything. Just explaining it all to me will help sort things out in your head.'

She got up and fetched a sheaf of notes from her briefcase. When she returned the television was off.

'Shoot,' said Fergus.

So she did, going through everything relevant that had happened or been found or said, not always in chronological order, but including her likes, dislikes, suspicions and fears. She told him about the divisional commander, Chandavarkar, Wallace, McKellar and Osborne. He listened without interrupting, his face giving no clue as to his thoughts. When she finished she saw how much information she had to work on. One way or another she had learned a lot about this mysterious, deadly bank. 'Well?' she said after a silence.

'Well,' he said. 'That's all rather a jumble. Different things have been flying at you thick and fast all day, so of course they're mixed up now. I think you should try to step back, look for the essentials. Let's take the crimes themselves,' he added quickly before she could interrupt. 'They are both brutal and, I would judge, unpremeditated. Forbes and Walkinshaw may be up to their arm-pits in money laundering, and fully capable of murder, but they would plan a murder down to the last detail if they were going to commit it themselves. Or, more likely, pay someone else to do it, making sure nothing would lead you to their door. So let's put them to one side, for the moment anyway. Davidson might have killed Parsley because of the homophobic bullying but I can see no reason for him to kill Thornton. They seemed to be getting on fine and Thornton was just about to take Davidson's place as Santa. I suppose Thornton's mum might have suddenly decided to kill him, but she clearly loved him and he would have had to say something terribly wounding to make her snap.'

'I felt she was hiding something, but I couldn't see her killing Bruce. I can see Davidson killing Parsley, though. Do you think we might have two killers?'

Fergus shook his head. 'Two deaths linked by time and place and killing method, a violent method, too. No, my money would be on a single killer.'

'If it was one of the directors that means Saddlefell or Eglinton.'

'Right. Eglinton had a relationship with Parsley – friendship, I mean. Might he have felt betrayed by Parsley's financial crimes? He had the best opportunity to kill him.'

Flick said, 'But Eglinton told Chandavarkar he first heard about the money laundering at the board meeting this morning. That's something we can check with the others. So why should he spontaneously kill his best friend? And why kill Thornton? It couldn't have been mistaken identity with him as he had been there when

Davidson changed his plan to play Santa and meet him instead.'

'So Eglinton has opportunity but no motive that we can see. Saddlefell keeps cropping up. He had opportunity and he has a temper on him, as I think our killer must have, but why should he kill Parsley or Thornton?'

'Parsley because of the financial crimes. Maybe they were worse than Saddlefell had been led to believe. If Thornton opened the door wearing the Santa suit, Saddlefell might have thought he was Davidson, who was threatening to blow the whistle, so a case of mistaken identity.' Flick was reluctant to drop Saddlefell as the prime suspect.

'But what doesn't ring true with that scenario is the way he called in Osborne to find Sir Paul's killer. And he must have got Osborne to hurry here when Parsley was killed. That would be odd if he had just killed Parsley, and maybe even ordered Sir Paul's death too.'

'We both know Osborne's a fool.'

'But not everyone does. Remember how he collected all the credit for solving the literary agent murders? That credit should have gone to you and Baggo. Have you spoken to him?'

'To Osborne? No. McKellar told me he'd caused a disturbance at the hotel's Christmas Fayre. Apparently Davidson had asked for a large gin and tonic to be beside his seat as he gave out the presents. Osborne's been off drink and when he played Santa he drank the gin and tonic. Then he went wild and supposedly assaulted a little girl. When the girl's father saw police in the hotel he wanted to get us involved but the manager sweet-talked him out of it. What are you laughing at?'

'That man can't help making an arse of himself.'

'Well he was my boss for too long for me to see the joke. I couldn't believe it when I realised he had been brought into this case.'

Fergus saw she was angry. He held her hand. 'Darling, I don't find your problems at all funny. I just find Osborne funny in an appalling sort of way. But seriously, tomorrow morning you should talk to him. He's got a good copper's nose and he's been coming at this from a different angle. He'll know he's in disgrace so you'll be able to play the "I'm in charge" card for all it's worth. It might even be fun, if you can make him squirm.'

'Maybe.' Flick sounded as doubtful as she felt. She would rather avoid Osborne altogether.

Fergus said, 'Let's look at the non-director suspects. Baggo probably gives Knarston-Smith an alibi for Thornton's killing, and anyway, if he had just agreed to help the police would he rush out and kill someone? Of course he must have felt wronged by Parsley and terrified that he might show Cynthia that photograph, so he has to be a possible for his murder. Anderson can be excluded as the CCTV shows she was in her room at the material times. I think the bankers' wives are unlikely. Belinda Parsley was all set to use divorce to free herself so why resort to homicide? Now, Eileen Eglinton was out about the time Parsley was assaulted, and she's one of those who could have killed Thornton but why should she want to kill either of our victims? Could she have been very angry with Parsley for some reason?' He paused.

'As we know, Simon says he didn't know about the financial crimes till today, so assuming she didn't know about them beforehand, what else could have angered her enough to kill Parsley? Besides, she's left-handed and we have a right-handed killer,' Flick said, glad to add to Fergus's analysis.

Fergus said, 'I can't see Sandi Saddlefell or Cynthia Knarston-Smith killing these people.'

'I agree. It would help if we could see a clear motive for someone with opportunity.'

'Something made our killer attack really viciously, probably something that made him react almost instinctively.'

'Him?'

'I believe so. More men than women bludgeon people to death. That's official,' he added, glancing sideways at her, 'as gender equality hasn't reached bludgeoning.'

For a moment he thought he had hit the wrong note then she smiled and cuffed his ear, misshapen after his rugby career.

'That's a statistic that could change soon,' she said.

'What about the rooms?' Fergus asked. 'You haven't told me where they are in relation to one another.'

'The Knarston-Smiths are in a room overlooking the golf course but in the spa block from which they can exit without going through the lobby. And they can go along corridors to the main part of the hotel. On Thursday night Knarston-Smith could have gone to his room then gone out again without us knowing. The only CCTV camera which would have picked him up wasn't working. The rest are in a first-floor corridor in the main block. All the directors have superior – God, how I hate that word …'

'Why?'

'Because Lady Sandi Saddlefell can't stop using it. She must be the stupidest, most affected person I've ever met.'

'I can think of a few who might give her a run for her money. Anyway, what superior things do the directors have?'

For the first time that evening Flick laughed. 'Rooms, you clot, rooms with balconies looking out over the golf course. As you go from the spa direction, they are next to each other in this order: Walkinshaw, Forbes, Davidson, who has been moved as his room is a crime scene, Saddlefell, Eglinton and Parsley. The lift is opposite Forbes's room and Anderson's room is beside the lift, facing the back. Why do you ask?'

'To get a mental picture. You know, assuming Thornton was alive when his mum left him, his killer moved quickly and decisively. He,' he smiled, 'or she must have a steady nerve.'

'You're right, and this has helped me get my thoughts in order. But I feel we need a game-changer, a smoking gun leading us to the killer and proving the case.'

'How are you getting on with your squad?'

'Okay, I think. I really like Wallace. McKellar is an asset with his local knowledge but he can be so insolent I want to lay hands on him.'

'He's been used to answering to older men from this

part of the country, men he respected instinctively. You have to earn his respect, and I'm sure you'll do it in time. It must be good to have Baggo with you, a familiar face.'

'But he's so irritating, looking for a joke in everything. Wallace seems to find him funny, and that encourages him. Why does everyone insist on calling him Baggo?'

'Because he's comfortable with it. I saw that up in Pitlochry when we met. It may help make him feel accepted. When you call him Chandavarkar it probably makes you sound stiff and formal.'

'It's a perfectly good name. Baggo sounds demeaning somehow.'

'He's happy with it, darling.'

Flick scowled. 'Anyway, he breaks the rules. I told you about that photograph.'

Fergus turned round and faced her. 'I sometimes break the rules, you know,' he said quietly. 'The way Baggo has played it he's maximised the chances of Knarston-Smith helping us as much as he can and at the same time saving his marriage.'

'But still, productions should always be properly logged as they are found. If they aren't you are likely to give the defence an open goal.'

'There are things you want to do that aren't regular and can be concealed by a white lie, but are not basically dishonest. I think what Baggo has done with the photograph is one of them. It's a bit like rugby. Some of the laws of the game are routinely ignored – like putting the ball into the scrum straight. Any top-class rugby player will do things he knows are illegal if the referee isn't looking – like holding the ball after he's been tackled. It's funny, you know, how rugby and golf are so different from that point of view. In golf everyone sticks to the rules. Should you not allow a bit of the rugby ethos into your policing?'

Flick looked at him aghast. She had not expected to hear what the divisional commander had said to her that morning and she certainly had not expected this from Fergus. Previously when they had talked about ethics he had said little apart from condemning cops who planted evidence or made up verbals. Now she knew why. 'I don't see it that way,' she said huffily.

There was so much he wanted to say about restrictive rules of evidence, ivory-tower judges and sheer common sense, but this was not the time for it. Flick believed that if a police officer compromised his or her principles in any way they were no better than the criminals they were pursuing, and for now at least he should not challenge that.

The less than companionable silence that followed was broken by the phone.

'It's nearly midnight,' Fergus grumbled as Flick answered.

Her face was grim as she listened to the slurred voice of Jamieson, the divisional commander, berating her efforts with a torrent of abuse.

'… I told you, I told you, to be careful with Saddlefell, and there you are, on national news, national news mind you, saying you hope for an early arrest then you lead Lord Saddlefell out covered in a blanket like a common criminal when you don't have a fucking case and you have to let him go after a couple of hours. What were you thinking of? And I get home after dinner to find messages from the chief constable, MPs, members of the House of Lords, Uncle Tom Cobley and all, asking one fucking question: what the fuck do you think you're doing? Christ knows what the papers will make of it tomorrow.'

'But …'

'And there's been another murder right under your nose so we'll have the media with us till we catch the killer. I'm not going to be made to look a fool because of you, Fortune. So tomorrow don't step an inch out of line, try and find something out and be ready to hand over the case to someone competent first thing on Monday morning. I'd take you off it now if I could but I'll have to speak to Maxwell's boss.'

'Maxwell?'

'I know he's your husband, but he's a bloody good policeman and that's what we fucking need. So do you understand? Tomorrow you find out as much as you can, collate everything you've got and on Monday hand it over. And don't do anything else.'

'But sir …' The phone clicked as the divisional commander rang off. Flick looked helplessly at Fergus.

'I could hear a bit of that. Don't worry. I'll refuse to take the case.'

'Could you do that?'

'I will anyway, and I'm pretty sure my divisional commander will back me.'

Flick put her head on Fergus's shoulder, he put his arm

round her and they remained like that till she was asleep. He gently roused her and tenderly helped her to bed. His shirt was wet where her head had rested.

* * *

'So what is the inspector really like?' Lance Wallace asked Baggo.

He had driven Baggo to his home, a modest detached house built with light brown sandstone on the main street of Dairsie, a village on the St Andrews to Cupar road. With its neat gravel path and small, tidy borders on either side, the whole impression was of solidity and order. Lance's wife, Jeannie, had been forewarned and greeted her guest as if Scotland's reputation for hospitality depended on it. Steaming plates of mince, tatties and peas which Baggo said tasted as good as a biryani, had been followed by Caboc, a soft buttery cheese coated in oatmeal and served on big, coarse oatcakes. Washed down by heavy beer, it relaxed both men after their traumatic day, Baggo having long since ceased to care about eating beef. After they had finished Jeannie had tidied up while Lance poured the special Glenmorangie. After some talk about the inquiry Lance asked the question he had really wanted to ask.

'The inspector? I like her, but she often does not give a good impression. She is very private and difficult to get to know. Her main problem is she does not have a proper sense of humour. She will generally laugh a bit after everyone else as if she needs them to tell her something is funny. I have found myself cracking jokes to wind her up. But she is decent, honest, brave and clever. She does not take advantage of her position and can talk to anyone. I met her husband during a cross-border inquiry, as she did. He seems a good bloke. How is she getting on here?'

Lance pulled a face. 'So-so, at best. She's seen as being too serious and a stickler for the rules. Of course she hasn't been with us for long.'

'It's hard for women in the police. I would find it daunting to have to order a lot of Scotsmen about. There's a sense of clannishness here that strikes me. Of course, I'm what most people still call a Paki. Cheers!' Hoping he had not given offence, Baggo raised his glass.

Lance ignored the Paki remark and the implied criticism of the Scots. 'What about this odd private eye who's going about the place creating mayhem?'

'Noel Osborne, known as "Inspector No", was in charge of Wimbledon CID. I got on alright with him, but it was a different story for Flick Fortune. If there was an irregular way to do something he'd do it. He'd cleaned up the East End of London years ago, according to him, and he'd done it with planted evidence, false confessions, the lot. He and Fortune hated each other and were always scoring points. She complained about his sexist attitude and he mocked her university degree and called her Felicity, which is her name but she never uses it. That drove her mad. He's an alcoholic and when he's drinking he's hopeless.'

'I hear that was the problem at the Christmas Fayre. I wonder what he'll be like tomorrow. Fancy another?'

The subtle, mature spirit made Baggo feel very good. He held out his glass. 'This is even smoother than Amrut, our Indian single malt from Bangalore,' he said.

Lance raised his eyebrows. 'I'm flattered,' he replied.

* * *

Osborne was aware of his head. It hurt. His mouth was dry. The phrase 'like a badger's arse' swirled about in his mind. His stomach felt tender. He needed a pee. He opened his eyes. He was face down on a bed, some vomit on the sheet under his head. Lights were on. A lot of small bottles were scattered about. There was something tight round his throat. Elastic. He pulled at it and a flowing white beard came round from the back of his neck. Gingerly he got up and tried to walk but his ankles were tied together. He looked and saw a pair of red trousers half on, half off. He was wearing a strange, red jacket with fur trimmings. The horrors of the previous day began to come back to him. He shuffled past the open mini-bar door to the toilet and peed, not caring where he sprayed. Using all his coordination he drank water from the tap as he could not find a glass. Then he went back to bed. He tried to put the lights out but could not master the complexity of the switches. Avoiding the vomit, he carefully put his head down and went back to sleep.

17

'It's a dreich day, so you'll need your breakfast,' Jeannie said, looking out at a dark grey morning. Baggo did not have to go outside to realise it was going to be a day when the cold dampness would reach his bone marrow. Briefly he thought of Mumbai and sunshine then concentrated on swallowing the porridge in his bowl. He found it as unappetising as the previous night's dinner had been delicious, but Jeannie was clearly proud of it and he had no wish to upset her. He was alert and ready for the day, having slept well in the Wallaces' nineteen-year-old daughter's room. She was at Aberdeen University studying English Literature, but if the posters decorating her room were anything to go by, her taste in music did not extend much beyond One Direction.

'Lovely,' he said after the last slimy spoonful had gone down. 'No thanks,' he added quickly as Jeannie offered him more. The two fried eggs and crispy bacon she put in front of him next were far more to his taste, and he ate happily while Lance cross-examined their seventeen-year-old son, Alan, about what he had done the previous night.

'You were late home. Where were you?'

'In St Andrews. At Willie Carlyle's.'

'So were Willie's parents in?'

'Aye.' Alan, who had come down to breakfast late and bleary-eyed, wearing a tee shirt, tracksuit bottoms and nothing on his feet, spooned his porridge as if on autopilot.

'Did they give you beer?'

'Aye.'

'And there were no spirits?'

'Naw.'

'And on Monday morning McKellar won't tell me about you trying to get into pubs?'

'Don't know what he'll say. Maybe he'll try and frame us.'

'Don't cheek me. Were you in a pub?'

'Only for a wee while, earlier. We just had a couple of pints.'

'Which one was it?'

'Didn't catch the name. Relax, Dad. We weren't caught.'

'You'd be seen, though. By people who know who you are.'

'By people who know who you are, Dad.' Throughout this exchange Alan had not lifted his eyes from his bowl of porridge. Now he glared at his father across the table. Jeannie wrung her hands in distress as Lance ignored his bacon and egg and out-stared his son.

'It must be hard to be the sergeant's son in a small area,' Baggo said, earning a silent nod from Alan. 'And hard in a different way being the father.'

'You can say that again,' Lance said through clenched teeth. He picked up his knife and fork and began to eat.

'I was very lucky,' Baggo went on, 'as my dad was in medicine, not the law, and it was not too embarrassing if I got caught doing something I shouldn't have.'

Jeannie said, 'Alan hopes to study law at university next year.' Smiling proudly at her son, she put a hand on her husband's shoulder.

'Lollipop Logan was there too,' Alan said huffily. 'He was totally pissed, he's younger than me and his dad's the sheriff.'

'I don't care. You are my son and as long as you live in my house it's my rules.'

'Why do you call him "Lollipop"?' Baggo asked, trying to divert the boy from a serious confrontation.

Alan looked at his mother, blushed and put the last spoonful of porridge into his mouth. 'Dunno,' he mumbled, sliding his bacon and eggs to his place.

'That breakfast will keep me going all day,' Baggo said, his imagination working on possible origins for the nickname. 'We should be moving, Lance. As I was dressing this morning I had a thought.'

'Right. We have a big day ahead. And you,' Lance turned to Alan, 'consider yourself grounded till further notice.'

Alan put down his cutlery with a clatter, got up and hurried out of the room. 'Fuck off, Dad,' he shouted before he slammed the door.

In an instant Lance was out of his chair, making after him.

'Stop!' Jeannie almost screamed. 'Stop, stop. You have your work to go to. And he's a good boy, really he is. All his mates go to pubs, as you know. It's hard for him being your son. Please try to understand.' She got up and stood between her husband and the door, her shoulders quivering.

Lance sat back down, breathing deeply. 'Sorry, Baggo,' he said.

'It is nothing I haven't seen before,' Baggo replied. About midway between father and son in age, he saw both viewpoints but identified more readily with the son's. He changed the subject. 'As I was dressing this morning,' he said, 'it occurred to me that there is one thing both victims have in common that no one has considered. They are both connected to Haleybourne Golf Club. Parsley was a member and Thornton was an assistant pro. Today I would like to go there and ask some questions, and I ask a big favour. Please could you get me to Edinburgh Airport so I can fly down to London and be there by lunchtime? I could go to either Heathrow or Gatwick but Heathrow would be closer.'

Lance scratched his head. 'Why are you so intent on going after the murderer? I thought your interest was the money laundering.'

'I'm sure the crimes are all related. And until we find the murderer and gather enough evidence it will be difficult to properly pursue the financial criminals. I do not want them to get off in return for giving evidence for the prosecution in the murder.'

Lance said, 'I see your point. I suppose it might give

us the breakthrough we need. If you dropped me in Cupar at HQ you could borrow our car, but we'd need it tomorrow. When will you be back?'

'I hope later today, but I might be delayed.'

'There's no way Sanderson, who organises the car pool, would lend one out to someone not in Fife Division.'

'What about Alan?' Jeannie asked her husband. 'He could drive Baggo through and come straight back. It could be a sort of punishment for last night.'

'Or this morning,' Lance said grimly. He saw Baggo looking eagerly at him and capitulated. 'All right,' he said grudgingly. 'Jeannie, you'd better call him. But make sure he hurries.'

* * *

'I'll ride in the back,' Baggo volunteered as Jeannie pressed a plastic box containing sandwiches into his hand. He made a mental note to bring a good present when he returned. Leaving most of his luggage, he had his computer over his shoulder and Knarston-Smith's memory stick beside the money clip in his trouser pocket. For back-up he had sent the contents of the stick and No's briefing from Saddlefell to a secure e-mail address, but he did not know what he would do with the clip. Perhaps, if he was positive he knew the identity of the murderer and there was not enough evidence … He preferred not to think about that.

Equally grim-faced and looking very much like father and son, Lance occupied the passenger seat while Alan took the wheel. It was a short drive to Cupar and it passed in silence until Lance hissed 'speed' as they reached the outskirts. Alan kept the speedometer at a steady thirty-five miles per hour until they slowed for traffic lights. Police HQ was at the far side of the town. Alan skidded as he brought the car to a halt outside the front entrance. Ignoring his son, Lance wished Baggo good luck as he got out. Baggo moved to the passenger seat and Alan revved the engine before screeching away.

'You drive well,' Baggo told Alan some miles down the road after he had safely avoided a tightly-packed group of lycra-clad cyclists with an apparent aversion to signalling.

Alan shrugged. There was a hint of a smile.

'My dad and I fought like cat and dog when I was your age,' Baggo said. 'He tried to teach me to drive. Did your dad teach you?'

'He tried.' Now the smile was real, if rueful.

'We came over from India when I was a bit younger than you,' Baggo continued. 'But in India the driving is dreadful. If you want to overtake you put your hand on the horn and go ahead. My dad had no idea about driving in England, but he thought he knew it all. He took me out when I was learning and we had terrible shouting matches. Once I was so angry that I got out of the car but he moved over to the driving seat and went home. It took me two hours to walk back – in the rain. Was it like that with you?'

'A bit.'

'I still argue with my father. He wants me to marry an Indian girl, a Brahmin like me and I don't want that, so we fight. But I never ever forget that he loves me and would do anything to help me. One night when our relationship was at its worst, I got into trouble. I hit an English boy who had called me a Paki and made fun of me. I broke his nose pretty badly and his friends said I had started it. The police came to question me, and my dad, who was a consultant at the local hospital, stood up for me and got me a lawyer he paid for himself. The charges were eventually dropped, but I learned two lessons. One, whatever we might argue about, my dad was always there for me, and two, when you are in the police you can have a massive influence on other people's lives. Your dad is a good man, and I can see he cares deeply about you. Part of his authority comes from his reputation, so having a son who flouts the law, even just going to pubs under-age, makes him look bad.'

Alan drove on in silence. Some miles further on he said, 'I know he cares, but ...'

'He has a difficult time in a small community where people know each other. Will you go away to university?'

'I hope to be accepted for Edinburgh. It depends on this year's Highers.'

'Good. Things will improve, especially when you reach eighteen. But in the meantime, cut him some slack and maybe he'll do the same with you.'

Alan said nothing but nodded. Baggo asked about school and the conversation became increasingly relaxed. By the time they reached the Forth Road Bridge Alan had laughed a few times. When he dropped Baggo at the airport he grinned. 'Thanks for the advice,' he said.

* * *

Flick sat on the edge of the bath, wiping her face. She had never looked forward less to a day's work. If morning sickness was not bad enough the cold, damp dawn leading to a short, bleak day depressed her further. She despaired of the little she had achieved in the inquiry. Chandavarkar had found out far more than she had, and she had needed Fergus's analysis to begin to make sense of the situation. Most of all, the small-minded resentment against her because she was young, female and English was getting her down. If only she could have the baby and never go near a Scottish police office again ...

'Get a grip and buck up,' she said out loud, rubbing herself vigorously with her towel. She hadn't got where she was by giving up. This was a hugely difficult, high-pressure inquiry and she had made real progress. In the short time between the alarm waking her and getting out of bed, Fergus had cuddled her and said, 'You are good at your job and I believe in you. Don't let anyone get you down.' It was something to hang on to. And maybe she should give a little, like calling Chandavarkar Baggo. If he didn't mind, why should she? He was an outsider, like her, but he had the gift of getting on with people in a way she never could.

In the car as she drove to Cupar for the daily briefing she thought about what she should say. About one thing she was determined, she would not tell them that she would be off the case within twenty-four hours.

The officers assembled for the briefing looked and

sounded as grim as they had the previous day. If any were pleased to get overtime they failed to show it. They fell silent for Flick, who began by taking them through the information on the whiteboard, now decorated with photographs of the characters featured. Then she called on different officers to report. McKellar confirmed that early on Friday morning Mrs Eglinton had booked a time on the Eden in the names of Eglinton and Parsley. A number of officers had tried to identify the chambermaid said to have told Osborne about the gold money clip in Saddlefell's possession. They had not been successful. Flick ordered them to keep trying.

Gilsland had with him in Cupar the computers seized in the search but had yet to find anything interesting on them. They were well protected by passwords and he admitted that it would probably be necessary to call in officers who were also IT specialists. He added that he was being careful in case a wrong move should delete everything. Wallace reported that nothing relevant had been picked up by the microphone in Forbes's room. He said that di Falco was continuing to question guests but had not learned anything of note.

Amy Moncrieff had visited Grace Thornton's friend, Ina Campbell, the previous evening. Mrs Campbell had been devastated to hear of Bruce's murder and alarmed to hear that his mother had visited him minutes before he died. At first she did not want to speak to the police, but when informed that Mrs Thornton had told them about their lunchtime meeting, had recounted what they had said.

It had been, Mrs Campbell explained, the first time Bruce's mother had mentioned his sexuality. With her husband refusing to admit the boy was gay, Grace had talked about Bruce being confused and needing to sort himself out. Though the two women had been best friends for decades, it had been very hard for Grace to describe the circumstances that had brought Bruce back to St Andrews without visiting the parents who had doted on him.

Ina had secretly entertained doubts about Bruce as he had never had a girlfriend. She assured her friend that it did not reflect badly on his parents, and that he still loved them. However he needed them to accept the truth, and it was that need for acceptance that created the barrier between them. There were many worse things in life than having a gay son. Gay sons were often more dutiful and loving than those who were conventionally married. Inside, Bruce would be longing to restore his relationship with his parents, especially his mother.

Ina Campbell had been uncertain about how much Grace had accepted, but she had been persuaded to visit Bruce and talk to him face to face. Ina had reassured her that if she showed some understanding, he would more than likely meet her half way. 'Did I do wrong?' she had asked Moncrieff, wringing her hands with anxiety. 'Is it my fault …?' That possibility in the forefront of her mind, Moncrieff had tried to be both non-committal and consoling.

'Well done, Constable,' Flick said when she finished, aware of sneers on the faces of a number of the men. 'You got that absolutely right. Now, we have a lot of material, and I want to have it all collated by the end of today, so every statement must be typed up and all information logged. We need to find out why these two people were killed, and to do that we have to keep talking to suspects, hotel staff, anyone who might tell us something. Remember, it's the small details that often unlock a case, so don't be shy about reporting things that seem unimportant. They may turn out to be vital. Let's make today count.'

Trying to appear more robust than she felt, Flick watched the officers file out. Amy Moncrieff lingered behind.

'Inspector,' she said tentatively.

'Yes?'

'Thank you for praising me there. It's sometimes difficult, you know …'

'Believe me, I know.'

'Well I'm really glad you're here. It makes a big difference for me.'

'Well, thank you,' Flick said, trying to hide her pleasure. 'Now get on and find our murderer.' As she watched Moncrieff join her colleagues, Flick wondered if the difference she made was as an example or a lightning conductor.

* * *

Flick spent the next half hour in her office, organising the material she would hand over. If she had failed to win the respect of the divisional commander she might at least demonstrate her worth to the person taking over. Dr MacGregor phoned to confirm what she already knew. Thornton had been first knocked down by one blow then killed by four or five blows to the back of his neck. The weapon had been his lob wedge, swung right-handed. MacGregor promised to have the report to her in writing within a couple of days. She could not bring herself to tell him she would be off the case. Minutes later the phone on her desk rang. She answered abruptly and found herself speaking to Murdo Munro.

'Good morning, Inspector. I hope you're well?'

'What can I do for you, Mr Munro?'

'I am presently in St Andrews with Lord Saddlefell and we have had an in-depth discussion. The long and the short of it is that he is willing to help your inquiry into certain activities within the Bucephalus Bank. He and I could be with you in twenty minutes or so and we would be happy to meet with you and Sergeant Chandavarkar.'

'Oh, good,' Flick said, surprise turning to wariness. 'We shall expect you.'

As soon as Munro had ended his call Flick phoned Wallace and asked where Chandavarkar was.

'He's flying down to London, ma'am, chasing up a lead.'

'This is very sudden. What sort of lead?'

'He's going to Haleybourne Golf Club, as both dead men had a connection with it.'

'But he's supposed to be investigating money laundering, not murder.'

'He thinks everything's connected, ma'am.'

'Well Saddlefell's coming in with Munro in twenty minutes to tell us something about the bank. Munro wants Chandavarkar to be there, but it'll just have to be us.'

This time the car in which Munro and Saddlefell arrived at Cupar police office was a top of the range Audi, Munro driving. Both he and Saddlefell wore suits and had an air of authority about them. They greeted Flick and Wallace politely but showed their disappointment when told that Baggo could not be with them. 'Is that a game-changer?' Flick heard Saddlefell whisper to his lawyer.

After a moment's discussion outwith the hearing of the officers, Munro nodded to Flick. 'We're ready,' he said.

Flick led the way to an interview room with recording facilities. She and Wallace sat on one side of the simple, off-white table with Munro and Saddlefell opposite. As she reached to turn on the tape Munro put up a hand.

'One minute, Inspector. Before this interview gets under way I would like to make clear the basis on which my client and I have come here. My client is anxious to assist your inquiries and is here voluntarily. He has information regarding certain irregularities in the Bucephalus Bank and we are concerned that the officer investigating these is not available. Nevertheless my client will give you a prepared statement. But he will refuse to answer questions. I hope that is clear, and that my client's cooperative attitude will be remembered as the inquiry continues.'

With scant control of the situation and realising that

Saddlefell was after some sweet deal, Flick would have liked to end the interview then and there but she could not risk losing useful evidence. Not reacting to Munro's remarks, she switched on the tape, specified the date and time and who was present then cautioned Saddlefell that he was not obliged to say anything.

Munro nodded at his client, who drew from his pocket some sheets of hotel writing paper covered in bold handwriting. Flick could see a number of crossings-out. Saddlefell cleared his throat and read slowly.

'I am here of my own volition to assist the police in their inquiries into certain irregularities within the Bucephalus Bank. Prior to 2008 our bank had been profitable and law-abiding. Like many others, our investment arm bought parcels of debt which we believed to be sound but which turned out to be toxic. Again like others, we misquoted the rates of interest we were being charged by other banks when reporting to the LIBOR authorities. I did not know we were doing this at the time. The person responsible was the late Hugh Parsley. Unfortunately, loans from other banks were not enough. Mr Parsley had given us far more exposure to American sub-prime mortgages than we had realised. The Sulphur Springs Bank in Atlanta was particularly supportive. In return Mr Parsley helped them in a money laundering scheme. Where that money originated I do not know, but one can guess it came from drug trafficking and other illegal activities. Mr Parsley used bearer bonds, which are illegal in America, to return the laundered money to the original owners. He also attracted a number of clients with questionable financial records to our bank and laundered money for them.

'This activity did not stop after we had resumed our customary stability. Mr Parsley continued to launder money and the bank made large profits. I did not know anything of this until recently. Mr Parsley was the director responsible and he was assisted by Gerald Knarston-Smith, a mathematical genius, who disguised all the transactions. We have "Chinese walls" in the bank and do not inquire into other directors' business. That prevents conflicts of interest but it also meant that I could carry on in ignorance of the true situation. Our auditors have not raised any questions about irregularities or possible illegality.

'I have recently learned that two directors knew about money laundering from an early stage. They discussed matters with Mr Parsley and also with representatives of Sulphur Springs Bank. They are Mr Forbes and Ms Walkinshaw.

'In the early part of September this year our late chairman, Sir Paul Monmouth, heard a rumour at one of his clubs and began to investigate. He spoke to me about the misstating for LIBOR, and was shocked that we should have done such a thing. Our bank has enjoyed a reputation for total integrity and Sir Paul was very proud of that. He could be quite dogged and I believe his sudden death at the end of September was not an accident. I persuaded my colleagues on the board to engage a private detective to investigate.

'Concerned by what Sir Paul had said to me and by his death, I made inquiries and uncovered what had been going on. I admit that I should have informed the authorities, but what I did do was to take effective action as acting chairman to stop all illegal activity without harming the bank's reputation.

'I regarded it as essential that we should make changes to the business, such as expanding the client base, to account for the likely drop in profits. Both Forbes and Walkinshaw agreed and said they would vote for me as chairman. Parsley was loyal to his old friend, Eglinton, who is very upright. As chairman Eglinton would have been bound to find out what had been going on and he would never have taken the steps that might be necessary to confine knowledge of the money laundering to those who already knew. In the week before we came here to St Andrews I talked to Parsley and made him see that his only hope of keeping out of jail was to have me as chairman. He agreed to support me when it came to a vote. I don't know if he told Eglinton before he died.

'I have done nothing illegal. As soon as I learned about the money laundering I stopped it. I have assisted the police from an early stage in their investigation.' He looked at Munro, who nodded, then he folded his papers and put them in his pocket.

Flick could not resist asking, 'Why did you lie to us about the time you went to bed the night Parsley was killed?'

Munro cut in quickly. 'I have made it clear that my client is not prepared to answer questions at this time.' He got up and opened the door. Ushering a smug Saddlefell out before him, he left without saying another word.

Flick switched off the recording. 'Do you believe him?' she asked.

'I'm not sure, ma'am,' Wallace said. 'It's a clever strategy. Could he really have been an active director all that time without having an idea that something fishy was going on?'

'It's strange, isn't it? But there have been a number of cases in which rogue traders have ruined a bank, or come close to it, without the people who should have known even suspecting it.'

'According to Eglinton, he and Davidson were kept in the dark for much longer. Baggo seemed to think that was possible.'

Flick said, 'I can see Munro's smart. We couldn't refuse to see Saddlefell and now he's on tape neatly giving Eglinton a motive for killing Parsley, while leaving himself with a motive for keeping him alive. And it all depends on a single conversation between him and the dead man.'

Wallace said, 'He admitted nothing except trying to keep the illegality under wraps.'

'And he's talking about it now only because he realises the police are well aware of what's been going on,' she said pointedly. 'He's claiming credit for stopping the money laundering, but if they realised the Feds and the SFO were on to them a month ago they'd have stopped anyway.'

'Do you think Baggo will want to use him and Knarston-Smith to convict Forbes and Walkinshaw?'

She said, 'I bet Saddlefell's dream result would be for him to go free in return for the prosecutors using him against Forbes, Walkinshaw and Knarston-Smith. You'll note he gave very little detail about how he knows what he says he does. I think he's making it up as he goes along.'

'You still fancy him as our murderer, ma'am?'

'I do. Even if Eglinton might have killed Parsley in a fit of rage if he was switching allegiance, I don't see Eglinton in a frenzy hitting him again and again. He had no reason to kill Davidson, or Thornton, come to that.'

'But we lack solid evidence pointing in any particular direction.'

'Yes,' Flick said. 'I wish we could get our hands on that money clip. That would wipe the smile off Saddlefell's face if we could link it to him. Make sure all possible leads on that are chased up.'

'What do you plan to do this morning, ma'am?'

She looked at him steadily. 'This morning when we get to St Andrews I'm going to hunt down the appalling Inspector No. It could be interesting.'

'Do you want me there?' he asked innocently.

Flick smiled. 'No thank you, Sergeant. I'll see him on my own.'

18

There was a flight to Heathrow at five past ten and Baggo secured a place on it by the skin of his teeth. He boarded the plane and found his seat in the middle of a row near the back of the plane. The window seat was taken by a middle-aged man whose nose was buried in a newspaper but the aisle seat next to him was empty. His hopes of unexpected comfort were short-lived because an obese man, panting with effort, crashed into the vacant seat and overflowed into the space Baggo had paid for and was entitled to occupy. 'Sorry,' the man muttered, appearing genuinely embarrassed. Feeling his right arm pinned to his side by rolls of fat, it was on the tip of Baggo's tongue to make a cutting remark, but he sensed something decent about the man. 'You're fine, mate,' he said, thankful that the flight would last only just over the hour.

The man had difficulty fastening his seatbelt and Baggo helped him extend its girth to the maximum. Sweating and fidgety, he was not a happy traveller. At take-off his whole body stiffened, he shut his eyes and Baggo felt a clammy hand holding his. 'Sorry,' the man repeated once they were through the clouds. 'No bother,' Baggo replied, deep in thought.

Although he felt his hunch was a good one, he hoped

he was not on a wild goose-chase. As his cover had been blown on a Saturday, he had delayed reporting to his superiors, but he knew that when he briefed them the next day he would be recalled immediately. He felt strongly that both the murders and the money laundering should be investigated together, otherwise quick-witted or well-advised criminals might slip through the net. Real progress was needed and he would not have much time at Haleybourne if he was to get a return flight that afternoon.

When the drinks trolley arrived the man ordered two miniatures of Johnnie Walker. 'Want one?' he asked Baggo.

Taken aback, Baggo said 'no, thank you'.

'Come on, I've been a nuisance to you,' the man said. 'Have a dram as we leave Scotland.'

'Do you have Amrut, the single malt from Bangalore?' Baggo failed to control his natural facetiousness. 'No, don't bother,' he said quickly as the flight attendant made to inquire in the galley. 'An orange juice would be fine. Thank you very much,' he said to the man.

As Baggo sipped his drink carefully, holding it in his left hand, the man introduced himself as Ron Barker and told him about his family (happily married, living in Woking with children at university), his job (events catering, trading as 'The One Ronnie'), and why he had been in Scotland (an investment seminar). 'They'd laid on pheasant shooting for today, but I didn't fancy that, though I love eating game, so I got them to book me on this flight. The girl at check-in said she'd try to put me next to an empty seat. Did you come along late?'

'Very,' Baggo admitted.

'Are you on business?'

'Yes.'

'Let me guess. You're in IT?'

Baggo could smell the whisky on his breath. 'I'm in the police.' That usually shut people up.

But not Barker. 'How exciting! Are you on a serious case?'

'Yes, but I cannot tell you much about it. Only that I'm heading for Haleybourne Golf Club.' Hoping to appear confidential, he tapped the side of his nose.

'Haleybourne?' Barker exclaimed, making the man in the window seat turn and stare. 'I know it well.'

'It is near Woking, I believe?' Baggo asked, hoping for directions. 'I will hire a car at Heathrow and I will need SatNav.'

'I'll take you there myself. I live in Woking and it's hardly out of my way.'

'Really, would you do so? It would help our investigation enormously.' Normally Baggo would not accept a lift from someone who might be over the drink-drive limit, but a lift from Barker would give him valuable extra time. Anyway, taking account of his weight, Barker would almost certainly be under the limit, providing he hadn't had a skinful the previous night.

They did not have to circle long before landing and even walking slowly, it took little time to reach Barker's car in the multi-storey. It was a large, silver Mercedes with cream leather upholstery. It purred majestically as it headed for Woking, its proud owner hardly drawing breath as he described how he had built up his business from nothing. Although impatient to make progress, Baggo was almost sorry when his luxurious ride came to an end. Barker insisted on driving him up the rhododendron-flanked drive to the front door of the clubhouse. Baggo thanked him profusely and looked around.

* * *

When Flick returned to the hotel all the paraphernalia of the Christmas Fayre had been cleared from the lobby, and where the previous day there had been carol singing, a loud Glaswegian voice could be heard.

'You can't force me to tell you that. It's none of your business. I know my rights.' The speaker had his back to Flick and was leaning across the table between him and di Falco. A shiny pink island of scalp on the top of his head was surrounded by turbulent waves of black, greasy hair.

'It's in case further information comes to hand and we discover you or your wife might be able to tell us something,' di Falco said, his tone reasonable.

'What will you do with the information once you no longer need it?' The Glaswegian sounded aggressive.

'Once it's no longer required by us or the lawyers it will be destroyed.'

'You can promise me that, can you?'

'I won't destroy it personally, but we have well-established procedures …'

'That are not always followed.'

'Why won't you tell us where you and your wife will be over the next week?'

'This is not a totalitarian state. My wife and I are innocently going about our business and I see no reason to give you that information.' He sat back, defying the young detective.

Di Falco shrugged and looked up at Flick, who walked round to his side of the table.

'I'm Inspector Fortune, and I'm in charge of this inquiry. I quite understand your position, Mr …?'

'Henderson.'

'Mr Henderson, we have to be very careful with data protection, but if we need a warrant, as this is a murder inquiry, we'll easily get one. And we'll find out all sorts of details about you and your wife, far more than we need to know now, including why you might not want to help the police in a serious case.'

As Henderson digested the implications of this, a tall girl perhaps in her early twenties rushed over. Designer clothes showed off her splendid figure. Long, shapely legs disappeared up a skirt too short to provide warmth and her blouse had more buttons unfastened than fastened. PC Amy Moncrieff was with her.

'Harry, darlin', this clever policewoman has found it!' she trilled, her accent from the West of Scotland.

'Oh good,' Flick said, sensing an advantage. 'What has she found?'

'My ring. I thought I'd lost it and all the time it was in the soap basket.' She pushed out her left hand. On the third finger a huge ruby on a gold band sparkled. It was the only ring on that finger.

'We've been talking to, er, Mr Henderson about your whereabouts over the next few days,' Flick told her.

'Oh that's alright. I've given Amy all our details, and she knows not to let on about our wee break here.'

'Why's that?' di Falco asked, smiling at Henderson.

'You know,' he said then got up. Shorter than Flick, he scowled at her, roughly took his 'wife' by the hand and made for the exit.

'It's amazing what money will do for your pulling power,' di Falco said to Amy as Flick left.

Some people need more help than others, Flick thought as she went to visit Knarston-Smith in his room.

* * *

She found him there alone. Cynthia had gone out, he explained. She had not said where or when she might be back. Despite the comfort of his surroundings and the fine view out of the window, from his demeanour he might have been in a cell already. He looked up at Flick with a mixture of fear and a desire to please. When she said she had some questions for him his shoulders sagged with relief. She guessed he might have a bag of essentials packed in case he was summarily arrested.

'On Thursday night after you left the Jigger Inn what did you do? I want the truth this time.'

He ran his hand through his hair, making it look more like a mop. 'Cynthia and I went upstairs, but Lord

Saddlefell had whispered that he wanted a word outside in ten minutes. I went down and we talked behind that mound to the right of the seventeenth fairway.'

Flick looked puzzled. Knarston-Smith got up from the bed where he had been sitting, went to the window and pointed it out.

'What was said?' she asked.

'He was just checking that I had printed out the papers for the meeting the following day. They detailed the money laundering and some other things. I had put them all in my room safe.'

'How was his mood?'

'He was cross about something. I assured him I had done exactly as he had told me and then I went back to my room leaving him smoking his little cigar.'

'When was this?'

'About quarter past eleven, I'd say. That's not exact, of course,' he added anxiously.

'Can you say when he came in?'

'No.'

'Had he been cross that evening?'

'He'd been tense, certainly. We all had a bit to drink and I suppose we became quite loud. Later on, in the Jigger, he was quieter and frowned a lot. I didn't know why. Sandi was going on about golfers' clothes.'

'When you went out later were you aware of anyone else about?'

'Someone coughed and we spoke more quietly, but I didn't see or hear anyone else.'

This information put the housekeeper's evidence

about hearing voices in context, and it left Saddlefell angry and alone, smoking a cigar in a place where he might have seen or heard Parsley and Eglinton making their way to the first green. He had lied initially about his rendezvous with Knarston-Smith, but once he knew the police realised he was lying, why had he not put forward some explanation? The answer, Flick supposed, was that he did not want to be caught out in another lie, but if he was innocent of the murder, and he knew the police were aware of the money laundering, why should he lie at all?

Flick had been gazing out of the window as she thought. Now she turned to Knarston-Smith. 'Thank you, Mr Knarston-Smith. Please stay in the hotel today. We may have more questions for you.' It was time to seek ex-Inspector No.

* * *

In some ways Osborne felt worse when he woke up, daylight exposing the horrors of the previous day and night. Moving gingerly, he went for a shower and let darts of hot water cascade over his head and shoulders. He took time to towel himself then attempted to tidy the worst of the mess. He collected the empties from the mini-bar in a bucket and wrapped some of the bedding to conceal the vomit. He ran the electric razor over his face and put on relatively clean clothes. He still felt dreadful, and a glance in the mirror told him he looked it. Most depressing of all was that the craving was back. If he hadn't emptied the mini-bar already he would have done so then and there. He decided that fresh air would help. He slunk unobtrusively out of the hotel by the Pro's Shop door, with an effort of will passed the Jigger's door and turned left, walking along the road beside the seventeenth and away from the town. The cold sharpening his senses, he sat on the low wall bordering the road and breathed deeply, then smoked two cigarettes, one after the other. Looking behind him at the hotel, he wondered what was the point of the small pond between it and the wall. 'Bloody stupid,' he muttered then decided he needed to warm up, so went back to the hotel.

He found a corner of the dimly lit library, sat down and ordered coffee. He took it black and strong and was refilling his cup from the pot when Inspector Fortune entered the room and sat down opposite him.

'Good morning, Felicity!' he said with a bullishness he did not feel.

She looked at her watch. 'Good afternoon, Mr Osborne.'

He did not respond. Neither wanted to speak first.

Flick broke the silence with a line she had rehearsed. 'You made a fool of yourself yesterday. You're lucky you weren't arrested.'

'Bollocks, Felicity. Anyway, my drink was spiked. Probably by the person you haven't caught yet. How is your inquiry going? Your first murder, is it?'

'We're making progress. But what are you doing here?'

'Earning an honest crust, Felicity, to add to my tiny pension.'

'Do you have information about the murders? It is your duty to help us if you can.'

Osborne grinned at her, all the time trying to work

out if Baggo had told her about Forbes's scheme to plant the money clip on Saddlefell. 'But I've retired. I'm not paid to do your job.'

'Don't play games with me, Mr Osborne.' Flick glared at him and leaned across the table, catching a whiff of stale alcohol. 'Tell me what you know now. If I find out you've been obstructing or hindering this investigation I'll have no hesitation in charging you. I've become quite an expert on the Police (Scotland) Act.'

'Ooh, that makes me quake. Ask me specific questions and I'll answer them.'

'Right. Why are you here at all?'

'The board asked me to investigate the death of Sir Paul Monmouth to see if there were suspicious circumstances. When Mr Parsley was murdered I was asked by Lord Saddlefell to come here immediately.'

'Have your inquiries got anywhere?'

'No. I was about to start interviewing when Thornton was killed and with your activities it has not been possible for me to do much.'

And your drunkenness Flick thought, but decided to keep quiet as he appeared to be cooperating. 'Did a chambermaid tell you about a money clip probably owned by Mr Parsley which she had seen in Lord Saddlefell's possession?'

Baggo hasn't told her, he thought. 'Yes.'

'What did she look like?'

His confidence soared. 'Oh, pretty, a brunette. Nice pair up front, a lovely pert arse, very slapable but not as nice as yours.'

Flick felt the colour rise in her neck and face. 'Have you seen her since?'

'No, don't believe I have. Can't give you her name, either.'

'You can do better than that.'

'How dare you say I could do better when your investigation is obviously getting nowhere fast? When I had my first murder I didn't have all the technology and fucking stupid gadgets you rely on. I had my personal radio, we had a forensic lab and a fingerprint lab and that was it. Apart from our common sense. My first murder victim was dismembered, fucking limb from limb, with grass stuffed in his mouth and his tongue cut out. Our suspects were vicious gangsters who wouldn't hesitate to kill, not bloody millionaire bankers who hate getting their hands dirty. But we persuaded people that it was better to have the police on their side, we got them to talk, and three guys went down for murder. Proper police work is done with people and common sense, not fucking gizmos and human rights. Now go away and write up this interview in fucking triplicate then use your brain.'

Flick tried to hide her fury. 'Well where is the money clip now?' she asked.

'If Saddlefell has any sense he'll have got rid of it.' An idea came to him. 'In fact, my guess is he'll have chucked it out of his window into that little pond outside the hotel. Watch out, mind, because they've stocked it with piranhas.'

Flick got up without a word and left. The encounter with No had not gone well. He smiled, scratched his crotch and slurped his coffee, not minding that it had gone cold.

* * *

Flick sat at the table in the police room, seething. Failure was one thing but to be mocked by No when before their encounter she thought she held the best cards was unbearable. She could not wait to be rid of this dreadful inquiry which was going from bad to worse. Wallace came into the room and sat opposite her.

'Don't worry, ma'am. We'll get to the bottom of this. They say the darkest hour is just before dawn. Did you learn anything from Mr Osborne?'

'No, except that leopards don't change their spots. He had some ridiculous theory that Saddlefell threw the money clip out of his window into the little pond between the hotel and the golf course.'

'Is it so ridiculous? If we drained the pond and looked for it, people would see us doing something. And it's possible we might strike gold.'

Flick shook her head but thought for a moment. If Jamieson heard that she had ignored a suggestion from Osborne, whom he clearly rated, her stock with him would drop further, and she wanted to be able to say that she had done everything possible during her time in charge of the inquiry.

'Right,' she said. 'Let's do it.'

'There is one other thing, ma'am. The manager of the hotel would like to have a word with you. He's concerned about our apparent lack of progress and the hotel is getting the wrong sort of publicity at the moment.'

Flick sighed. She picked up the phone and arranged to go straight through to the manager's office. This time she asked Wallace to come with her.

The manager, Leonard Taylor, was in his early forties. Fit-looking, with blond, receding hair cut very short, he wore a charcoal grey business suit and a green tie. He rose to shake Flick's hand, a polite smile on his face. 'Thank you for coming to see me, Inspector,' he said.

After showing his visitors to comfortable chairs and ordering coffee he sat in an armchair and explained his concerns. 'Frankly, this is not good for business. We offer five star luxury, excellent food, a spa and golf. We want our guests to feel safe and secure, and I am aware of a number who have become very anxious, particularly after the second murder here in one of our rooms. Obviously your investigation takes priority, but the police presence is intrusive and our guests are finding it hard to relax. May I ask how you see things going from here?' The smile was disarming and the tone was reasonable but Flick knew that a representation to her superiors was not far away.

'We are very grateful for the help you have already given us and we are making progress,' she said. 'Our interviews with staff and guests not involved with the bank are nearly complete. We will be able to give you a better idea tomorrow, but before we scale down the police presence in the hotel there is one thing you could help us with.'

'What is it?'

'We need to drain the small pond between the hotel and the golf course. We have reason to think the murderer may have thrown something quite small into it.'

Taylor looked surprised but unruffled. 'Certainly. We drain it regularly. We might do it now if you like. It's best done on a Sunday as there's no play on the Old and you won't be bombed by sliced drives from the seventeenth tee. Shall I set that up now?'

'Yes, please,' Flick said.

'I'll phone the duty engineer. But before we start we'll have to make arrangements for Jack and Tiger.'

'Jack and Tiger?' Flick asked. Were there really piranhas in that innocuous looking little pond?

Taylor grinned. 'Yes. The resident goldfish. It's a pretty high-tech operation but first we use an old-fashioned net to put the two fish in a tank until their fresh water is ready.'

Flick managed a smile, finished her coffee, thanked Taylor and left.

'Let me know when they're ready to start draining,' she told Wallace.

* * *

The first thing Baggo noticed was that the car in which he had arrived at Haleybourne was in a completely different league from those in the car park, an assortment of mid-range Fords, Mazdas and Skodas, some of them a few years old. The clubhouse had been a grand, rambling house in its day, but the ivy strangling its red brick walls failed to hide crumbling pointing and some loose bricks. The paintwork on the front door and round the windows was peeling and the tall chimneys had a precarious look. A bald man, in what looked like gardening clothes, emerged from a side door and pulled his caddy-car across the car park to the first tee where an older man was swishing his club impatiently.

Baggo identified the pro's shop, a wooden building beside the first tee whose window offered ten per cent off all purchases of new equipment. ERNEST MILDENHALL PROFESSIONAL was written in crisp red letters above. Baggo noted that the building appeared better maintained than the clubhouse. It was clean with shiny white gloss paint on the window frame and door jamb. Feeling self-conscious wearing a leather jacket with his computer case slung over his shoulder, he pushed the door open and went in.

An assortment of golf clothes and equipment was attractively displayed. Behind the counter stood a man who could have been a sprightly seventy-five or a prematurely grey forty-something. He had a strong, well-tanned face and stooped slightly. His air of authority marked him out as Ernest Mildenhall. Beside the till was a pile of books entitled *Mr Chips*. The cover showed a dark-haired Mildenhall executing a short pitch. In a corner of the shop a man gripped an iron club, an expression of intense concentration on his face. A stocky young man, smartly-dressed like his boss, was describing how the club was weighted. Grateful for Lance Wallace's thorough note-taking, Baggo guessed the young man might be Bruce Thornton's friend, Tony Longstone, but if he was to get him to talk freely he would have to get him on his own.

'Can I help you?' Mildenhall asked, not entirely welcoming.

'I am hoping to take a lesson,' Baggo said. 'I do not have my clubs with me, but I was advised to come here. I have just started the game and I am as keen as mustard.'

Mildenhall gave him the ghost of a smile. 'We can arrange that. When do you want your lesson?' Baggo detected a trace of West Country burr.

'Now, please. I have come out from London specially.'

'Did you not think to phone to make an arrangement?'

Baggo pulled a face. 'I am very sorry. I wanted to see this place before I committed myself. You see I hope to join somewhere. And I plan to buy clubs to use when I am in Britain,' he added.

'All right,' Mildenhall said. 'Tony, you give this gentleman a lesson and I'll help Mr Alford choose his new irons. That will be fifty pounds for half an hour, please.'

By the time Baggo had paid by credit card Longstone had put on a waterproof jacket and fetched a club and a bag of balls. Baggo smiled at him. 'I will need to borrow a club, please. Do you have a five iron that I may use?'

Longstone looked puzzled but went to the back of the shop and returned with a club. 'Right-handed, I presume?' he asked.

'Oh yes,' Baggo said and they set off. It was warmer than it had been in Scotland and a watery sun made the day quite pleasant. It was a good day for golf.

As they walked together towards the practice area Baggo pumped Longstone for information. In its heyday one of the leading clubs to the west of London, Haleybourne was going through difficult times. The clubhouse was a listed building. Heritage watchdogs had blocked a series of proposals to bring it up to contemporary standards and the roof had needed fixing. The considerable cost of doing that had, however, been dwarfed by the cost of repairing flood damage to four holes adjacent to a river, flood damage that had been repeated two years later, with no guarantee that it would not recur. In order to spread the cost of all this the committee had reduced membership fees to entice new members and for a time the course had been overplayed. The more discriminating members had resigned and many of the new influx had not stayed. With a constantly changing membership, a vulnerable course and an out of date clubhouse the soul of the club had been lost and more new members were sought.

Despite the decline of the club, Ernest Mildenhall had continued to prosper. Renowned for his prowess at chipping, he wrote articles for golf magazines and was in demand as a teacher, even coaching a small number of tournament professionals who found the short shots a bit fiddly. He was a gifted retailer and his business was good enough to keep himself and two assistants fully occupied.

As Longstone hesitantly described the club's problems, Baggo wondered why Parsley should want to belong to such a place. He had lived in Wimbledon, probably two hours' drive away, and it lacked the class and facilities he would have insisted on.

They arrived at the practice area and for ten minutes Longstone adjusted Baggo's grip and stance and tried to improve his pivot.

'Ooh, can we have a rest?' Baggo sighed, putting a hand to his lumbar spine. 'I was sad to read about the assistant here who was murdered in St Andrews.'

Immediately Longstone went on the defensive. 'Are you a journalist?' he asked sharply.

Baggo decided that honesty was the best policy. The professional seemed to be a straightforward young man. 'No. I am a policeman, and I am trying to find out why your colleague died and who killed him.' He produced his warrant, which Longstone examined as if he had not seen one before.

'Right,' he said slowly. 'Mr Mildenhall said I wasn't to speak to journalists. Can I help you?'

'First, can you explain the black eye he had?'

'Oh yes.' He shook his head ruefully. 'That was me trying to balance a driver on my finger. See?' He took the five iron from Baggo and placed the end of the grip on his right index finger so that the club was vertical then took away his other hand. The club wobbled for a while but remained balanced on his finger until he grabbed it. 'Anyway, it didn't work and I caught Bruce just above his eye. He was very good about it but Mr Mildenhall was furious.'

'Is he a good boss?'

The pause was eloquent. 'He is, providing you stay on the right side of him. He's taught me a lot. Bruce too.'

'Did you see much of Bruce away from work?'

'No. We got on well, but we didn't live near each other, so we didn't socialise much.'

'Did you know anything about his private life?'

'No. He didn't say much about that.' Longstone frowned. 'I saw on Twitter someone was saying he was gay, but I don't believe it.'

'Why not?'

He shrugged and looked uncomfortable. 'He wasn't the type, know what I mean? And some of the things he said …'

'He said anti-gay things?'

Longstone was blushing. 'Well, we all do, in the shop. I suppose we take our lead from Mr Mildenhall.'

'What sort of thing does Mr Mildenhall say?'

For a moment Baggo thought he would refuse to say more, then he said, 'He describes men who are you know, girly-like, as "great fucking pansies". It's the worst thing he can call someone, I think. Was Bruce gay?'

'Yes, and he was finding it very difficult, not only here at work but also at home. His parents could not accept it.'

'Was he with a man when …?'

'He was in an hotel room he shared with his lover, but no, at the time he was killed he was about to play Santa Claus at a Christmas Fayre. But I have another question. Was he cross-eyed or anything like that? Did he look at you properly when he spoke to you?'

Longstone screwed up his face. 'There was nothing unusual about him,' he said definitely.

'Is there anything you can tell me that might help identify his killer?'

'I don't think so. I liked him and I'll miss him,'

Longstone said softly. 'He was hoping to play some events on the Challenge Tour next year. I think he might have gone all the way. He was always working on his short game and he was deadly round the greens. Deadly ...'

Baggo changed the subject. 'Can you tell me about Mr Hugh Parsley? He also was killed at St Andrews.'

'Are their deaths connected? Was Mr Parsley ...?'

Baggo could not help smiling. 'I think their deaths may be connected. That is why I am here. But no, Mr Parsley was definitely not Bruce's lover.'

Longstone nodded, as if he were pleased. 'There's not much to say about Mr Parsley. He didn't come very often and changed his shoes in the car rather than go into the clubhouse. He always seemed to play with his wife, who wasn't a member, and they went round in a buggy. He just came into the shop, paid for his wife's ticket and the buggy and went out. They often played just a few holes.'

'So he didn't have friends among the other members?'

'No. They seemed very snobbish, the Parsleys. In the shop we called them Mr and Mrs Posh.'

'Is there anything else you can tell me about them?'

'Well, they usually arrived in different cars, always top of the range. And they talked a lot while playing, as if they were both very busy and this was a chance to catch up with each other. They've been here more often in the last few months than during the rest of the year, though the course hasn't been in great condition.'

Baggo thought for a minute then phoned Lance Wallace on his mobile. 'Where are you right now?' he asked.

'In St Andrews.' There was excitement in Lance's voice. 'We've made a breakthrough.'

'I think I am on to something too. Please get someone to use a mobile to take photos of all the women on the whiteboard and send them to me on this phone ASAP.' He turned to Longstone. 'Thank you, Tony. You've been most helpful. I must ask you to stay here with me till a colleague phones back. While we wait, what were you saying about my pivot?'

19

A steady drizzle carried on a biting North Sea wind made Flick wish she was indoors. For what seemed an eternity Ally Hay, the hotel engineer, had been trying to catch Jack and Tiger using an angler's net while she, Wallace, McKellar and two constables watched with a mixture of amusement and impatience. For all their usual dignified progress round the pond, the large, fat goldfish could put on a turn of speed when avoiding a net. Eventually both were deposited in a plastic crate with enough water to keep them alive. They briefly thrashed their tails in anger then calmed down.

'Jack after Jack Nicklaus?' Wallace asked.

'Aye,' Ally replied, '"the Golden Bear" as he was called. He's the one with the gold on top of his head. Tiger's the paler one, which is funny, I suppose. We used to have Bobby, after Bobby Jones, but the heron ate him.'

'The thing we hope to find is quite small,' Flick interrupted the idle chatter. 'Can you filter the water as it escapes?'

'Oh yes,' Ally replied, 'you'd be amazed at what we find in there. Lots of golf balls from the seventeenth, obviously, but also rings, bracelets, credit cards. A few things don't get in there by accident, know what I mean?'

'I think I do,' Flick said.

Ally went to a tiny iron door set low in the hotel wall and used a key to open it. He pressed a button, turned a dial then pressed a second button. A dull thud came from the pond and the surface began to move.

'I've put it on the narrowest filter, so it'll take a bit of time, but nothing will escape,' Ally said.

As the dark water seeped away down an underground pipe, Flick scanned the windows of the hotel. If No was watching, she could not see him. On the first floor she saw Sandi Saddlefell and Eileen Eglinton staring down from their rooms. Either of them, or Belinda Parsley, whose room was to the right of the Eglintons as she looked at them, could have tossed a money clip from their window into the pond. There was a small strip of roof above the ground floor but it would have been easy to throw a small missile over it.

'What do you do with the golf balls?' Wallace asked as numerous white blobs appeared at the bottom of the pond.

'We keep a few, sell a few and give a few to charity,' Ally said.

The water, which had been about four feet deep, was nearly all gone and on the bottom Flick guessed there must have been at least a hundred golf balls. 'Is it alright for these two constables to climb in and sort through what's left?' Flick asked.

Ally nodded. 'No problem. There's thick plastic at the bottom. If we let water escape it would affect the water table and the links supervisor would be raging. The fairway's lower than we are here.' He pointed towards the golf course.

The two younger constables went into the pond and began to hand balls out to Wallace and McKellar, who put them into clear plastic bags. Another bag was for rubbish and Flick held a small evidence bag just in case.

'Put that back!' she shouted at one of the constables in the pond who had slipped two balls in good condition into his pocket.

Sheepishly he pulled them out and placed them on the bank. When Flick turned away he made a face at her, earning a scowl from Wallace.

It did not take long to clear the pond. There were three bags of balls and one of rubbish, mostly bottles and cans. There was a layer of silt on the bottom and Flick ordered the constables to search it by hand. There was no point in half measures.

'Here's more rubbish,' the ball-taker said with disgust, chucking a round, dark object towards the appropriate bag.

'Let's have a look,' Flick said as McKellar bent to pick it up.

It was a pair of woman's tights wrapped and tied round something heavier. Flick replaced her leather gloves with plastic ones. Carefully and slowly, she untied the knot and unwrapped the sodden fabric. Inside was a golf ball, made by Nike and in good condition.

Wallace held out an evidence bag and she dropped it in. The tights bore no label, but were brown and thick. Flick held them up and saw they were large size. She bagged them and, suddenly impervious to the cold, she sat on the low wall between the hotel and the course and thought.

She thought of three women, one taller and generally bigger than the others; a tall, thin man practising his putting in his room without a ball; a golf club store with only one left-handed set, belonging to a man; a man signing autographs using a gloved hand.

'You play golf, don't you, Wallace?'

'Yes, ma'am.'

'And right-handed players usually wear a glove on their left hand?'

'Yes.'

'So left-handed players will use a right hand glove?'

'Yes.'

At this point his mobile rang. It was Baggo. Wallace moved away to take it. When it was over he made a quick call to Gilsland in Cupar then came back to Flick, who continued to sit on the wall deep in thought.

She asked, 'Do you ever get right-handed people who play golf left-handed and vice-versa?'

'Absolutely. Phil Mickelson's the best example. He's right-handed but golfs left-handed. They say Ben Hogan may have been left-handed.'

'Who's he?'

'A terrific player from the past, but there are lots more examples.'

Flick nodded. Wallace sat beside her on the wall as the constables continued their fingertip search of the pond bottom.

It did not take them long. 'There's nothing there,

ma'am,' McKellar said. 'Shall I get Ally to fill it up again?'

'Yes,' Flick said, then added half to herself, half to Wallace, 'So no money clip. But why, and why Thornton?'

Wallace's phone rang again. It was Baggo. Wallace listened for a while then turned to Flick.

'It's Baggo. He may have the answer to your questions. I'll put my phone on speaker. The inspector's listening,' he added to Baggo.

'Inspector, ma'am, the late Hugh Parsley came to play golf at Haleybourne with a woman who was not his wife but whom he passed off as his wife. They had long, intimate conversations as they went round in a buggy together. Neither of them were known here otherwise. I have with me Mr Tony Longstone, a colleague and friend of Bruce Thornton's and he has positively identified the woman he had known as Mrs Parsley as …'

'Eileen Eglinton,' Flick cut in.

'Gracious, yes. We have reached the same conclusion by different routes.'

'Please ask Mr Longstone one thing. Does Mrs Eglinton play right or left-handed?

After a pause Baggo said, 'I see the point. Yes, she plays right-handed. She must have killed Thornton because he recognised her. He expressed condolence for the death of Mr Parsley and addressed the remark to her. The real Mrs Parsley was also there and thought nothing was strange apart from the fact that Thornton did not look at her when talking to her. Mrs Eglinton was so concerned about the truth coming out that she killed him at the earliest opportunity.'

'What are you going to do now?' Flick asked.

'I am going to catch the first flight to Edinburgh. Now that we have solved your murders, I must catch my money launderers.'

Wallace ended the call. By now the pond had been refilled through small pipes in the sides. Ally tipped the crate over the water and Jack and Tiger were unceremoniously returned to their home.

'Right,' Flick said to Wallace, 'get these tights and that ball to the lab ASAP. There may be fingerprints on the ball and I bet Parsley's blood was spattered over the tights. I hope they'll find some trace of it despite the water. Now, let's get her.'

* * *

Flanked by Wallace and McKellar, Flick knocked for a second time on the Eglinton's door.

'Y'er wasting yer time. They've gone oot,' Sharon told them as she tried to steer her cleaning trolley past them.

Flick rounded on her. 'When?' she demanded.

'Ho, I dinnae take note. I've mair to dae than that.' Seeing the anger on Flick's face she added, 'Weel, maybe ten minutes ago.'

Flick looked at Wallace. 'Go downstairs and find out where they've gone.' Turning back to Sharon she said, 'Please open this door for us. This is an urgent police investigation.'

Unhurriedly, Sharon folded the towel she was holding and put it on the trolley. She took her pass key and opened the door. It was clear that the room had not yet been made up, but it was not untidy. On one side of the bed was an autobiography of Bobby Jones. On the other was a biography of Harold Macmillan and a slim, battered paperback, *St Andrews Ghost Stories*. Flick had read this collection of far-fetched tales spawned by the Royal Burgh's often bloody history. It was not her sort of book but gave an intriguing perspective on her new home town. The Eglintons had made no attempt to pack and there was no evidence of a hurried departure.

'Don't touch this room, please,' Flick told Sharon. 'We may need to search it.'

They left Sharon muttering rebelliously and went downstairs. Wallace was with the porter, who was on the phone. 'They took a taxi ma'am, and Joe here is talking to the taxi company. Joe says they were wearing coats. They said they were going into town.'

'Thanks, mate.' Joe put down the phone. 'The cab dropped them off at the end of North Street about five minutes ago.'

After Wallace had thanked Joe, Flick told him to get as many officers as possible searching for the Eglintons. 'No sirens or flashing lights, though,' she added. 'We don't want to spook them. McKellar, you come with me. Your local knowledge may be useful.'

* * *

Shocked by the notion that the grand woman he knew as Mrs Parsley had murdered his friend, Tony Longstone gave Baggo his contact details then the number of a local taxi company. As they walked back to the pro's shop Baggo told him what the next steps might be.

'Will I have to give evidence?' he asked.

'If there's a trial, almost certainly, and it'll probably be in Scotland,' Baggo told him. 'I advise you not to talk about it too much,' he added.

By the time they reached the shop the taxi had arrived. 'Thank you for improving my pivot!' he shouted as he climbed in.

As the taxi driver tried to avoid the potholes in the golf club drive, Baggo phoned Lance Wallace.

'They've gone, the Eglintons have gone,' Lance told him. 'I'm trying to organise a search of the town.'

'Have you listened to the bug in Forbes's room today?'

'There was nothing interesting overnight, apart from you-know-what. This morning we haven't had time.'

'But with the murderer identified this is the time to push forward on the money laundering. They may be rattled. I am heading for Heathrow now and I should reach St Andrews by early evening. Do you have anyone at the hotel who might listen to the bug now?'

'DC Di Falco's still at the hotel. He's supposed to interview departing guests, but tell him I said he should help you.' He gave Baggo di Falco's number.

Baggo's call interrupted di Falco and Jocelyn the under-manager in a conversation about their favourite films. Bored with quizzing guests, he was delighted to do something more exciting. He readily understood the instructions on operating the device and what he should listen for. He promised to phone back as soon as possible.

'Come on,' he whispered to Jocelyn. 'Come and see some real police work.'

* * *

North Street runs west to east and is a continuation of the Cupar road. A cinema, some flats and fine old university buildings along its left side, it reaches the cathedral wall and does a right U-turn to go back on itself as South Street. Unlike the nearby castle, which was battered by French guns in the sixteenth century, the huge medieval cathedral, in its day the premier ecclesiastical building in Scotland, was ruined by poor architecture, storms, a fire, lack of money and looting. A number of houses in the vicinity were constructed using sandstone removed from the cathedral. Today the stark ruins of this formerly magnificent and important building are preserved by Historic Scotland. What remains of spires, arches and windows is surrounded by a well-kept graveyard in which the different tombstones indicate the length of tenure of their corpses. Many of these grey slabs lie flat on the ground, to be peered at by visitors. Others are more elaborate, such as the engraved stone set in the boundary wall marking the resting place of Young Tom Morris, the brilliant golfer at the end of the nineteenth century who died tragically young of a broken heart. The whole area is enclosed by a high, thick wall built as fortification in medieval times and built to last. Towers and turrets break up the wall and more modern sections close any gaps that have occurred over the years.

Also made to withstand the ravages of time, at the west end of the ruined cathedral, St Rule's Tower stands tall, square and strong. Erected in the twelfth century, it is some thirty-three metres high and the top can now be reached by a spiral stair containing one hundred and fifty-one steps.

If the bloodstained history of St Andrews was not sufficient, the historic parts of the town have spawned a number of ghost stories. A beautiful girl, dressed in white and mummified in one of the towers along the wall, is said to haunt the cathedral. The ghost of Prior Robert of Montrose, a good man stabbed by an evil monk and cast off the north side of St Rule's Tower, has been seen leaping onto the parapet and jumping from the top of the tower.

Flick had little time for such fantasies; they were simply local colour, but having seen the book of ghost stories beside the Eglintons' bed, she had little doubt that, having been dropped at the end of North Street, they would head for the cathedral. Following her hunch, she threw the car into a space beside the narrow Monument Gate and rushed in. She looked round desperately. The drizzle had stopped, the wind had softened to a mere zephyr and there were even fleeting hints of pale sunlight. Few visitors were inspecting the cold, damp fragments of history that afternoon. A couple wearing raincoats walked beside the north boundary wall, perhaps seeking the haunted tower. Neither of them was tall. A tall man wearing a tweed cap and a raincoat came round a corner of St Rule's Tower and stood at the entrance. He was joined by a big woman in a thick coat and trousers. She was bare-headed.

'It's them!' Flick hissed to McKellar as the woman appeared to insert something before entering the tower. The man did the same.

'After them!' Flick said, breaking into a run.

'We'll need tokens to get in,' McKellar said at her elbow.

'Can we not …?'

'No. I'll go round to the shop and buy them. You could stand by the door in case they come out.'

'Okay,' she said, trying not to show her impatience. 'I'll tell Wallace where we are.'

McKellar was away for five minutes. By the time he joined Flick at the door of the tower, she was highly agitated.

'What can they be doing here?' she asked, not expecting a reply but seizing a token.

The tokens persuaded the revolving metal bars to let them through. They found themselves in a dank stone chamber, well-lit by electricity and with stone steps leading upwards. There was no sound from the stairs.

'They must be up there,' McKellar whispered, aware of a slight echo. 'This is the only way up and down.'

'Shush,' Flick said unnecessarily and she set off up the spiral staircase. McKellar followed her but began to struggle. The stones were black and wet and worn. They carried on up and round, up and round, tiring thighs and making both officers breathe heavily. Flick was now several steps in front and increasing the gap between them. As her body began to hurt she thought of other things. She remembered it was about this time of year, just before Christmas, that Prior Robert had been murdered at the top of this tower, if you believed the story. Anyway, this space, these stones she brushed past as she ascended, had seen centuries of life back to when human existence was nasty, brutish and short.

At last she came to the top step, a wire mesh door ahead. She took a deep breath. Suddenly fearful, she pushed the door open and stepped onto the wooden decking at the top of the tower. The first thing she saw was Simon Eglinton sitting on the waist-high parapet on the north side. He was posing for a photograph, looking serious. The photographer was his wife. Angling a mobile phone, she stood some six feet from him. She looked up when she heard the mesh door. An expression of fury twisted her face. She dropped the phone and lunged towards her husband.

Historic Scotland, anxious for the safety of their visitors, had erected a stout fence of wire mesh topped with wood a couple of feet back from the parapet. Both Eglintons were on the wrong side of that fence. Instinctively, Flick moved forward to stop Eileen. She leaned over the fence and grabbed her thick, tweed coat by the left arm which was stretched forward as if to push Simon over the edge. Then Flick pulled backwards and to her left. 'Get down,' she yelled at Simon.

Eileen Eglinton swung round and punched hard with her right hand. Flick squealed as the blow landed on her left eye. Her grip on the coat loosened. Swinging her left arm powerfully, Eileen pushed Flick backwards, causing her to slip on the wet decking and sit down heavily, her back against the door from the stairs.

Flick shouted at Simon, 'She means to kill you.'

Simon, who had got off the parapet, looked at his wife incredulously. He moved towards her as if to embrace her. 'Eileen, what … what … ?' he stammered. Eileen made no move towards him. She stood still, glaring at Flick, rage and frustration on her face. Slowly, Simon climbed back over the fence and hovered indecisively in the middle of the decking.

'She killed Parsley and Thornton,' Flick said, 'and she was going to kill you.'

Simon turned to Flick, shaking his head. 'No, Inspector, it was I who killed Hugh Parsley. Eileen just tidied up. And I don't believe she killed that boy. You've got it all wrong.'

'Simon, be quiet, for God's sake,' Eileen snapped.

Flick felt pressure on her back as McKellar pushed the door behind her. She sensed that Simon, in particular, was more likely to talk if she was alone. 'Let's all stay exactly where we are and talk,' she said loudly. 'Of course you know I am a police officer and, while you're not obliged to say anything, anything you do say may be used in evidence. You are both entitled to see a solicitor before speaking further.'

McKellar took the hint and ceased to push against Flick's back. He did keep the door ajar so he could hear what was said.

Simon shook his head at Eileen. 'Darling, I have to tell her. I can't let you take the blame.'

For a moment husband and wife stared at each other across the safety fence then Eileen leaned back against the parapet. She said nothing.

Simon paced up and down on the decking, not looking at either woman, talking as if to himself. 'You know how we spent Thursday evening. Hugh and I went out late to practise our putting. We were both drunk and it was very silly. We went to the sixteenth green but couldn't see so walked to the first, where there was a bit of light, and our eyes were getting used to the dark. At one point we swapped putters. He was very rude about my old-fashioned blade and I replied in kind. It got more heated than it should have. Then, out of the blue he said, "I can't support you as chairman. I'll be voting for Saddlefell." I said, "You can't mean that." We'd always laughed at Saddlefell, with his preposterous wife and Yorkshire vowels. He said, "I mean it, old friend. I have to." He turned his back on me and walked away. Couldn't face me, I suppose, after all I'd done for him and his career. Then with the drink, the red mist descended. I took that ridiculous putter of his and swung it as hard as I could. It hit him on the right side of his head and he went down. I killed him, Inspector. I knew it then. And I panicked. I picked up my putter and ball and went up to the room. I told Eileen everything. She went out to make it look as if some local madman had done it. That's why she hit him a few times, wiped for fingerprints, threw the putter and ball and that ball scoop thing into the burn and took some cash from his wallet.'

He stopped in front of Flick and looked down on her. 'The next day I wanted to admit it, but Eileen … Anyway, I remember telling you I hoped God would forgive whoever was responsible, because I never would. And I meant it. I'll never forgive myself as long as I live, even after discovering what Hugh had been up to. I'd never have believed he could have got mixed up in money laundering. But you've got it wrong about Eileen. Completely wrong.'

Flick said, 'Your wife was meeting Hugh Parsley secretly at Hayleybourne Golf Club. We believe Bruce Thornton recognised her and she felt she had to kill him before he called her Mrs Parsley again.'

'Don't be absurd.' He turned to Eileen.

A resigned look on her face, she said, 'It's true. I wanted to keep it from you and you'd be better dead than in prison. That's why I was going to push you over the edge. You'll hate me when you learn what's been going on behind your back, and I can't bear that. But now you'll find out anyway. I might as well tell you myself, so you'll get the truth.'

Simon took a step towards her but she waved him back. He reached out a hand to support himself on the fence then his long legs seemed to give way under him and he slumped down to sit on the decking to Flick's right.

Eileen looked at Flick, curling her lip. 'As they said in some television programme, "Listen very carefully. I shall say this only once."' She paused. No one smiled. 'I have been meeting Hugh regularly for years. No, not for sex. He tried it on once and I told him to put it away and grow up. What we met for was something much stronger and more enduring, something I could never have got from you, my love.' Suddenly tender, she looked adoringly at Simon. 'We met to scheme. We schemed to make money, to become powerful, and for you to become chairman of the bank. You believe most people are good. You assume they are honourable until they show they are not. Hugh and I saw the world as a jungle, with rules to be used or broken as circumstances dictated. And the main thrill, as any huntsman will tell you, was the thrill of the chase, the excitement of breaking rules and getting away with it.

'Of course it all started in 2008. Where do you think Hugh got all these contacts, people with illegal funds to launder? From me and my father. He may be old but he still goes to the House of Lords regularly, keeps his ear to the ground and enjoys a bit of scandal. After the crisis had passed Hugh and I couldn't stop. I loved hearing about the American gangsters we were dealing with through Sulphur Springs, rumours about concrete coffins and real-life offers that couldn't be refused. We had a dream of you being chairman of a wonderfully respected bank, while all the time the sharks, Hugh and I, would circle underneath and make your bank massively successful. That's what we planned when we met, and it was our secret. Just ours. But he hadn't told me he was switching allegiance to Saddlefell. I knew things were beginning to unravel, and I suppose Saddlefell nobbled him, offering him protection in return for his support.

'It was Sir Paul who spoiled things when he began sniffing about. He was an old hypocrite. You should hear my father on some of the stunts he pulled when he was starting out. Because he had been a chancer in his day and could be like a terrier, he was dangerous. I said to Hugh, "It's a pity he couldn't have an accident." A week later he did. Hugh had mentioned his name to one of our American gangsters and they had friends in the East End. It was frightening …' Her voice trailed off. 'I was sorry about that little poof, Thornton, but he was collateral damage. I couldn't let him live. I was going to throttle him, but the golf club came to hand.' She smiled at her husband. 'You were sleeping off the gin you'd had at lunch and didn't realise I'd been out of the room.'

Incensed by the woman's callous superiority and managing to keep her voice level, Flick said, 'Bruce Thornton's parents are mourning a son who died estranged from them. They are in a living hell and you are responsible.'

Eileen turned her cold eyes on Flick. The two women glared at each other in silence. Speaking as if to a careless servant, Eileen said, 'I don't know what made you drain that pond. I was sure my tights would disappear for good there. I couldn't risk flushing them down the lavatory.' She paused before adding, 'Oh, and Hugh was still breathing when I found him, so of course I had to finish him off.'

While Simon sat wide-eyed and open-mouthed, Flick wondered at this statuesque woman who sat on the parapet, back ramrod-straight, lower jaw protruding, a sort of twenty-first century cross between a Hapsburg empress and Lady Macbeth.

Very deliberately, Eileen began to rock to and fro, leaning beyond the parapet.

'Don't, Mrs Eglinton,' Flick said, keeping alarm out of her voice. 'Your husband, whom you love very much, will never forgive himself if you go over. And during the next few months he will need you as he hasn't needed you for years. Please don't do the selfish thing. Do the brave thing.'

Eileen continued to rock back and forward. Flick knew that a movement towards her would probably make her lean back too far. She hoped Simon would sit still, and he did, as if he was frozen. At last Eileen stood up and looked round the panoramic views, breathing deeply. Moving laboriously, she climbed over the safety fence. 'No handcuffs, please,' she said. Flick got up. The mesh door opened and McKellar, followed by Wallace and two constables, came onto the decking. 'No handcuffs,' Flick repeated and with one constable in front and one behind, Eileen Eglinton made her way down the hundred and fifty-one steps and into captivity.

'I don't know you. I never knew you.' Simon's voice sounded hollow and forlorn. Flick doubted if Eileen would have heard him.

'We won't need handcuffs for him, either,' Flick said and Wallace and McKellar escorted Simon down.

'What will happen to him, ma'am?' McKellar asked later.

'It'll depend on whether the pathologist can say which was the fatal blow. From what he said to me, they were cumulatively fatal, so they'll probably both go down for murder. Did you notice that Simon said he struck Parsley only once? If that's right Eileen must have hit him on the back of the neck as well as on the face.'

'To mak siccar, as we say in Scotland, meaning make sure,' McKellar observed. 'But if I may say so, you handled that situation very well, ma'am. It's just a pity we couldn't get what they said on record.'

'Oh but I did,' Flick said. She took her mobile from her pocket. 'I switched it to record mode. And I cautioned them both before they spoke. It's worthwhile doing things by the book,' she added.

McKellar smiled but said nothing.

An hour later, after both prisoners had been processed, Flick sat in her office, deeply satisfied but very, very tired. She put a hand to her stomach and worried.

20

The taxi was another Mercedes, but this one was dirty, with scrapes along the passenger side, a dented front bumper and a worryingly noisy engine. 'So tomorrow it rain and day after it wind,' the driver told Baggo. An East European, he used the journey time to practise his broken English. Sitting on a stained tartan rug in the back, Baggo checked the time. He had used his mobile to book a flight to Edinburgh leaving Heathrow at quarter past two, and hoped he would make it. The driver had no sense of urgency, hardly increasing his speed despite his passenger's entreaties. The man also chattered non-stop, frequently looking over his shoulder. His gut churning and waiting anxiously for di Falco to phone, Baggo fidgeted with his computer strap and shut his mind to the driver's prattling.

'Quiet, please!' he said abruptly as his phone sounded. It was di Falco.

'I have good news and bad news,' di Falco said.

The good news was that the bug had paid off. About half past eleven that morning Forbes had received a phone call during which he listened and said little. He ended the call by saying, 'This is serious. I'll have a word with Nicola and we'll come round to your room in quarter of an hour.' He had then phoned Nicola Walkinshaw, telling her it was an emergency and asking her to come and see him immediately. When she was with him, Forbes told her that Webb had just heard from his right-hand man in Atlanta. Hours earlier, in what appeared to be a well-organised operation, the Feds had mounted a dawn raid on the Sulphur Springs Bank and removed a lot of records. Worse, Webb's divorced brother, who had missed a family Thanksgiving he said due to illness, had in fact spent the last three days talking to Federal agents, and had probably incriminated not only Webb but also Forbes and Walkinshaw. They agreed that both had, at different times, spoken to Webb and his brother about buying commodities or overseas stocks to avoid the money laundering being done using only bearer bonds. In the UK all the actions were authorised by Parsley and executed by Knarston-Smith, and their involvement would not appear from the records. But they had been party to activities illegal under American law and it looked as if the Feds might be able to prove it. 'The words "Federal Penitentiary" make my blood run cold,' Forbes had said as he and Walkinshaw left the room, presumably to see van Bilt.

The bad news was that all three had disappeared. On hearing the recording, di Falco had asked Jocelyn to discreetly find out where in the hotel Forbes, Walkinshaw and van Bilt were, but they were not in their rooms, or any of the bars or restaurants, or the spa, or the Pro's Shop. Joe the porter had not seen them leave by the main door and they had not checked out. As di Falco spoke, Jocelyn was phoning the local taxi companies to see if any of their drivers had picked up a fare in town.

Baggo heard a female voice. Di Falco shouted, 'A Golf City taxi has just dropped off two men and a woman at Edinburgh Airport. One of the men was American. The other was a "wee, fat posh shit". Forbes didn't leave a tip.'

Baggo said, 'Well done! I should land in Edinburgh about half past three. Try to find out what flight they are booked on. I am arriving at Terminal Five now. I shall ring you back before I board. Oh, and get Gerald Knarston-Smith to the phone. I'll need to speak to him.'

'Keep the change,' Baggo snapped as he scrambled out of the car, slamming the door and shutting off the driver's wordy thanks for a ridiculously generous tip. With no time to spare, Baggo ran to the check-in desks, flashed his warrant and, with profuse apologies and smiles, barged to the front of the queue. 'Cutting it fine,' the clerk commented disapprovingly as, with a trace of reluctance, she handed over his boarding card. Using his warrant again, he went to the express lane at security where a yellow-vested special needs helper moved aside grudgingly and a man in a wheelchair cheerfully waved him past. At the gate boarding had started, but he needed to speak to Knarston-Smith.

Di Falco answered on the first ring. 'As far as I have been able to find out, they're not booked on any flight this afternoon. Do you think they're using false names and passports?' he asked.

'Perhaps. Keep trying, and persuade the Edinburgh police to detain them if they find them. I'll have to go soon, so can I speak with Knarston-Smith?' Baggo smiled at the attendant at the desk and walked slowly down the arm to the plane.

'Mr Knarston-Smith, we believe Forbes and Walkinshaw are doing a runner with van Bilt,' he said as soon as he heard Gerald's breathless voice. 'Can these bearer bonds be traded electronically?'

'Yes, it's through ...'

'Never mind how. Could Forbes and Walkinshaw trade using their mobiles?'

'Yes. They'd both need to be on line at the same time and use the right passwords. One director on his own could not activate a trade away from the office.'

'I believe they are certain to try to transfer huge sums in bearer bonds or take a large amount of money out of the bank. They may be doing that right now. Can you stop them?'

'Yes, I think so.'

'If necessary get DC di Falco to persuade Saddlefell and Davidson to help you. But hurry. There is no time to lose.'

'I'll need access to a computer.'

'Get the hotel to help. I'm sure they will. Now please hand the phone back to di Falco.'

In a couple of sentences he gave di Falco his instructions. He rang off as he entered the plane.

* * *

They did not have long to wait before take-off. During the

flight Baggo was like a cat on a hot tin roof. Declining refreshment, he smiled sweetly at the neat, bird-like flight attendant with elegantly thin calves but she told him firmly that, policeman or not, he might not use his phone and that there was no way he would be allowed into the cockpit to use the radio. As he squirmed in his seat, ignoring the grunts from the man beside him, he used the time to ask himself what the three fugitives would do, where they might go and how they might get there. By the time the captain announced ten minutes to landing he thought he knew the answers, but he had no idea how he could try to stop them.

The plane broke through the cloud above the patchwork of East Lothian then headed out over the dark, cold waters of the Forth. As it swept round, Baggo could see the famous rail bridge, its floodlights shining through wispy cloud and advancing dusk. Soon they were lower, over golf courses. He could make out a figure in a bunker. The Scots were hardy people, he thought, mad about their golf.

The landing was smooth and the plane taxied towards the terminal. Baggo phoned di Falco before the seatbelt sign went off, ignoring the flight attendant's glare.

'It's a private charter,' di Falco told him, confirming his fears. 'It was booked late this morning in the name of the Bucephalus Bank, and they've filed a flight plan. They're heading for Caracas. The plane's a Dassault Falcon 50 EX, which is a long-range corporate jet. I tried to stop them but as we don't have a warrant the flight controllers wouldn't listen and take-off's scheduled for quarter to four.'

Baggo's heart sank. If they reached Venezuela and managed to take a lot of money with them they would be untouchable. Citizenship could be bought and Venezuela did not extradite its own citizens. He had less than quarter of an hour to stop them. 'I will need back-up to arrest them. Please contact the Edinburgh police,' he said then rang off.

The plane came to a halt. The captain said something about an arm. Baggo peered out of a window. The floodlights were on. He could see a number of planes belonging to different airlines. Passengers were disembarking from one, using mobile steps. A truck-like vehicle approached the rear door of a different plane and stopped beside it. The rear part, the size of a small cabin, rose from the vehicle until it was level with the door of the aircraft, a bridge was extended and someone wearing a yellow vest pushed a person in a wheelchair into the aircraft.

Baggo's plane moved a couple of hundred metres, but the doors did not open. Increasingly frustrated, he looked out of the window once more. This time he saw a jet, smaller than most commercial planes and without the markings of an airline. A door front left of the fuselage was open. A woman with black hair was climbing steps leading up and in. She was followed by a short, rotund man.

'I need to get off this aircraft!' Baggo shouted at the bird-like attendant. 'This is very urgent. Serious criminals are escaping justice as we speak.'

The attendant stared at him as if calculating whether

he might make trouble. She went to the cockpit and was admitted. She came out a minute later and nodded towards Baggo. Then the captain announced that because of difficulties in the allocation of arms, passengers would be asked to disembark using steps. Any passengers who might find this difficult should speak to one of the crew. At once the daughter of an elderly lady put up her hand, causing her mother to scowl.

It took more precious minutes for the steps to be positioned. Waving his warrant, but no longer smiling, Baggo was first down. He looked over to where the Falcon had been, but it had gone. He scanned the airport anxiously then saw the Falcon trundling towards the east end of the runway where three aircraft queued ready for take-off. He knew he was too late, but nevertheless prayed silently to the Hindu god, Shiva, who defeated demons by dancing on them.

As he pictured the god dancing on Walkinshaw and Forbes, the disabled lift vehicle approached. 'Thank you, Shiva,' he said aloud and stood between the vehicle and the plane, his hand held up to stop it.

'I am a police officer on urgent business and I am commandeering this vehicle right now,' he shouted at the startled driver as he climbed into the cab beside him. 'Here is my warrant,' he added, pushing it in the man's face.

'First, please tell me if there is anyone in the cabin that rises up,' Baggo ordered.

The man was in his fifties, balding and though overweight, not obese. He was unshaven and his skin was pale. In a Scots accent he said, 'My mate Jamie is there.'

'Tell him to get out now.'

The driver hesitated.

'Now, or serious criminals will escape.'

The driver used an intercom. 'Jamie. There's an emergency. Get out now.'

Baggo added, 'And tell him to call the police. Come on, we must move.'

'Are ye alright, Archie?' Jamie asked.

The driver paused. 'Aye, I'm alright. The guy with me is polis. But call some more. I think he needs help.'

Baggo heard a metal door open then shut. A younger man appeared beside the cab and looked anxiously at his colleague.

'Come on,' Baggo shouted. 'Make for the middle of the runway.'

He watched carefully as Archie drove away from the clutter of planes and airport vehicles near the terminal. 'How do you make the cabin go up and down?' he asked.

'You press this button.' Archie pointed to a red button in the middle of his dashboard.

'And you drive this like a car?'

'Aye. You can see the gears and the wheel. The pedals are normal.'

'Thank you. Please put on the lights and get out. You have been very helpful.'

Archie brought the hoist to a stop. There was about thirty metres of paving between them and the runway. Archie switched on the headlights then turned to Baggo. 'I fear ye'r going to do something bloody daft,' he said.

'You could kill someone doing what I think ye'r going to do.' He climbed out of the cab.

'I know what I am doing,' Baggo said, sliding along the bench to the controls. Shaking his head, Archie slammed the door.

A British Airways plane thundered along the runway in front of him, heading west to rise over the fields of West Lothian. The Falcon was next up for take-off. Timing would be crucial. Go too early and the pilot would harmlessly abort, too late and what followed would be too terrible to contemplate.

The Falcon turned so it faced down the runway. It began to move. Baggo pushed the red button and pressed down on the accelerator. The mechanism lifting the cabin creaked and groaned, indicating it was working. Baggo was now on the runway, just short of the broken lines down the middle. He turned right to face the Falcon and took his foot off the accelerator. The vehicle stopped. He did not think the Falcon could get up in time to fly over him and there would not be room for it to pass. If it carried on without deviating its left wing, full of fuel for the trans-Atlantic flight, would hit the disabled cabin. Baggo could see the pilot waving an arm. He closed his eyes, suddenly afraid he had made the biggest blunder of his life, and perhaps the last. He thought of his mother and father.

He heard a loud screech and a roar to his left. He looked behind him and saw the Falcon bumping across the long grass on the far side of the runway, muddy gouge marks in its wake. It came to a halt and sat, lop-sided and ridiculous, like a great bird of prey with a broken wing.

Stunned by the success of his plan, moments passed before he decided to approach the Falcon, ready to arrest anyone who emerged. Blaring sirens and flashing blue lights announced the arrival of three police cars. It was Baggo who took most of their attention and they eyed him with suspicion even after seeing his warrant and hearing his explanation. Once inside the terminal it was apparent that Baggo's stunt had made the airport authorities incandescent and they wanted every available book thrown at him. Phone calls to Fortune, Jamieson, the Serious Fraud Office, the Federal Reserve and finally Scotland's Chief Constable persuaded the Edinburgh police to take no action against him. After all, he had secured the arrest of serious financial criminals and no one had been hurt. Jamieson, in particular, sensed kudos from his division's assistance in what turned out to be a highly successful operation, and perhaps even a goodwill trip to the States.

At one point, van Bilt, Forbes and Walkinshaw were led along a corridor in which Baggo was standing. When she saw him, Walkinshaw's face remained stony. She passed him then turned and struck like a cobra, her long, purple nails raking his cheek and narrowly missing his left eye.

Once she had been restrained he went up to her and whispered in her ear, 'Only worth five? I reckon today was worth a ten.'

21

Much later that evening, Baggo and Lance Wallace took a dram together and compared notes. In Cupar, the Eglintons had refused to answer questions and were being held before appearing in court on the Monday. After much deliberating and posturing it had been decided to regard the financial criminals as detainees of the Fife Division. They had been taken to Glenrothes where they had declined the services of local solicitors and said nothing in response to Baggo's questioning. Other officers from the Serious Fraud Office were due to travel north and, with them, Baggo would escort the prisoners to London later on the following day.

'Belinda Parsley was really upset when she heard Forbes had gone without her,' Lance said.

'She will get over it, I bet,' Baggo said. 'I think she will come to realise she has had a lucky escape. And she will not be poor.'

'What about Saddlefell?'

'He will get his knuckles rapped for not coming clean when he learned what was going on, but with Davidson and Knarston-Smith he prevented Forbes and co from transferring any bearer bonds. They tried while waiting to board in Edinburgh. Your man, di Falco, is smart.'

'And he knows it. My spies tell me he's made a big hit with that pretty under-manager at the hotel. What do you think will happen to the bank?'

'Someone will take it over and make money out of it.'

'Davidson?'

Baggo shook his head. 'I think he is fed up and wants out. People like him are called BOBOs – Burnt Out But Opulent.'

It had been a long day. As they got up to go to bed, Lance asked, 'Did you say anything to Alan? He was, well, a lot better this evening.'

Baggo shrugged. 'I told him a bit about myself. And I said he should cut you some slack. As you should him. He is a fine fellow and going through a difficult phase.'

* * *

The next day was fine and dry and crisp. As he was not due to travel south till late afternoon, Baggo took the bus into St Andrews. He wanted to buy Jeannie Wallace something good to thank her for her hospitality. The previous evening she had cooked another fine dinner and the way she had fussed over his lacerated cheek had made him feel quite heroic. Before visiting the shops he went for a walk beside the famous Old Course, its fairways silver with frost. Crossing the Swilken Burn into which Hugh Parsley's putter had been thrown, his hands in his pockets, he felt the money clip he had kept there for the last two days. He drew it out of his pocket and re-read the inscription, SHAFTED BY HP. That would apply to a lot of people, he thought. With a satisfying plop he dropped it into the muddy water flowing towards the bleak North Sea.

* * *

On Tuesday morning Fergus Maxwell brought Flick tea in bed. Though reassured about the baby, she had nevertheless been ordered to take a week off work. The Monday papers had been full of her triumph and the sitting room was made fragrant by a large bunch of flowers from the divisional commander.

Fergus did not bring Flick the Tuesday paper. On an inside page there was an article in which former Detective Inspector Noel Osborne claimed credit for tipping off 'his protégé' where she might find a vital clue, 'Needed my help, she did. So I helped her out of the kindness of my heart.' The article went on to say that years ago he cleaned up the East End of London and finished with the quote, 'I like St Andrews. It's a real pukka place. I might even buy a property here.'

Flick would inevitably hear about this, but Fergus was not about to spoil things for her now. Anyway, Osborne moving to Fife was something that would never happen. He hoped.

ACKNOWLEDGEMENTS

This is a work of fiction and if any of my characters bear some resemblance to real people it is coincidental. That includes those characters I have put into the Old Course Hotel, an excellent establishment with good food, an efficient and friendly staff and a superb setting. I hope I might have captured something of its welcoming ambience, but while some details are accurate others are not, and that is deliberate. I thank for their help Sarah Middlemas, Debbie Rose and (although I did not tell him why I wanted to see the club store) my friend from boys' golf many years ago, the professional, Neil Paton. I also thank Historic Scotland for information over the phone. I am grateful to Matador for their professionalism and understanding. Most of all I thank my wife Annie for her encouragement, criticism and constant support. All errors are of course mine.

ACKNOWLEDGEMENTS

Since retiring from a law career which included sitting as a judge in High Court murder trials, Ian Simpson has been writing crime fiction. In 2008 one of his books was shortlisted for the Debut Dagger by the Crime Writers' Association. He has also written newspaper articles on legal topics. He was brought up in St Andrews and for a time as a youth held a handicap of three.